THE
DIABOLICAL
BONES

BRONTË SISTERS MYSTERIES

The Vanished Bride
The Diabolical Bones

THE DIABOLICAL BONES

A BRONTË SISTERS MYSTERY

Bella Ellis

BERKLEY

New York

BERKLEY
An imprint of Penguin Random House LLC
penguinrandomhouse.com

(Penguin colophon)

Library of Congress Cataloging-in-Publication Data
Names: Ellis, Bella, author.
Title: The diabolical bones / Bella Ellis.
Description: New York : Berkley, [2021] | Series: A Brontë sisters mystery; 2
Identifiers: LCCN 2020019722 (print) | LCCN 2020019723 (ebook) |
ISBN 9780593099155 (trade paperback) | ISBN 9780593099162 (ebook)
Subjects: LCSH: Brontë, Charlotte, 1816-1855--Fiction. |
Brontë, Emily, 1818-1848--Fiction. | Brontë, Anne, 1820-1849--Fiction. |
Women authors, English--19th century--Fiction. | GSAFD:
Biographical fiction. | Mystery fiction.
Classification: LCC PR6103.O4426 D53 2021 (print) |
LCC PR6103.O4426 (ebook) | DDC 823/.92--dc23
LC record available at https://lccn.loc.gov/2020019722
LC ebook record available at https://lccn.loc.gov/2020019723

First U.S. Edition: February 2021

Printed in the United States of America
1 3 5 7 9 10 8 6 4 2

Jacket art: woman (left) © LML Productions / Arcangel;
women (middle and right) © Magdalena Russocka / Trevillion
Jacket design by Emily Osborne
Book design by Alison Cnockaert

Dedicated to my dear friend Julie Akhurst

THE
DIABOLICAL
BONES

The night is darkening round me,
The wild winds coldly blow;
But a tyrant spell has bound me,
And I cannot, cannot go.
The giant trees are bending
Their bare boughs weighed with snow;
The storm is fast descending
And yet I cannot go.
Clouds beyond clouds above me,
Wastes beyond wastes below;
But nothing drear can move me;
I will not, cannot go.

—Emily Brontë

Haworth Parsonage, April 1852

❧

Charlotte could not conceive of a place more beautiful than Haworth and the surrounding countryside in the spring.

The trees were heavy with blossom, the moors green and fecund with new heather, still tender and soft underfoot, dotted with the little white clouds of cotton grass that danced in the brisk breeze. And yet, as much as Charlotte was glad to be at home, recovering after a long illness and with nothing but time and the freedom to write, it could not be denied that even now, all these long months later, months filled with travel and acclaim, she felt trapped: a prisoner of isolation.

Still, even with the trips to London, the company of Thackeray, Mrs. Gaskell and, yes, dearest George Smith, she felt always as if a part of her heart were missing. No, that wasn't quite right: as if three-quarters of her heart were missing, each one taken on to heaven before her by her late brother and sisters. If only some miracle could return them home to her, then perhaps she could laugh more, perhaps she could love more and, most important, perhaps she could write more. Indeed, there were some long, stormy days and nights when she felt such a craving for support and companionship as she could not truly express. It was as if her loneliness were whittling away a little bit of her, day by day. When the prospect of marriage, of being loved, had come to her, in the form of Mr. James Taylor, all she had felt was ice in her veins.

With the playful wind cooling her cheeks, Charlotte walked on, her mind wandering so far from her route that it was with some surprise she stopped outside the highest dwelling on the moor, Top Withens Hall. She paused for a while, even now a little reluctant to draw nearer to the cold grey edifice that looked more like a haunted ruin than a busy home and farmhouse.

Top Withens's gargoyle sentinels looked down on her just as fiercely now as they had on that dark afternoon. Was it really six years since the bitter Christmas when Charlotte, Emily and Anne had trudged through the snow to this very gate, unaware of the hidden horror that lay beyond? Despite the mild sunny afternoon, Charlotte shuddered at the memory; she had never forgotten what it felt like to stand in the presence of unadulterated evil.

And yet for all the fear and misadventures the three of them had endured in the pursuit of truth, at least she had had her family around her. Even in the darkest moments of her life, it had been her brother and sisters who had given her strength.

Take courage: those had been Anne's last words to her, and take courage she must, for there was no alternative but to continue. Charlotte took one more long look at Top Withens, searching for any remaining traces of the infestation of wickedness that had once thrived here, but to her relief, she could find none. These days Top Withens was a quiet house occupied by a quiet and decent family man.

But in December of 1845, things had been very different.

1

❧❦❧

The scream ripped through the frozen air, sharp as a knife.

Liston Bradshaw sat bolt upright in bed, his quick breaths misting in the freezing air. Outside a snowstorm raged, and the wind tore around Top Withens Hall, imprisoning it in a howling, furious vortex of noise. When the dreadful cry sounded for the second time, Liston stumbled out of bed, dragging on his breeches and shoving his bare feet into his boots. Careering down the stairs into the hall, he heard his father's violent shouts.

"Begone with you, demon, begone!" Clifton Bradshaw railed at thin air. Liston arrived to see his father swivelling this way and that, a rusty old sword from above the fireplace in his hand, as he jabbed at and threatened empty spaces. His eyes were wild with fright and red with drink. The hounds barked madly at his side, in turn cowering from and snarling at some invisible threat. "Show yourself, and let me fight you!"

"What is it, Pa?" Liston asked as the latest scream died away, and he searched out every dark corner for the phantom intruder. "Why are we cursed so?"

"I'm mortal afraid that she has come back to claim my soul," Clifton told his son, his voice trembling.

"Who? Is there someone outside?" Liston went to the door, grabbing a poker from the fireplace.

"There's no one outside, fool," Bradshaw spat. "This fury comes from within the house. It comes to take revenge."

When the wailing came again, it was heavy with a piercing, plaintive sorrow that soaked the very air in grief. His father was right. There was no mistaking it: the cries were coming from the oldest part of the house, from the rooms that his father had shut up on the day Liston's mother died, and none had set foot in them since.

"Mary." Bradshaw's face crumbled as he spoke his dead wife's name aloud, dragging the sword across the stone flags. "Mary, why do you hate me so? Please, I beg you. Tell me what you want from me!"

"Pa?" Liston called after him uncertainly.

"Are you coming, or will you be a milksop all your life?"

Liston swallowed his misgivings and followed his father into the perfect dark.

The dull jangle of heavy keys, the clunk of the stiff lock opening and the creak of the old door echoed in the night, and Liston held his breath. His mother's mausoleum had been unlocked.

The rush of air that greeted them was stiff with ice.

Liston shuddered as he stepped over the threshold into the old house. Thirteen years since his mother had gone to God. Thirteen years since his father had shut off these rooms, keeping the only key on his belt at all times, even when he slept. In all that time there had been no fire in the grate, not even a candle lit at the window.

It was as cold and silent as the grave.

"Mary?" Liston was stunned to hear his father's voice thick with raw and bloody sorrow. "Mary, is it you? Are you coming back to me, my darling? Mary, answer me!"

As they entered what had once been his mother's bedchamber, it was as if time stopped. The storm quietened in an instant, and suddenly every corner was lit up by the full moon, almost as bright as day. The ancient box bed crouched in the corner, as if it might pounce at any moment. The few things that his mother had owned were still laid out on the dressing table, and a howling wind swept in through a shattered window, leaving jagged, frosted shards glinting in the moonlight.

What had happened here?

Bradshaw fell to his knees on the dust-covered floor, tearing at his hair. "Mary, I'm here. Come back to me. I beg you. Please, please, tell me you forgive me."

For the space of one sharp inward breath, there was silence. Then the screaming began again, so loud that Liston felt for a moment it was coming from within him. Furiously his father grabbed the poker from him and dug it into the gaps of the drystone chimney breast, forcing out one stone and then another. Dropping the poker, he frantically began to pull the loose stones out, until, at last, a great cascade of them tumbled onto the floor, making the rotten boards tremble.

The shrieking stopped, as if cut short by a smothering hand.

Warily Liston took a step closer to see what his father was staring at. There, tucked into a sooty alcove more than halfway up the chimney, was something bundled and bound into a blackened cloth parcel of considerable size.

"Fetch it down, then," his father commanded him, and though he felt a sense of dread in his gut unlike any he had ever known, Liston obeyed his father. Though it was large, the parcel was light as a feather, shifting in his arms. As he laid it down, all the fear Liston felt drained suddenly away, and he was left only with horror.

"Out of my way." Bradshaw elbowed his son to one side, taking the knife from his belt, slicing through the bindings and revealing to the night what had been hidden within.

"Dear God in heaven, deliver us from evil," Liston whispered as he fell back on his heels at the sight.

"I'd say that God was nowhere to be found when this occurred," his father replied.

For contained within the desiccated cloth were the skull and bones of a child.

2

December 1845

Anne

Though the fire was banked and burning brightly, and she was wrapped in her warmest shawl, Anne had never felt so cold, not even during her father's lengthy sermon in church yesterday. At least on a Sunday, there was the rest of the congregation to create a community of warmth among them. On this freezing December Monday, however, the air was thick with frost, without and within, as evidenced by the filigree etched onto every window. And the paper that Anne had laid out on her writing desk was still as pristine as the last fresh snowfall.

"Emily, you have yet to write to Ellen and thank her for her letter," Charlotte told her sister from her seat at the table, a neat pile of correspondence before her. "As it is, Ellen is vexed with me for not visiting Brookroyd recently. I find myself having to beg her not to scold me further! Please don't compound the matter with ill manners. If you write a note now, I can enclose it with my letter. Perhaps she will forgive me, for honestly her letter is as prickly as the holly leaf on the mantel, and quite unfair. A person cannot help that they are occupied with writing, detecting and disastrous brothers, not that I have told her about the first two. And now we are marooned in the midst of all this snow. I am surprised that Ellen cannot understand that which is quite plain."

"Ellen is your oldest and dearest friend, Charlotte," Anne reminded her sister mildly. "Do not hold her regret at not seeing you against her. Think of all that she is managing, with her brother ill again and sent to the asylum."

Charlotte pursed her lips, just as Anne knew she would. If there was one thing Charlotte did not like, it was to have her own shortcomings revealed to her.

"Well, at least I have written to her, Anne, and sent your regards as you requested," Charlotte said primly. "Emily is ignoring her completely, and that, I would say, is the worse transgression."

"Heavens!" Emily replied, with a deep sigh as she stood at the window peering into the freezing air. "Cannot you see I am occupied?"

"Occupied?" Charlotte snorted. "By standing?"

"By *thinking*," Emily said. "Though I realise this is an endeavour that you are largely unfamiliar with. I have received a request that though on the one hand it would give me great pleasure in its execution, it would also require me to be . . . *social* . . . and nice to those I am not at all interested in. In short, other people."

"You should decline immediately," Charlotte advised. "If I recall, and I do my best not to recall, your last social engagement resulted in us moving to Brussels."

"That is not true!" Anne laughed. "Emily, what request has been made of you?"

"One Lord and Lady Hartley," Emily said, handing a letter headed with a coat of arms to Anne as if it were imbued with some terrible plague, "most often of London, but sometimes of that ghastly gothic folly Oakhope Hall, wish me to play at a musical evening they are arranging for some charitable cause. Apparently, word of my prowess as a pianist has somehow reached their notice."

"Lord and Lady Hartley?" Charlotte whipped the letter out of Anne's hand and was examining it intensely before Anne was able to read one line. "But, Emily, they are very great and important people. You must know that."

"I know that they are very rich," Emily said. "And I know that some, Charlotte, dear, equate riches with status."

"Their wealth is an aside. Lady Hartley is a famous philanthropist. Her charitable work has eased the suffering of many a poor soul here in the North, where she grew up. I have heard it said she converses with Thackeray, and Mrs. Gaskell . . . and has even been received by Her Majesty the Queen. You must accept!"

"Must I?" Emily turned to look at her older sister. "There will be dozens of accomplished young women of good families lining up to play a pretty piece. What on earth does she want with a Brontë daughter?"

"'What does she want with *you?*' is a more pertinent question," Charlotte said, unable to hide her regret at not receiving such a prestigious request.

"You should have practised your lessons more, Charlotte," Emily said. "It seems the great Lady Hartley has no use for someone who is expert in talking."

"But you will do it," Charlotte said. "Imagine what an acquaintance with the Hartleys might do for us. And just at this moment when we have sent our poetry out into the world. It might make all the difference to our success, Emily. To have our work put before the eyes of important personages, to have their patronage, could change our fortunes entirely."

"Sister dear," Emily sighed. "I care no more for who sees our rhymes than I do for writing ridiculously superfluous thank-you notes for thank-you notes' sake. All that will happen is that I will write to Ellen saying 'Thank for your letter,' and then Ellen will write to me, thanking me for my letter, and then I shall be obliged to write her and so on for all eternity. To save us all some precious time, I shall trust that Ellen knows me well enough to know that I am always most thankful!"

"I do believe that we are all rather strained by being so much indoors," Anne interjected quickly, noting how the colour rose in Charlotte's cheeks. "Perhaps if we took a walk around the table, put all thoughts of letters and recitals aside for a moment and shared our ideas aloud . . . ?"

Anne often wondered what would become of her sisters if she was not present to mediate with them. Though Emily and Charlotte loved each other fiercely, they each took a perverse delight in irritating the other. Charlotte knew that Emily would always resist anything Charlotte asked her to do, and Emily was perfectly aware that Charlotte would not be able to rest until she was certain that everything had been properly done. They goaded each other out of boredom, competition and a new sense of unease that neither of them would admit to. For Anne was certain that this most recent skirmish had nothing to do with the banks of snow that seemed to engulf them, or their continuing lack of paid employment. She was sure that it was because just recently, after a series of polite refusals, Charlotte had sent their collected poems to the publisher Aylott and Jones, asking if they would consider them for publication. There were eyes outside their own on their work once more, and soon they would know if there was any merit to their efforts. It was terrifying.

Emily could barely speak of it without having to storm off in a fluster, and as for Charlotte, well, it did not help that last month she had written to Monsieur Héger, after waiting the six long months he had bade her, and now she was in a state of torture, desperate for a reply. Anne had hoped the passing time, the distraction of detections and their book might divert her sister from her devotion to that individual, but still her longing for his favour lived on within her, like a fever that would not abate. The wait for the post had become a fraught affair that had so far resulted only in double disappointment, and now this Lady Hartley business would only distress and vex her more, for Charlotte would so dearly have loved to move amongst those rarefied circles that Emily cared for not one jot. Christmas was meant to be a time of family, of communion, companionship, contentment and prayer, and yet . . .

What they all needed—what Anne herself longed for—was adventure.

"When the world looks like this, I wonder if it will ever thaw again," Emily said eventually as the moment of tension eased. "I believe I prefer it, despite the cold. I can almost imagine it unsullied by man entirely. In fact, perhaps Keeper and I shall go out for a walk and enjoy a few minutes of believing I am the only human being left alive."

"You cannot go out in this cold, Emily," Charlotte said. "You will catch your death."

"Well, at least that would be more interesting than this interminable period of sitting still. There has been no detecting for weeks," Emily lamented. "Nothing of any note anyway, and frankly I'd rather not detect at all if all I am being asked to investigate is the disappearance of a cow."

"Cows matter a great deal to some people," Charlotte countered. "Mr. Hawthorne was delighted to have Gracie returned to him, and

I do believe he will think twice about gambling her away again in the future."

"Yes, and that was all well and good," Emily sighed. "But it's not quite the same as our summer adventure, is it? Why, we haven't been terrified for our lives on any single day or night for the last four months."

"I was rather concerned by my last cold," Charlotte said.

"Perhaps it might be more helpful for us to talk about the fears and anxieties that concern us regarding our submission to Aylott and Jones," Anne suggested. "For if we voice our feelings, share the burden of our worries, we may lessen them."

"Don't be ridiculous," Charlotte said.

"What a horrifying prospect," Emily said, adding thoughtfully, "Perhaps we should advertise Bell Brothers and Company in the paper—spread word of our services further afield. I'm sure that Bradford is rife with immorality of all kinds."

"There is a good deal more law enforcement in Bradford," Charlotte said, disconsolate. "Constables everywhere you look spoiling the fun."

"Soon we will have word of our book of rhymes," Anne persisted. "Our names, or rather the names Currer, Ellis and Acton Bell, will be out in the world, for praise or condemnation. And should it be praise, then, well, we should have material ready. For, sisters, we will never make a living from detecting. But we may from our writing."

Emily sat down in a sulk, her gaze trained on Charlotte.

"She will not stop talking about it, will she?" she said, jerking her head in Anne's direction.

"She's clearly very nervous," Charlotte said. "As her older sisters, we should try to calm her."

"It would soothe me a great deal if you would first calm yourselves," Anne said. "Stop fighting like a pair of sparrows and face what truly ails you. If we concentrate our efforts in our novels, then we will all feel much more settled. I am going to write about a governess." Anne smiled as she recalled the idea that she had been unwinding in her head for the last few days. "My heroine shall be ordinary and plain, decent and good and at the mercy of wicked children and unpleasant gentlemen."

"Who on earth would want to read about a governess?" Charlotte said. "I was thinking about writing about a young woman who is exceptionally bright and brilliant, and how she finds herself drawn to a much older professor. . . ." Charlotte's cheeks pinkened at the thought of it.

"Clearly you both need reminding that we are attempting to write fiction and not our autobiographies," Emily sighed, shaking her head. "We are the architects of Gondal and Angria. If we cannot conjure up something truly remarkable, then we should not try at all."

"Very well, then, what revolutionary idea are you proposing?" Charlotte asked.

"I do not know," Emily admitted, dropping her chin. "If I go out on to the moors, they talk to me in song and verse, and I can write a hundred poems in a day. But this dreary business of putting one word after another to make a book—it's much more laborious than one would imagine."

"Well, then." As much as they infuriated her, which was a very great deal, Anne was pleased to see the tension between her sisters begin to ebb away. "Let us walk and talk around the table as I suggested, and see what arises."

But Anne had scarcely pulled back her chair when there was a quiet knock at the door and their housekeeper of many years, dearest Tabby, entered, her pallor greyish, and her mouth set in a thin, firm line that spoke of deep discomfort and unease.

"Tabby, are you quite well?" Anne asked her, taking her hand and drawing her to her chair. "Whatever is the matter?"

"I am not," Tabby said. "For there has been a discovery made—a most diabolical one. A discovery of a body, and I am very afraid that if something is not done about it, all that we know and love will be engulfed by evil."

3

Charlotte

"I would speak to your father," Tabby said, agitated. "But with his eyes so bad and it being almost Christmas, it hardly seems right. And young Mr. Nicholls is a decent enough fellow, but he don't have the grit—he don't have the strength of mind or the stubbornness. Not like you girls."

"Really, Tabby," Emily said with a smile, "I do believe that is the nicest thing you have ever said to us."

"Tell us all you know, dearest Tabby," Anne said, "and let us soothe your fears."

However, though it was a kind promise, it was not one any of them was able to keep.

"It's scarcely believable," Charlotte said. "That Clifton Bradshaw should have made such a tragic discovery in the first instance, but then to propose simply leaving the bones out for any to gawk at until he can bury them on his own land in the spring is indefensible.

Has he forgotten that a human soul once dwelt within that wretched skeleton?"

" 'Tain't no surprise to me," Tabby said unhappily. "Those Bradshaws have always been a bad lot—since creation, I shouldn't wonder. Who else'd build their house right up there on top of the moor, where nowt but the hidden folk should live?"

Charlotte patted the distressed woman's hand in a bid to comfort and quiet her, though she herself was drenched with cold horror.

"What the world of Men has forgotten is that there is always a price to pay for everything they take from the land, a balance to be made," Tabby went on. "Haven't I always told you that the hidden people, the children of Adam and Eve, inhabit those hillsides where the Bradshaws farm and plough? Didn't I say there'd be trouble?"

"You did," Charlotte said soothingly.

"Created in original sin and hidden by God as His punishment, but always there, inhabiting rocks and woodland, moors and rivers, always there but never seen. In the old days, folk would leave out offerings to them to keep away ill fortune, but times have changed, and the old ways have been lost. I always knew there would be a heavy price to pay for such arrogance, and I don't know how, but I just know these bones are the start of it."

"Top Withens is a very ancient house," Charlotte said. "The bones could have lain there concealed for two centuries. Though Mr. Bradshaw is very wrong in his treatment of the remains, take some comfort, Tabby, that they are the remnants of some tragedy long since played out."

"Perhaps," Tabby said. "But if I know one thing, it is that as long as that poor soul's remains are so badly done by, then there will be nowt but ill fortune and unease, and not just at Top Withens—it'll spread like a blight across the land. You mark my words." Tabby's voice fell away, causing Charlotte to lean in to her, searching out her troubled gaze.

"All will be well, my dear Tabby," she said. "We will rectify this awful situation as soon as we are able. If only the weather wasn't so very inclement. Top Withens is almost unreachable at present."

"Nonsense!" Emily cried. "Charlotte, you behave as if we were camped in the Arctic, not our little English village. The snow is deep, indeed, but we can follow the shepherds' paths up to Top Withens with no fear of getting lost. Tabby, we shall speak to Mr. Bradshaw and bring him around to the correct way of thinking before you are abed."

"Will you really, my child?" Tabby said with such relief that Charlotte could see there was no point in trying to argue her case, or point out that it would be a fine Christmas gift for Papa if his three daughters were lost to snow, as many others had been before them. Still, Tabby was Tabby, as precious and dear to them as a mother, and none of them could bear to see her so troubled.

"We shall do more than that," Anne said with surprising enthusiasm at the prospect of losing a toe or two to frost. "We shall take those bones and carry them away with us. I will bring such wrath down upon those in residence at Top Withens that they will wish the house had crumbled over their heads."

"I'm not entirely sure that is the best way to approach the Bradshaws," Branwell said, as he entered the room. "Forgive me—I stood a moment in the hallway, listening to your talk, while deciding if it was your usual feminine prattle or something worth engaging in. I believe it is the latter."

Despite his smile their brother looked exhausted; his face had a bluish pallor, made all the more stark by the supernatural flame of his hair. "They talk of nothing else but the bones in the Bull, and indeed it is a distressing situation. To think of a child, abandoned like that . . . lost forever . . ." Branwell trailed off for a moment as he slumped into a chair at the table. "As strong and as able as you are, sister, Clifton Bradshaw is not a man who will easily bend to the will of a woman, or even three of them. His son, Liston Bradshaw, however, is a friend of mine and a fine fellow. I shall accompany you to Top Withens for Tabby's sake."

"You hardly made the trip to that chair, Branwell," Charlotte said. "Are you sure that you are up to an expedition?"

"Quite sure. Besides, Top Withens Hall is a house of men, and it takes a man to know how to talk to them, and, though you may call yourselves by the names of men, that doesn't give you men's strength and courage."

"There's something else you should know before you go up there," Tabby said very gravely. "For I cannot send my angels and Branwell into the lion's den without arming you against what may lie in wait for you."

"Am I not an angel?" asked Branwell, mildly affronted.

"A fallen one, perhaps." Emily smiled at Anne.

"What is it, Tabby?" Charlotte asked as the others gathered nearer.

"Some do say . . ." Tabby began, lowering her voice as if she was afraid she might be overhead, "that on the night his wife was taken from him, Clifton Bradshaw was so full of fury and grief that he sold his soul to the devil, as vengeance against the God that robbed him of his love, and that's why he's had the luck of the devil ever since."

4

Emily

There are many who would not be able to fathom that what Emily Brontë loved most about the moors that surrounded her home was that at any moment they might bring one's existence to a sudden end. A single misstep, an unplanned detour, one careless moment on a clifftop path, and the likelihood of unwittingly delivering oneself into the jaws of death was remarkably high. This was never truer than in the grip of wintry weather, which had held dominion over their little corner of the world for more than three weeks now, as it continued to snow with no sign of a thaw. Bitter it was, but also sublime, all the noise and clamour of the world muted to a hush of peace and soundless calm. Emily would be sorry when spring eventually broke the deadlock, but even then the thaw would cause a deluge of meltwater to flood down the hills and valleys into the villages. For in Yorkshire even the onset of summer could be treacherous.

All four of them had dressed as wisely and as warmly as they were able, given their means. Even so, after just a few minutes of walking, the cold had wormed its way in under every layer of Emily's clothing. It was as if it were a living thing that sought to feed upon her warm blood, steadily permeating her entire being, until she believed she could feel its icy touch even in the marrow of her bones.

Despite his self-inflicted fragility, Branwell led the way, and on this one occasion, Emily was content to let him. Before the Mrs. Robinson business, her brother had seen nothing in walking twenty miles in a day, and he knew the footpaths just as well as she. These days he was made more of gin than he was of flesh, and his pace was slower and a great deal more laborious than it would once have been, but he had not lost his goatlike agility or unerring sense of direction. If only he could have utilised those attributes in his personal life, Emily thought, then perhaps he would not still have been wondering, waiting for news of Mrs. Robinson, certain that somehow at the right moment she would summon him to her side, when it was quite clear to everybody else that Lydia Robinson was doing her very best to erase her brother's existence from Robinson family history.

Emily suspected that her brother had considered the secrecy of the love poems he had submitted to the *Halifax Guardian* to be a great success. Of course, it was obvious to anyone who happened upon the verses who they had been penned by and whom they were for, for Branwell was not quite so practised at artifice as he liked to think. No doubt he prayed that his mistress would see his passionate words and sacrifice all to be with him. In fact, Emily had hawkishly observed, the result of his efforts had been the arrival of small sums of money, in a bid to quiet him. But Branwell was not a man given to hiding his passion away, no matter what it might cost him, or any of them for that matter.

When Top Withens Hall came into sight at last, it stood out against the monotone background like a black crow perched on the highest branch of a tree, swaying in the wind and yet sure-footed and certain of its right to be there.

The few remaining living human souls who occupied it kept it as warm as they could, which was no easy feat in most houses, let alone one that was precariously positioned. Heat escaping through the rafters had melted the snow, exposing the slate roof tiles, and candlelight flickered hesitantly at three of the visible windows, all of which were shrouded in frost.

"Infernal-looking place," Charlotte said as the four of them paused to catch their breath, the incline levelling out at last. "If hell was a frozen place, this is how I would picture it."

"How any can live here and stay decent, I do not know," Anne added, her dear face made red raw by the cold. "It's a cruel place, and such an unkind home makes for cruel occupants."

"Liston Bradshaw is no animal," Branwell admonished them, rubbing the blood back into the tip of his nose. "He might be less educated than you or I, and have had fewer chances to see the beauty in the world, but for all his father's brutality, Liston has a kind heart and a good mind. You will like him."

"For my part, I admire it, if not like it exactly," Emily said. "There's something to be said for the first to choose a desolate place for their home—an admirable stubbornness that appeals to me. Though it has a rather ominous presence, as if the house itself is watching us."

"That, my dear," Charlotte said, heading on towards the gate, "is because you would love nothing more than to live in a cave like the Ponden Hermit, and never speak to another human being again."

Charlotte was not incorrect. Emily admired the spirit that had been unafraid of digging foundations here, on the wildest and most inhospitable location for a hundred miles around. Up here there was no shelter of any kind, no higher peak to prevent the freezing north wind from pouring in through every crack and fissure in the house. Or to stop it from bending the stunted trees to its volition, making them a permanent testament to its ferocity.

The old wrought iron gate, which once was meant to proclaim the entrance to a house of note, and which had been torn almost off its hinges sometime over the winter, swung and creaked in the wind like a hanged man. At each gatepost and on every corner of the hall's roof stood roughly hewn, ghastly-looking gargoyles, each standing sentinel over one of the four corners of the earth. The front yard was a quagmire of snow, ice and frozen mud, and though the gate was no longer a barrier to entry, the all-pervading sense of misery that seemed to form droplets in the dank air certainly was.

It was rare that Emily ever wanted to turn back from any moment, reckoning that the dark and difficult ones were as necessary as the ones that brought comfort and joy. Yet at that moment, she hesitated; every instinct she possessed looked into the shadowy windows of Top Withens Hall and whispered, *Beware.*

As they entered the yard, a pack of hounds of every shape and size flew to greet them with a frenzy of barking and bared teeth.

"Get back 'ere, foul beasts!" Clifton Bradshaw roared at the animals as he appeared from within the house, hastily putting on a filthy-looking coat. "Shut your noise, or I'll whip you till you bleed." At once the animals cowered and whimpered, rolling meekly over onto their backs, and he strode towards their small party. The dogs were terrified of him.

"Good day to you, sir, ladies," Bradshaw said, affecting something approximating a smile, his cold, cracked lips stretched painfully thin over yellowing teeth. "No guests were expected on such a day."

"We aren't visiting socially," Anne told him, having to raise her voice to make herself heard over the wind. "We have come as representatives of our father, the Reverend Patrick Brontë, to demand that you give over the remains found on your premises to the church so that the poor soul may be able to receive a Christian burial at once."

Emily couldn't be sure, but she wouldn't have been surprised if her sister had stamped a furious foot on that last word. For a moment Clifton looked bemusedly into her sister's face, then exploded into rough and raucous laughter that echoed all around the yard, distressing the animals in the barn and scattering the dogs at his feet.

"Listen here, little girl . . ." Bradshaw began, and Emily felt a rage that began in her toes propel itself through her veins like a short, lit fuse.

There would have been no telling what choice and decidedly unladylike words might have erupted if Branwell hadn't halted her in her tracks long enough for her to think better of speaking her mind.

"Mr. Bradshaw, sir." Branwell offered him his hand. "Please excuse my sisters. They are sensitive creatures, emotional through and through, and are apt only to see the tragedy of the situation, not the scientific or historical value of your discovery. Please, will you excuse their womanly weakness and invite us inside? My sisters are fragile, and I do believe we all may perish if we stay outside in these conditions a moment longer."

Clifton looked at Branwell, then at the three cloaked women who accompanied him, before turning on his heel and kicking a small lurcher out of his way as he strode into the house.

"If you must," he said. "Be quick about it."

Bradshaw turned on his heel and strode into the house. After a moment the three sisters and their brother followed him, deep into the devil's den.

5

Charlotte

The interior of the hall was altogether brighter and more welcoming than Charlotte had expected. At one end of the large room, an elderly woman busied herself with overseeing a young maid at the fire in the making of what smelled like mutton stew. At the other a huge dresser stood against the wall, and all manner of animals roamed around their feet, including more dogs and several cats. Even a hen wandered around the old lady's feet, oblivious to the fierce-looking cleaver that was embedded in the butcher block nearby.

Swinging from the ceiling were haunches of pork and mutton tied up with bunches of herbs that gave the room a pungent but not unpleasant scent of sweet and meaty smoke, combining with the perfume of heating spices. The room was clean, the floor swept and scoured; the pewter that lined the great oak dresser that took up almost a whole wall shone as if freshly polished. Though the room was not dressed for Christmas, as other homes might have been at the time of year, it hardly seemed the home of the half-wild heathen Tabby had warned them of.

"Bess, Molly," Bradshaw barked, gesturing at their bedraggled party when the old lady turned at the sound of her name. "People."

"Oh, aye. Now, then, lasses"—the old lady blinked at them—"take off ye cloaks and draw closer here 'fore you freeze to death!"

"Thank you," Anne said, "Mrs. . . . ?"

"Nay, you know me, mistress. I am your Bess! Perhaps the cold has frozen your head, hey?" Bess laughed merrily.

"Don't mind her, misses," Molly said as she took their sodden cloaks. "Bess is half in heaven already, and it is my job to mind her, though she does not know it."

"I see," Charlotte said. Though she longed for the respite of the fire, she stood her ground, determined that Clifton Bradshaw would hear her. Such a brutal man fascinated and repelled her in equal measure. His coarseness horrified and disgusted Charlotte, and yet in some slight way, she rather admired him too. Here was a man who let convention be damned.

"I'll not take orders from any on my own land, not even the parson's offspring," Clifton told them before they could speak. "The bones are my property, and I shall bury them here at Top Withens as soon as the ground has thawed enough to dig. You may not take them, but you may see them if you wish. Then you can see they are being treated decent and tell the village folk to cease mithering on about what is none of their concern."

"Sir," Charlotte said, "every soul deserves a Christian burial, and surely—"

"Will you see the bones or not?" Bradshaw cut across her, unmoved. "Those apartments have been shut up these last thirteen years, and I have no care to venture there again until I must. But Liston will take you."

"We will," Branwell said. "Yes, we would like to see the bones."

Charlotte glanced up at her brother, but he shook his head imperceptibly, warning her to remain silent, to be patient and wait. Knowing that on this occasion Branwell was right, Charlotte complied, though it was very hard to do so.

Clifton went to the foot of the central staircase and hollered up it. "Liston, get down here—people want to see the bones!"

Instantly the timbers above their heads creaked, and the sound of heavy footsteps could be heard as Liston Bradshaw half walked, half tumbled down the stairs to answer his father's call, still wrapped in the blanket in which he had presumably been sleeping, his long, dark hair a wild and tangled mess, his cheeks ruddy from slumber. The moment he saw the ladies in his home, however, he stopped midstair, hastily tucking in his loose shirt, and combing his wild mane back from his face.

"Misses Brontë," he said, two bright spots of pink appearing on his cheeks as he took in the sight of polite company. "And, Branwell, old friend, forgive me—I did not expect visitors on such an afternoon as this!"

"They've come to see the bones, not you, you fool," Bradshaw growled at his son. "They cannot leave well enough alone down there—always sticking their noses in where they are not wanted, nor needed."

Liston seemed to make a determined effort to ignore his father, clapping Branwell on the upper arm. Branwell returned the gesture before they shook each other's hand enthusiastically, like two young stags playing at being fully grown, while Molly watched on like a wide-eyed doe.

"You take them up there," Bradshaw instructed his son. "I'm occupied with"—he gestured at a pile of ledgers on the table—"business."

Charlotte noted the shift in his demeanour with interest. Suddenly there was a shadow of something else that haunted his expression—a wariness, perhaps even guilt. Was it possible that Bradshaw had some scrap of conscience that they would be able to appeal to?

Liston's pleasure and surprise at seeing Branwell and his sisters fled the moment his father mentioned taking them to see the bones, and a great mantle of visible misery settled over him at once.

"Branwell," he said in quiet appeal, "this is no sight for ladies."

"Nor is it a sight any of us seeks, friend," Branwell murmured just loud enough for Charlotte to hear. "We have come to offer refuge to the lost and may need your help."

Liston's dark eyes went from Branwell to Charlotte, who nodded once.

"You shall have it," he whispered. "For in truth I cannot stand to know that the poor soul lies up there all alone a moment longer."

"Sisters?" Charlotte called Anne and Emily, who had gathered near the fire. "The matter is at hand."

6

Anne

Anne felt no small amount of apprehension as she followed the rest of the party, led by Liston Bradshaw, into the oldest and, until recently, locked-away part of Top Withens Hall.

It was the dense and sorrowful atmosphere that weighed the heaviest on her slender shoulders, for there were ghosts in every corner—not the spectral sort that Mr. Dickens liked to write about, but rather the remnants of memories that told of a distant, happier life. A group portrait of Clifton, his wife, and Liston, even from beneath the veil of cobwebs and dust shrouding it, showed a close family full of pride in and warmth for one another. On a windowsill a vase was placed, surrounded by scattered desiccated petals; a shawl was draped over the end of the bannister as if it had been left there only a few moments before, its owner expecting to return to gather it up at any moment.

It seemed to Anne that the moment Mary had died thirteen years ago, Clifton Bradshaw had locked away every trace of the cordial family life that had lived there and buried it along with his wife.

How sad it was, Anne thought, especially for Liston, who would have been aged only twelve when his mother passed away, on the brink of manhood, but still young enough to need his mama. Anne barely remembered her own mother, but at least their papa never sought to erase her memory, or how much they had all loved her and longed for her. In this way, at least, Maria Brontë was present every single day.

Liston halted rather abruptly ahead, his hand on the latch of the chamber, head bowed. Even under the blanket that he wore as a makeshift shawl, Anne could see that he was trembling.

"Shall we go in, my friend?" Branwell asked gently after a moment, placing his hand on Liston's shoulder. "For if it must be done, 'twere well it were done quickly."

Liston took his hand from the latch and stepped back, turning his face away from the room beyond.

"I cannot." He shook his head. "I cannot go in and face it again."

"You need not," Branwell assured him.

"This was my ma's chamber," he told them. "Even to look upon the closed door is to remember the worst hour of my life, never mind the terrible discovery that lies behind it. It is difficult to find the will to open it once more."

"I understand, Liston," Anne said sombrely. "Yet we must make ourselves unafraid. We have come on behalf of that poor lost soul, and on behalf of our father, the Reverend Patrick Brontë, and under the protection of our Christian faith. We are armoured with all the courage we need."

Nodding, Liston opened the door and stood aside.

First Branwell, then Emily and Charlotte entered the room. As she was about to go in, Anne heard something like a gasp, something like a sob, come from one of her sisters, and she stopped at the threshold, looking up at Liston, caught in a moment of uncertainty. Liston offered her his hand, but Anne shook her head.

"This is a task I am equal to," she asserted, more to herself than to Liston, and went in. Behind her she felt Liston follow, though he stayed by the door.

Snow gusted in through the broken pane of the mullioned window. It was so cold it felt as if they were standing out on the hillside, and quite a drift had formed on the rotting floorboards. The sisters reached for one another's hands as Liston drew ragged but heavy curtains over the gaping glass and, once the howling draught was muted, lit some candles, though they threatened to gutter and blink out at any moment. Only when each of them was assembled around a small table did Liston remove a sheet that had been kept in place with loose stones. In silence and shock, they observed the remains.

Anne was unprepared for the swell of grief that rose within her, for she had not anticipated the skeleton to be so small in stature. She had not been prepared to see the bones of a child of perhaps ten years.

Her voice wavering a little, she began to say the Lord's Prayer. As her resolve strengthened, her siblings fell in with her, and between them they created a fortress and built it over this child, and she knew somehow, without having to ask, that each of them, with every word they recited, resolved to do right by this lost soul, no matter what it cost them.

Eventually their prayers fell silent, and Anne straightened her shoulders. There was no time for more tears now.

"Liston, do you have something other than that dirty cloth— perhaps a blanket, something *kind*—in which we can wrap the child?"

Liston pulled the blanket from his shoulders and offered it to

Anne, who laid it over the body before beginning to tuck the cover around the bones, creating a kind of swaddling.

"There, there, little one," she cooed softly as with great tenderness she worked. "You need feel no more fear. We are taking you out of this place, and soon you will be home and in the arms of God, where you will find eternal peace and never-ending love."

7

⮠✦⮠

Emily

It was Branwell who lifted the bundle in his arms with such care that Emily saw a shadow of the man her brother might have been, perhaps still could be. That man was honourable and decent, protective and kind, a man who would cherish his wife and care for his children.

"What shall we do now?" Branwell asked Anne.

"We will take the child home to Haworth," Anne told her sisters and brother. "We'll ask John Brown to open the schoolroom and keep the child there until we are able to talk to Papa, and to your Mr. Nicholls, Charlotte. Then, at the first opportunity, we shall arrange a Christian burial, and we shall cover the cost as best we can so they will not suffer the indignity of a pauper's grave. Though we will never know the name of this poor innocent, nor the cause or date of their death, at least then we can be sure that they will be commended into God's grace under our care."

Emily nodded in agreement, proud to see such clarity and determination in her little sister, for here was a woman with the strength and fortitude to lead the way, while the rest of them strayed from certainty when faced with such tragedy.

"Liston, old man." Branwell turned to his friend, who had watched them gather the child up without protest. "You are certain to pay a price for allowing us to take away the remains. Your father is not a man to stand interference, and I know, from all you've told me, he is inclined to violence."

"I love my father, but he has done wrong by this child, Branwell," Liston said. "Perhaps he will raise his fist to me, but I am a man grown. I can stand up to any."

Even as he spoke so defiantly, Liston looked unbearably young and uncertain.

"There is something more," he said, frowning deeply. "Pa wanted to keep it hidden, and until this moment I didn't see that it mattered, but the truth is, there is a date. At least we know a year that the body could not have been hidden before."

"Liston, what do you mean?" Emily asked him. "If there is anything that will help us to name the child or add any detail to the burial, then you must reveal it."

Emily watched as Liston went to the fireplace, stepping over the rubble that had once formed the chimney breast. Reaching into the cavity where the bones had been found, he brought out something small enough to be entirely enclosed within his fist.

"This were round its neck," he said, delivering it into Emily's hands.

Emily frowned at the object that lay lightly in her palm.

"A medallion," she told her sisters as she closely examined the object under candlelight. "Here on the front an engraving of the Virgin Mary, and the date eighteen thirty. And on the back these symbols and stars, and another date that appears to be roughly etched: eighteen thirty-two. Here." She moved her palm around for all to see.

"Eighteen thirty-two is but thirteen years ago," Anne said. "The child was placed here much more recently than we assumed."

"Well within living memory," Charlotte added.

"It was the year my mother died," Liston said heavily. "The year my father locked away this room and all the secrets it contained. Do you suppose . . . ? No, I cannot say it aloud."

"Say what aloud, Liston?" Emily asked him.

"That my father may have known that the bones were interred within this room?"

Liston looked so lost, so afraid that he might be speaking the truth, that Emily wished she were able to reassure him. She was not, however.

"We cannot know," Emily said. "At least not yet, Liston. But my family has a knack for detecting the truth, no matter how well it might be hidden." She looked in turn at all gathered there as she spoke. "From this moment on, we must assume the circumstances of this child's death to be most heinous and wicked. And regard this room as the scene of a murder."

8

Emily

Emily covertly observed Liston Bradshaw from under her lashes as he ate a bowl of mutton stew with great gusto. Branwell had insisted Liston join them for dinner with Papa, and Papa's curate Mr. Bell Nicholls and she and her sisters had concurred at once. After all, Liston had willingly courted his father's fury at their bidding, and the night outside was as dangerous as any ever was. In truth, now she was safely home, as the gales wound ever tighter around and around their little house, she couldn't quite believe that all that had occurred wasn't some fantastical creation of her imagination, a gothic Gondal tale, even if the aching chill remaining in the tips of her toes was conclusive evidence that it was not. So very practised was she at spinning worlds out of thin air that sometimes she did rather forget which version of her life was reality. Then again, perhaps it didn't matter which was which, not when each felt exactly as true as the next.

In any event, the least they could do was to offer Liston sustenance and shelter. To say that Tabby was not best pleased by their guest was something of an understatement. So convinced was Tabby that the sins of the father *should* be visited on the children that she regarded Liston rather as though he were sprouting horns from the top of his head and a rather delightful tail was swishing nonchalantly away at the back of his chair. Liston was not often seen in the village, so it came as something of a surprise to Emily to note that the Bradshaw boy was of a most pleasing countenance, his long, thick dark hair swept back from his pale Yorkshire complexion, and eyes as dark as a raven's wing. He looked as he lived, free from society in the heart of the wilderness, and Emily envied him.

"With your permission, may Liston stay with us tonight, Papa?" Branwell asked after some minutes of weary silence. He covered his father's hand with his for a moment, his thoughtful touch joining his near-blind father to the sound of his voice. "He may sleep in my room—I'll take the floor. Not even one so well acquainted with the shepherds' paths as Liston should make the journey to Top Withens at such an hour in these conditions. Besides, after his father discovers what he has done, returning may prove difficult. No one knows how to hold a grudge like Clifton Bradshaw."

"It will be difficult, but it will be done on the morrow," Liston said at once, with a resolve that Emily found intriguing. "I must return to Top Withens and face my father's wrath. Pa is a . . . a hard man, but though it must seem strange and remote to most, Top Withens is my home; its earth is in my blood and lungs. If I can't return there, then I shall die, like a fish dragged out of a river."

If those words had been spoken with any less intensity or certainty, then Emily would have been tempted to laugh at such a proclamation, but it was clear by the hot flush on his otherwise fair skin that Liston was deadly serious. Here was a man who loved the land he had grown up on as if it were his mother; indeed since his own mother was taken, perhaps it had been. That was a devotion that she could understand. But there was something else to Liston that she hadn't yet quite fathomed: a kind of wariness. He looked like a haunted man, as if there were a shadow at his back that had not been cast by him. Perhaps he knew more of his father's deeds than he had yet been able to speak aloud. He would have been a child when his mother died, about twelve years old, not old enough to have any control over his life, but of an age to detect wrongdoing.

"You each did a good thing this day, my children," Papa said finally. He turned to look at each of his children as he spoke, though Emily could not be sure that he could distinguish her from her sisters. The deep Irish rumble of his accent hadn't faded, though, and she always took great comfort in it, even when it was about to deliver a lecture. "Even so, you should have come to me first, for the duty you carried out this afternoon is mine or my curate's. No matter how the Lord decides to test me by taking my sight, I am the defender and the shepherd of this parish and shall be until the day I am in my grave. To make decisions and allowances for me is to disrespect me. Am I clear?"

"Yes, Papa," Emily and her sisters muttered in unison, joined a moment later by Branwell.

"Sight or no, I am in my prime, and I am certain that Arthur and I could have retrieved the poor child between us, and in doing so completed our duty as men of God. Branwell behaving so impetuously is one thing, but young women were never meant to be curates or parsons—it is not in God's plan."

"Of course not, not when curates are all so utterly hopeless," Emily muttered, catching the eye of Anne, who repressed a small smile in return. Despite the sadness of their mission, there had been a kind of camaraderie between the four of them today that was almost as it had once been when they were children: all of them together, even Liston, as they made their way home with his stout pony at their sides. They had been a band of confederates and adventurers: it had given them purpose and solidarity anew.

"What I should very much like to see you do, Emily Jane, is lend your musical talent to the great lord and lady who requested your presence at their charitable musical evening at Oakhope."

"How did you . . ." Emily began.

"I am rather well acquainted with Lady Hartley," Mr. Nicholls said somewhat smugly. "It has been my great pleasure to assist her in distributing her charitable beneficence when she is in the county. Today I received a letter from her informing me of the invitation. You must be incredibly flattered, Miss Brontë. Not least because Lady Hartley has never met you."

"That may well be a deciding factor in why the request was issued in the first place," Charlotte muttered. "In any case, you agree, Papa? Emily must say yes, must she not? It would reflect very poorly upon our family name if she refused, would it not?"

"I am inclined to agree, Charlotte," Papa said. "However, Emily is her own person, and the decision must be hers alone. I have always treated you each as agents of your own destiny. This matter is no different."

Charlotte audibly harrumphed as the table fell into silence once more, a moment of quiet that Emily found most soothing. It had been such a day that she could no more think of regal ladies' recitals than she could of writing of the strange events—at least not yet.

For now they were tasked with discovering who had concealed the death of the lost child behind the chimney breast in a room that was supposed to have been locked these past thirteen years.

In any event there was no way that Mr. Arthur Bell Nicholls, with his heavy brows sheltering earnest eyes and his straight, sensible nose would have seen the mystery in the bones. Emily was sure that he was a man who lacked even the smallest morsel of imagination. If his face was a true reflection of his mind, then he surely must have been the very dullest creature on this earth. God forbid that

Charlotte should ever think of reciprocating the fellow's adoration for her, for if she did marry the man, Charlotte would surely be dead of boredom within the year, though Emily supposed her sister would get access to Lady Hartley's drawing room.

"Today's task was most certainly not one Lady Hartley would approve of," Mr. Nicholls said, doing his best to be stern and, Emily was certain, husbandly. "One might question the wisdom of taking your sisters on such an endeavour, Branwell."

Before Emily was able to bite back, Branwell answered, "Sir, I regret to inform you that my sisters took *me*, and indeed they carried out the whole dreadful business with a great deal more robustness and fortitude than I or perhaps any man could have done." Branwell's smile was wry. "As for myself, today's exertions have illustrated quite clearly that I am not the young man I used to be, for each limb is as heavy as stone."

"Today you were marvellous," Emily said, only because she believed it to be true. "You led the way as you always used to, with all of us following behind. And after all was said and done, you guided us safely home, Mr. Liston and his trusty friend Piper the pony included. You are a remarkable fellow, Branwell, when you allow yourself to be."

For a moment Branwell held Emily's gaze, a silent message of affection passing between them. It was impossible not to note the pallor of his cheek or the blue shadows beneath his eyes, the hollows around his bones that grew increasingly deep over the weeks. She thought of the skull of the child she had seen today, and suddenly it was as if she could see her own brother's skull grinning across the table, stripped of all that remained of him.

"My dearest Branwell, please," she said with an urgency and emotion that took all seated around the table by surprise, "won't you be our captain again, brother dear? Won't you release the hurt and ignominy of the past year from your heart and return to us, for though you are very foolish and almost always wrong, we need you so very much. And if you are ours once again, then we shall keep you safe from harm. I swear it."

There was a long moment of silence as the four took one another's hands, remembering one another as they had been long ago when the summers were endless and there was never a care in the world.

"Emily is quite correct: it is time, my son, to return to your life." Patrick broke the moment, his tone kind but stern. "You have suffered pain, but the pain you have suffered is of your own making. You may have peace, happiness and your own home, but not without accepting your responsibilities. It is your duty, my son, to realise the promise that has always been yours, the potential that your family has sacrificed so much to support. To waste your gifts is a terrible sin. Look at your sisters, see the seemly and orderly way they live their lives and take inspiration from them."

"Papa," Charlotte said gently, seeing the pain on their brother's face. "Emily has never once been seemly, and I know full well that I am not orderly. The best of us is Anne, and even she was prepared to take on Bradshaw with her own dear hands today. You have raised brave, good children, Papa, but not seemly ones. And besides, perhaps even yet it might be one of your daughters who saves the family's fortunes."

"In any case," Anne interjected, looking at Liston, who had been rapt with attention throughout, "perhaps we might spare poor Liston these family squabbles, for these are private matters, and we embarrass him."

"Not so, Miss Anne," Liston said, with a shy smile, "for I do love to hear a family speak so to one another, with kindness and even in disagreement with . . . well, with love, I suppose. It ain't . . . it's not a way of life I am familiar with, and to see it played out so gives me great comfort and hope that one day I may find a wife who would willingly make a family with me as loving as this one."

"You are always welcome at the table, my boy," Patrick said, nodding at Liston, "as is your father and every sinner in search of redemption. For it is never too late to seek God's forgiveness if your heart is pure."

"Well, on that note, Liston, may I suggest that you and I brave the cold and seek out a well-earned ale or two? After all, the Bull is virtually on our doorstep. It would seem inconsiderate not to." Branwell rose from his seat.

"Branwell, don't mock Papa so," Charlotte admonished her brother.

"I do not mock him," Branwell said cheerfully, bending down to kiss his father on the cheek. "Papa says it is never too late to seek redemption. That leaves me plenty of time to have another drink and sin a little more."

9

Charlotte

All their party had stood sentinel as the small bundle had been carried from the church into the back room of the schoolhouse, where it was determined it would be best kept until a funeral could be conducted. It was somehow more seemly and comfortable than the cellars beneath the King's Arms that were commonly used as a mortuary. Charlotte tarried a little longer after her family returned to the parsonage, taking her time to light a few lanterns. It might have seemed foolish to some, but when she had been a child mourning the loss of her mama and feeling so desperately alone, there had been no greater comfort than the thought of a lamp keeping the dark at bay.

John Brown waited patiently for her outside, and when she had completed her task, he locked the door behind them. Bidding Mr. Brown good night, she fixed her gaze on the window of the brightly lit dining room, where her sisters were waiting for her, and at once was pinioned by a near suffocating weight of premonition. Suddenly she somehow *knew* with terrible certainty that to continue further with the mystery of the bones would put all of them into great danger. It hardly made sense, yet she was filled with such dread as she had never previously known. Caught between that lonely lamplit schoolroom and her own dear little house, she felt trapped.

A choice had to be made, and she was not at all certain what it should be.

"I cannot see how this mystery can ever be resolved," Charlotte said as she entered the dining room. Emily was reclining on the sofa, staring upwards, her stockinged feet resting on top of Keeper's broad head; Anne busied herself picking dead leaves from the holly that garlanded the mantelpiece. "That the bones were concealed at some point during the last thirteen years is all we know for certain. There are no footprints in the mud to follow, no hidden hideaways to discover. Despite your assertions at Top Withens, Emily, I believe that we have done all we can here. Tomorrow the child will receive a Christian burial, and thereafter we should let the matter be closed."

"I believe that you are incorrect," Anne said rather quietly.

"I suspected you might," Charlotte said wearily. The more Anne grew in confidence, the more troublesome and less compliant her opinionated sister became.

"Indeed, I believe that if any are able to find the root of this great wrongdoing, then it is we three. We learnt a great deal from the Elizabeth Chester business, and though our subsequent endeavours might not have been quite as stimulating, we have learnt a great deal more since. We are experienced detectors now who have divined the best way to coax information out of an individual. We excel at observation, paying attention to every detail lest one of them is the key to the matter. And we are clever—exceedingly so. Not even to try would vex us all, so instead of beginning with what we don't know, which I own is a considerable amount, let us start with what we do."

"I admit this matter fills me with a sense of great unease." Charlotte took a seat at the table, the little spaniel Flossy sitting beside her, nuzzling her head under Charlotte's palm until Charlotte's fingers found exactly the spot under her ear where she liked most to be scratched. "It will sound fanciful to you, I am certain, but did you not feel that there was a kind of sickness within Top Withens Hall? For all of Old Bess's housekeeping and Liston's good nature and clear devotion to the place, it was almost as if the building itself was full of some kind of malice."

"That does sound fanciful," Emily said, sitting up suddenly, "but yes, I had much the same impression. However, the reason we visited was a very grim one, Charlotte. Should we have called by on a summer's day without knowledge of the bones, I daresay we would have had a quite different impression. And no ghosts spoke to me while we were there, so I must assume there are none."

"A terrible feeling is not a rational reason to turn away from the work that is required to resolve the truth," Anne said firmly. "Indeed, that something awful happening should elicit awful feelings seems entirely sensible."

"Perhaps," Charlotte said, "but we must also think of our real work, our purpose. Perhaps Aylott and Jones will agree to publish our words, and thereafter we may be called upon for more. Should we not answer the calling that will bring forth our novels and thus, with God's grace, grant us a living that will allow us to stay together at home with Papa? Don't you agree, Emily?"

"You are frightened, Charlotte," Emily said, not unkindly. Even so, the observation cut through her sister most keenly.

"I am not," Charlotte countered. "I simply want my life to move forward, to be done with the tedium of teaching, the fear of poverty and homelessness. I want to have the time and freedom to write every day, simply because I cannot do otherwise. Detecting delays that moment from being realised."

"We all want that, but we have a duty to do what is right," Anne reproached her mildly, "to ourselves as much as to others. We have never been women who look away from injustice, Charlotte."

"And what can we three do that is any different from what the constable or the courthouse might?"

"We can care about a lost child no one has ever missed or looked for," Anne said.

"And we shall seek out every trace of information there is," Emily said. Charlotte was not surprised that Emily was in agreement with Anne; Emily never seemed to be afraid of anything, so certain was she of her own immortality. "We will talk to anyone we can find who was involved with Top Withens in eighteen thirty-two and listen to their stories. We can trace the many rumours about Bradshaw to their root, and sift through all the facts we can gather, seeking out the nuggets of truth that will reveal it all. For that, Charlotte, is the very business of being a detector."

"But there is no more information!" Charlotte was frustrated with her sister's glib assertions. "Do you propose we seek to conjure up a ghost and question it?"

"There are no ghosts; I already told you," Emily said. "However, we may yet be able to question the dead."

"Oh really, Emily, how so?" Charlotte asked rather shortly.

"By a close examination of the remains, drawing and annotating every detail so that we may have a record to refer to once the burial is complete."

"Emily, you cannot mean . . ." Anne began, her eyes wide with horror. "You mean to make the bones an item of . . . reference? That is a desecration!"

"Medicine learns from the dead," Emily said. "Think what we learnt from the single bone we discovered at Chester Grange. And what better honour could we do the child than allow their own body to shed some light on their fate? I am convinced. We must go to the schoolhouse and examine the remains with analytical care, as Mr. Goddard of the London detectives did. He was the first to note that a tiny mark on a bullet can lead back to a weapon, then to the perpetrator. We may not know what we are looking at—yet—but we must look nevertheless."

"Then we must all go," Charlotte said to Anne, for it seemed that the choice had been made, and she gained a little comfort from knowing that whatever happened next, it was out of her hands. "For if we don't accompany Emily, and she discovers something important, we shall never hear the end of it."

And yet as they headed out of the door and into the dark, Charlotte felt the danger that had been lurking since the moment they had entered Top Withens Hall draw just a little closer.

10

❦

Anne

The night bristled with ice as they left the parsonage by the back door with Keeper at their heels, the spare key to the schoolhouse tucked into Anne's sleeve.

"I am not sure that hound is conducive to discretion," Charlotte whispered as Keeper immediately launched himself into a thick drift and rolled around so frantically that he created his own localised blizzard.

"He's just pleased to be out of the house," Emily replied in equally low tones. "Give him a moment, and then he shall be our loyal protector, as silent as the grave and as deadly as a wolf."

Her assertion was somewhat undermined, however, by Keeper's joyful salvo of barks as he shook himself free of the snow, immediately racing off into the dark, chasing down an intoxicating scent.

"You can't hold it against him," Emily said as she watched him vanish into the dark. "Who wouldn't want to run through the pristine snow under the bright moon, given half the chance?"

Anne smiled; despite the grave circumstances, it was uplifting to see the simple pleasure the dog took in life. It gladdened her heart to remember that for every dark corner and unjust hurt in the world, there was a place of light, hope and goodness. Ensuring the latter outweighed the former was surely every person's greatest task on this earth.

Tucked under her arm she had all the equipment she deemed necessary for their examination: her drawing box and writing slope. They carried a lamp each and a can of hot, strong tea that Emily had prepared to help steel their nerves. Anne had fetched the spare schoolhouse key from Papa's bureau, feeling a terrible thrill as she concealed it in her sleeve. Surely God would forgive a little sin if it led to the greater good?

But just as Anne was about to turn the key in the lock, she heard a sound to strike dread into her heart: the voice of one Arthur Bell Nicholls.

"Ladies," he questioned them with an air of authority he did not wear with a great deal of comfort, "may I ask what you are about at such an hour?"

"You may not," Emily said. "Good night to you, sir."

"If I may be so bold . . ."

Emily sighed heavily, and Anne bit back a smile. She would never be as openly contemptuous of Mr. Nicholls as her sister was, but it was true that his laborious effort at gentlemanly conduct was surely one of his least appealing characteristics. Much as had Papa, he had worked diligently to free himself from a life of poverty in Ireland, but unlike Papa, though undoubtedly a good and well-intentioned man, he had all the gravitas and moral authority of one of Tabby's jellied calf's feet.

"It is close to midnight," Mr. Nicholls said. "I feel duty bound to say, as your father's second, and your voluntary protector, that it is rather dangerous for three young women to be abroad unaccompanied. I am afraid that I must insist—"

"But we are not afraid, Mr. Nicholls," Anne replied sweetly. "Indeed, we are in sight of our home, guarded very closely by Keeper, or shall be when he returns. And besides, who should we be afraid of meeting in the night, when the only suspect abroad is you, sir? Unless you are suggesting we should be fearful of you, Mr. Nicholls?"

"I, well . . . I . . . I . . . that is to say . . ." Anne felt sorry for making him feel so ill at ease—only a little, but even so, the remorse was there.

"The truth is," Mr. Nicholls said when he finally found his voice, "that I find myself unable to sleep. This whole business, the discovery of the bones at Top Withens, the pure evil of it, all the talk in the village of the devil, is playing on my mind. It is as if you brought a great darkness down off the moor with you this night—" Mr. Nicholls stopped himself, as though just now remembering the tender minds of the three ladies he was talking to. "So it occurred to me to sit with the deceased and offer up prayer until the dawn rises and all is prepared for burial."

"Well, you can't," Emily said bluntly. "Off you go, back to bed."

"Arthur." Charlotte stepped in front of them both, elbowing Emily back a step or two, and the sound of her voice speaking his given name brought a look something like ecstasy to his stupidly sensible face. "What Emily lacks the social graces to express adequately is that we three have already resolved to do the same. We have come prepared and in readiness for a long night of . . . observation. And I do believe that some may feel it inappropriate if we were to spend all night with an unmarried gentleman."

"I see. Yes, I see, Charlotte," Arthur said, though Anne was fairly certain that he would have agreed with absolutely anything that Charlotte said, no matter what it was. "Of course, of course, you are very much correct."

"That you thought of such a thing is admirable and shows your great character," Charlotte told him. "But let us keep watch this night. And perhaps, sir, if you return to your room, you may keep watch over us?" Charlotte gestured to John Brown's cottage, where Arthur lodged.

"It would be my great honour, Charlotte," he said, taking her gloved hand in his.

Anne felt a pang of sorrow for the curate when her sister removed her hand at once and despatched him with a return to her usual formality. "Thank you, Mr. Nicholls. Good night to you, sir."

"You should both be ashamed of yourselves," Anne hissed at Charlotte and Emily as she opened the door at last. "You, Emily, speaking to poor Mr. Nicholls as if he were the village idiot, and you, Charlotte, playing on his affections to manipulate him."

"Mr. Nicholls does not have any extraordinary affection for me," Charlotte said as they entered the room. "It is simply that he holds all of Papa's children in great esteem, as is proper."

Under normal circumstances Anne would have expected Emily to have made the best of this situation to tease Charlotte until she had at least made her sister stamp her foot and turn red in the face. Not tonight, though, for as they set down the lanterns, the gravity of the situation fell over them as heavily as a mourning veil.

The remains of the child had been laid on a small table, the school desks and benches pushed to one side. The lanterns Charlotte had lit earlier had gone out, and it was particularly dark until Anne walked into the middle of the room, holding her lamp aloft.

"We promised this poor soul prayer," she said, "and we shall pray as we work. Emily, how shall we proceed?"

"Charlotte, you make a written note of everything you see," Emily said. "Everything, no matter how small or inconsequential it might seem: the number of teeth in the skull, any marks or fractures in the bones or skull, measurements of each bone—and label them as per Papa's medical dictionary. Anne and I shall draw every detail until we will have created a full record." She hesitated, meeting Anne's gaze. "We shall be required to pick up the bones and examine them from all angles. You begin at the head, Anne. I shall begin at the feet."

Since she had wrapped the child, Anne took it upon herself to unwrap the bones, and as she did, she heard the faintest chime of something metallic fall on the wooden floor. Anne didn't remember Liston concealing the medallion in the bundle, yet there it was.

Reluctantly she picked it up.

"This must be drawn and recorded too," she said. "Then it can be buried with the child." Her sisters nodded their assent, and they set about their work, each one considering this the most important task they had yet undertaken.

To Anne, their softly murmured prayers were as luminous as any lamp, circling them in a halo of warmth.

The night wore on, still and in near silence as they laboured, each one of them taking great and tender care over every bone. After a while it felt almost as if they were at prayer, lost in their communion with thought and every minute detail of what remained of the child. Yes, Anne believed, as devastating as this task was, it was a prayer not to death, but to life, and how very precious and miraculous it is.

And then a sharp bang came from the main schoolroom, and the sound of footsteps scuttling away.

"What on earth . . . !" Anne gasped, twisting in her seat to stare into the shadows. They all froze as they heard the locked schoolhouse door rattle insistently, as if some poor spirit were desperate to escape.

"Could it be . . . ?" Charlotte did not complete her whispered sentence, which remained for a moment misting in the cold air.

"Whatever it is, it wants to be free." Emily took up a lamp, and Anne hastened to join her as she swept what little light they had away to investigate, opening the door into the school hall.

"Lift the lamp a little higher," Charlotte murmured to Emily. The room appeared empty, the neat rows of benches and slates left ready for the morrow. Anne was just about to let out a sigh of relief when she heard a movement in the far corner, and the shadowy figure of—of *a child* darted towards the door.

"Oh dear God!" Anne cried out as the poor creature vainly clawed at the locked door. "We must set the poor spirit free!"

Without another thought, Anne progressed at speed to the door, fumbling for the key that she had tucked into her sleeve, until Emily took three steps closer and the lamplight fell upon the supernatural child.

And they could see at once that it was no ghost at all, but rather the scrawny and sleep-crumpled personage of one Master Joseph Earnshaw, a boy from the village who often ran their more discreet detecting errands for them.

"Joseph Earnshaw! What is the meaning of this escapade?" Anne grabbed the boy by his ear and dragged him into the pool of light, where the three sisters encircled him. The boy looked terrified. "What are you doing out of your bed in the middle of the night? I am sure if your mother and father found you'd gone, they'd be beside themselves with worry!"

"I only meant to be a minute, miss," Joseph said. "I made myself stay up till I thought the whole village would be asleep. It's just . . . well, I wanted to see the bones, miss. And I wasn't expecting you to be here. I came in through the back window, but when I thought I was discovered, I took fright and tried the front door, which turned out to be locked."

"Well, you've learnt a grave lesson tonight," Emily told the quivering boy sternly. "When you are escaping the scene of the crime, you never exit through the front door."

"Come to see the bones, Joseph?" Anne admonished him, horrified. "What a little ghoul you are. Are you not familiar enough with death, Joseph? Haven't you lost your own sister and brother before they could walk? What on earth could you want to see such an awful thing for?"

"You were looking at them, miss," Joseph defended himself robustly. "And you are drawing them and writing about them. I saw you all from my hiding place, peering at the body."

"For scientific purposes," Charlotte told him. "Not because we wish to, but because we must. To try to discover the identity of the poor child. You have no such reason to be here, young man."

"I know, miss." Joseph's shoulders slumped. "I am just interested, like you, miss. I ain't never seen no one murdered before. I couldn't stop thinking about it, and it scared me, so I thought it was better to go and look rather than have all these imaginings going on in my head."

"Well, in the first instance," Anne said, her tone a little more gentle, "we do not know that the child was murdered, not yet. And in the second, I suppose there is some logic to your reasoning. Nevertheless, you are to go back to your bed this minute, Joseph Earnshaw. Do you hear me?"

"Yes, miss," Joseph said demurely.

"Though I must say, your vocabulary is coming on very well," Charlotte said. "If you stay at your studies, and in your bed every night, you may have a very bright future before you."

"Thank you, miss." Joseph straightened his shoulders a little.

"And," Emily said, "if you are very wise, you will not tell a soul of what you saw here, and in return we shall not tell your parents of your misdeeds, which will no doubt save you a walloping. Is that clear?"

"Yes, miss," the boy agreed.

Anne unlocked the door and shooed Joseph out into the night, keeping watch until he vanished into the narrow two-up two-down cottage he lived in with his family just at the top of Main Street.

"He's a caution, that boy," Anne said, shaking her head.

"And yet," Charlotte said, "despite his terrible impertinence, I find I rather like him."

"He has spirit," Emily said, "which is so much preferable to being one."

At last their work was complete. Silently Charlotte compiled her notes, and Emily folded their drawings into her sketchbook as Anne carefully returned the medallion to the bones and rewrapped them in the blanket.

As she locked the schoolhouse door, Anne was pleased to see Keeper bounding out of the snow towards them, and somehow there, yapping at his feet, was Anne's dog, Flossy, as though Keeper had deliberately returned to the parsonage to liberate Anne's little friend. She bent down to embrace the damp creature, hugging her close.

"Ah, our loyal protector," Emily said, ruffling Keeper's ears. "I knew you wouldn't let us down." Anne was weary, but felt a sense of peace as she and her sisters bid one another good night. That was until she felt the touch of something cold slide against her skin. Feeling some strange object trapped in her sleeve, she shook it out into her palm.

It was the medallion.

11

✎∾❀∾✎

Anne

The service was short, the interment brief, and a simple marker stone set in the furthest corner of the crowded graveyard was all there was to say that that day a child had been buried. Scarcely a week went by when a local infant wasn't interred by Anne's father, or these days more likely by Mr. Nicholls. And yet Anne hadn't wept so hard standing by an open grave since they had buried her father's curate William Weightman almost three years ago now. That day she had done her best to hide her tears, afraid that her sisters would see how she wept to watch a man she had never had a hope of and yet had hoped for lowered into the ground. The sorrow was of a different nature, but just as intense.

They hadn't expected any more mourners, save themselves and Liston, and yet just before her father had begun to speak, a fine carriage drawn by six beautiful black horses pulled up, and the coachman, a tall, top-hatted gentleman, handed down a fine lady wearing a feathered black bonnet, the veil drawn down over her face. However, Anne and her sisters did not need to see the woman's face to know that Lady Hartley herself had seen fit to attend the interment.

"Such a fine woman," Charlotte whispered as Lady Hartley took her place amongst the small collection of mourners, standing beside Mr. Nicholls with her head bowed. "To go out of her way to be here, at the burial of a forgotten child. One can tell she is so much more than merely a title and money. She is a woman of immense character and decency."

"It does indeed show a kind of humanity," Anne had conceded, "for her to trouble herself with what so many in her position might consider inconsequential."

As Papa had begun to speak, the snow had fallen, like a soft embrace, cradling the child and bearing him away to a place of peace at last.

After it was done, Anne put her gloved hand on Emily's, as Mr. Nicholls escorted Lady Hartley in their direction.

"She cannot come into our house," Charlotte whispered, "not on this day, when it looks only one step above a pauper's hovel."

"It is our home, and I love it more than I could any castle," Emily said. "However, I agree. I do not wish for another person in our house today."

"Reverend Brontë, Misses Brontë." Lady Hartley curtseyed, and the sisters followed suit in unison. "I do hope you don't find my presence intrusive. My coachman, Hemming, and Mr. Nicholls informed me of the discovery of the bones and of your intervention. I simply couldn't let the day pass without paying my respects to the poor abandoned soul, and to offer you each my sincere thanks for not letting the matter rest. Too many human souls are cast aside like rubble in this dreadfully cruel and inhumane world. To know that such care has been taken over one so humble is indeed inspiring."

"We were very glad to do it, Lady Hartley." Charlotte nodded. "No soul should ever go without a Christian burial."

Lady Hartley smiled. "You may know that Lord Hartley and I do our best to improve the lives of local children. I wonder if I might trouble you to call on me before I return to London to discuss how I might best help you with this matter of the bones and any others that need my attention."

"We should be honoured, madam," Charlotte said, doing her best—rather poorly, Anne thought—to hide her delight at the invitation.

"Thank you, Miss . . . I believe from the way Mr. Nicholls describes you, you must be Charlotte. Arthur admires you very much."

"Oh well." Mr. Nicholls coughed rather profusely. "If you'll pardon me, Lady Hartley, I believe I will escort the reverend to the parsonage before the cold gets to his bones."

"I am indeed," Charlotte said as Mr. Nicholls guided her papa home. "This is my sister Anne, and I believe you already know of Emily."

"Ah yes, Emily. I do so hope you will accept our invitation to play at Oakhope. I hear you have a great talent."

"Other matters have rather overtaken me," Emily said, nodding at the grave. "But I suppose that I must, as Papa and my sisters are so very keen for me to agree."

"I'm delighted." Lady Hartley smiled. "I must take my leave, but once again, I am delighted to have made your acquaintance."

"You suppose you must." Charlotte shook her head at Emily as the carriage pulled away.

"I agreed to do as you wish, didn't I?" Emily asked.

"You did," Anne said. "And with such good grace and humour, one might have mistaken you for a great lady yourself."

"Well, greatness is something one is born with," Emily said. "I suspect I was born with rather more than most."

———

Now all of them, save Papa and Mr. Nicholls, crowded into the small kitchen, warming themselves by the bread oven and eating Charlotte's favourite seed cake, while Tabby muttered furiously under her breath about the incursion into her sacred space.

"Why not sit in a room tha' has for sitting?" she demanded once or twice but to no avail. No one wanted to be at the front of the little house, where they could see the freshly dug grave steadily disappearing below the latest fall of snow.

"Do you plan to return to Top Withens today, Liston?" Anne asked the young man, who was especially quiet, standing in the corner looking rather lost and out of place.

"Aye, I suppose I do, Miss Anne," he said, though there was no pleasure in his voice at the thought.

"What will happen? Will your papa be very angry?" Anne asked him.

Liston shrugged. "I'd say so, more'n likely," he said. "No matter, as I must go back—my horses and my sheep will need feeding, and my pa don't pay much mind to the dogs except to take a stick to 'em. . . . I expect he's drunk himself to sleep. With a bit of luck, I won't have to face him today."

"I shall come with you," Branwell offered. "We may face your father together."

"I cannot ask that of you," Liston said. "If Pa is sensible to the world, he will be a vile man that no one decent should have to encounter."

"Which is why Branwell is the perfect companion," Emily said, grinning at her brother, who smiled wryly in return.

"Or we could all come with you," Anne offered. "Perhaps your father would be more temperate in the presence of ladies."

"I am certain that would not be the case," Liston said ruefully. "I do remember a time when I was a little lad and my ma was alive when Pa was gentle and kind as could be, to her above all. I think sometimes her death robbed him of his heart, and he buried it alongside her. I am afraid you would be offended if you were to see or hear him this day, Miss Anne."

Anne thought of the medallion that she had placed in the tea caddy in the dining room, without mentioning it to her sisters, for fear it would unsettle them. She had thought of dropping it into the open grave, but it seemed to her, perhaps foolishly, that the child had rejected the object. And now she was utterly uncertain what to do with it. Perhaps she could return it to Top Withens and never think of it again?

For she would like very much never to think of it again.

"I do believe Anne is right," Emily said. "Though the snow is yet falling, we should return to Top Withens Hall alongside Liston. It will serve a double purpose: to buffer Liston against his father's fury and to act as a distraction while the other matters are discreetly looked into."

"What other matters?" Charlotte asked. Of all of them, Charlotte seemed the most worn through by their recent hours of activity, her tiny frame crumpled and creased. Anne worried for her. Charlotte was so powerful in her nature, her thoughts and speech that it was easy to forget she was perhaps the most delicate of them all, the smallest and slightest made.

Before she continued, Emily glanced at Liston as if she was uncertain of sharing her thoughts with him.

"We must examine the chimney breast again," she said, "in daylight and with a good lamp. There may be more evidence that has yet to be seen. From the broken glass that fell into the room, we can surmise that the room was broken into. That is no small undertaking, given that that side of the house faces out to what is almost a sheer drop of rock. If the forced entry is tied to the bones—and it seems very likely that it must be—then it may be that Bess or even Clifton Bradshaw himself can identify a time when it might have occurred."

"Pa says it must have been my mother," Liston said dourly. "He said he reckoned it was her spirit fighting her way back out of the cold grave and into our home to scream us awake."

"Say what you may about your father, Liston," Emily said, "but he does have a natural talent for the gothic."

"That's 'cause he's the devil," Tabby said stoutly, taking them all by surprise, "or in the devil's pocket anyways."

"Come now, Tabby," Anne said. "Liston, please reassure dear Tabitha that your father does not deal with Satan."

Much to Anne's surprise, Liston was silent for a long moment, his cheeks colouring brightly.

"I knew I spoke the truth," Tabby said, tossing a handful of salt over her left shoulder before spitting on it.

"I wouldn't say he was in league with the devil," Liston said. "He was devout once, but something happened before Ma passed. He changed his views, and now he don't believe in such things as heaven and hell. Indeed, after Ma died there was a time when the house was often alive at night: comings and goings, carriages and horses, chanting voices and strange music. Those nights Bess would come and sit in my room and keep me there like she was guarding me. I tried to ask her about it once, before her mind began to wander back to happier times, but she would not speak of it—gave me a clip round the ear for asking."

"This is a bad to-do and no mistake," Tabby said unhappily. "The son of a devil in my kitchen and your father a parson."

"Tabby, Liston is not the son of a devil," Anne said, "but in any event we shall take him out of your kitchen directly and escort him back to Top Withens as Emily suggests."

"Mrs. Aykroyd, I will go at once, but, Branwell and Misses Brontë, if you want to return to seek further knowledge about this matter, I will aid you. But I pray you do not come tonight. I would not have my good friends witness my pa this eve—it would shame me."

"Then we shall visit you tomorrow as soon as the sun is up," Anne said, looking up into Liston's face with a good deal of warmth. "You have shown great fortitude, sir, and you shall not be abandoned by the Brontës. I swear it."

Later, as the fire made the dining room cosy, and the shutters closed out the night, the sisters sat together at the table, Anne writing and Emily comparing the drawings she had made with a book on anatomy she had acquired. Charlotte could not seem to settle to any occupation.

"I shall not accompany you to Top Withens tomorrow," Charlotte said, frowning deeply.

"You shall not?" Anne asked her. "Do you still feel weak, Charlotte, dear? Perhaps you should take to bed now."

"I do," Charlotte said, "but I have another plan."

"Which is, sister?" Emily asked—she was always fascinated by plans, it seemed.

"To take our observations, our drawings and notes to Celia Prescott in Bradford. If anyone might see what we do not, it will be she; I have already written to her to tell her of my arrival."

It was a good idea, Anne thought, and she could see that Emily did too, even though she might secretly be vexed that she hadn't thought of it herself.

They had first met Mrs. Prescott, the wife of a Bradford doctor, when they had been searching for any trace of the missing Elizabeth Chester. It had been immediately clear to clever, quick Celia that the sisters had been visiting her under false pretences, and the moment she had been drawn into their cause, she was a willing collaborator. Celia had studied medicine alongside her husband, and she lacked only the formal qualification required to call herself a doctor.

"It is very far to go alone in this weather," Anne worried.

"I shall take a coach from Keighley," Charlotte said with a little wrinkle of her nose, "though it is such an odious mode of transport. I already asked John Brown, and he says there will likely be a service tomorrow as the main roads are passable."

"Excellent," Emily said. "And tomorrow night we three shall meet again to see what we have discovered."

"You make us sound like Shakespeare's witches," Charlotte said with a small smile that showed she wasn't entirely displeased with the idea.

"Well," Anne said, "I am almost certain that hard toil and great trouble lie ahead for all of us before this adventure is completed."

12

❧ ❦ ❧

Charlotte

Charlotte's sisters had told her she looked so depleted, and so frail, as they met in the shadowy hallway before dawn that morning, that Emily insisted Branwell accompany her to Bradford rather than go with them to Top Withens Hall.

"I am perfectly capable of going alone," Charlotte insisted firmly. "I have lived my life as an independent woman of independent will. My physical appearance is not the sum of all my parts."

"Of course it is not," Emily said. "But you are very short and small. I fear you might be carried away by rogues or highwaymen. A particularly sturdy one could tuck you under his arm or pop you in his pocket, and none would be the wiser."

Charlotte did not seem unduly concerned by such a prospect. "I am travelling to civilisation, to the home of a friend, in the company of people," Charlotte replied.

"And that is why you should take Branwell," Emily insisted. "People are terrible. At least Branwell is the devil you know, as is Clifton Bradshaw. We will have Liston at our side, and Bradshaw is no match for our Anne since she became opinionated. So it is settled. You will take Branwell."

"Very well," Charlotte sighed. "But you can be the ones to drag him out of bed."

Branwell had not ceased complaining about his eviction from the warm haven of sleep since they had departed, so when at last they had made their frozen way to Celia Prescott's doorstep, Charlotte was exceedingly relieved.

"Why, Hattie, good day to you." Charlotte smiled warmly at Celia's housekeeper, who returned her greeting with a stone-cold and highly suspicious glare.

"And I thought it was cold on the coach," Branwell muttered. "Did Mary Shelley write this character?"

"You might remember me," Charlotte ventured. "I visited with my sisters last summer? Mrs. Prescott and I remain correspondents? Perhaps she speaks of me from time to time."

Hattie's demeanour didn't alter one notch.

"Dear lady," Branwell said, stepping forward, "please, would you be good enough to invite us inside before we are frozen to death?"

At that, Hattie stepped aside, watching Branwell closely as he entered, quite possibly surmising, Charlotte thought by the foul look on her face, that if it came to it, she could best Branwell in a fight.

"Be patient and let me talk," Charlotte murmured to her brother before turning to Hattie. "Mrs. Prescott might not be expecting us, I'm afraid," Charlotte told Hattie. "I did write yesterday, but perhaps the weather delayed the post? If she is at home, I would be very grateful if we might speak with her."

Hattie thought for a moment and then shrugged. "Missus!" Hattie yelled into the house, her eyes still fixed on Branwell and

Charlotte. "That small lady from Haworth is here to see you, and she has a sort of man with her."

"My name is Miss Charlotte Brontë—" But Charlotte was cut off before she could introduce Branwell.

"Miss Charlotte Brontë, she says!" Hattie yelled at the top of her voice.

"And my brother, Mr. Branwell Brontë." Charlotte couldn't help but finish her introduction, even though she knew what was coming next.

"And this other feller is her brother!" Hattie shouted.

There followed a short and intensely awkward silence as Hattie remained exactly where she was, staring at Branwell and Charlotte in turn as they waited for a response from within the house. Charlotte breathed a sigh of relief as an inner door was opened at last.

"Charlotte! My dear, I'm so delighted to see you," Celia said as she emerged from the parlour. "I was just resting my eyes, as my dear husband would say, though in truth I was sleeping deeply, for Hattie and I were out quite late, offering aid and comfort to Bradford's ladies of the night. Please forgive me. I must look a sight."

"You look quite lovely, Celia," Charlotte said, for save a stray curl here and there, it was the truth. Mrs. Prescott looked very well, her complexion good, her cheeks rosy and her dark eyes bright and alive. Branwell was almost certain to fall in love with her at once.

When Charlotte and her two sisters had first visited her last year, they could hardly have known just how closely Celia Prescott and her husband were involved with the dreadful circumstances at Chester Grange, but it was largely thanks to Celia's medical expertise and forthright honesty that they had been able to resolve the matter. Charlotte felt confident that this would be the case again, and she was glad to call Celia a detector by association.

"My dear Celia"—Charlotte took her friend's hands—"please

forgive the intrusion and allow me to introduce you to my brother, Mr. Branwell Brontë. I did write to notify you of our visit, and I should have waited for you to confirm, but the matter in hand, though committed many years since, feels quite pressing."

"Mr. Brontë," Celia said, smiling at Branwell, who bowed, "Charlotte always writes so warmly of you."

"Does she indeed?" Branwell sounded genuinely surprised. "Then I can only commend my sister for her determination to see the best in people."

"Please, come through to the parlour." Celia gestured for them to follow her. "Hattie, please bring tea, dear. And if you can refrain from bawling the names of our guests like a street-corner fishwife, then I shall consider myself most lucky."

"Last time you was vexed because I didn't call you when there were visitors," Hattie said. "You should settle on an opinion and stick to it, madam."

"You are quite right," Celia said. "Tell me when we have visitors, but at a volume that cannot be heard three streets away. Perhaps if you came to where I am to relay the information?"

Hattie gave Celia a look that was pure resentment before offering a halfhearted curtsey and departing. Charlotte feared the arrival of tea might now be uncertain.

"Hattie lived a very troubled, colourful existence before she came to reside with us," Celia explained to Branwell as she led them into her sitting room. "I rescued her from a life of violence and immorality, and in the process alienated most of polite society in Bradford. Even so, I do love her very dearly, and though you might not guess it, she loves me too."

"You are quite extraordinary, Mrs. Prescott," Branwell said so warmly that Charlotte made a point of taking the seat next to her friend on the sofa as quickly as she was able.

Charlotte had visited this very room before with her sisters, and there was a pang of renewed envy at the sight of it, especially on this December's day when it was dressed so prettily for Christmas. Lush swaths of holly and ivy tied with bright ribbons garlanded picture frames and windowsills. On the mantel was collected a group of the new, fashionable Christmas cards. This, combined with the rich colours of the room and the fire burning merrily, made Charlotte think it must be very lovely to be the mistress of such a home. It was true she was driven by her passion for words and her very strong desire to make her talent visible to the world, yet this domestic haven—evidence of a simple, loving life lived well—was something Charlotte often dreamt of for herself.

"Now." Celia planted her palms on her knees. "Tell me all. For I must say I find your visit, as welcome as it is, doubly intriguing for the very fact that you made it on such a day as this."

"Madam, I completely concur," Branwell said. "I myself had hoped to stay close to a fire all day today, but my sisters are very persuasive and determined, by which I mean rather terrifying."

"So tell me," Celia asked eagerly, her eyes shining, "have you brought another tooth for me to look at? Or a bone that requires identifying?"

"I'm afraid it's rather more—how shall I put it?—detailed than that," Charlotte said, lifting the bag Branwell had carried for her onto her lap. "We do not bring you fragments, Celia, but a complete set of human remains. A body was discovered interred within the chimney breast of a home local to us. All that remains is skeletal, and it is very small in stature, so we believe it to be the body of a child. We have come to you in the hope that you might be able to tell us something more about the poor soul. Their age. Perhaps, if it is possible, a suggestion as to how death occurred? The child was buried yesterday but we made extensive illustrations and notes first."

"Oh, my dear." Celia frowned. "How terrible! If I may help you, I will. To have gathered such information shows great foresight; often there are stories to be told in the very last of what remains of us."

Charlotte had been afraid that Celia would be horrified, distraught at her request, and she was grateful that her friend was a woman of science and reason who viewed the establishment of fact as the most certain path to the truth.

"Tea, ma'am." Hattie entered, the door swinging open with a resounding bump against the corner of the sideboard as she brought in the refreshments on a tray. Unlike the first time she had served tea to Charlotte the previous summer, she lowered the tray carefully and steadily, and Charlotte was pleased to see that lemon and milk were present on this occasion.

"Hattie makes great progress," Celia said. "In the last few months, I have seen her begin to talk and even laugh again. And when I think of the poor silent woman she was when I brought her into my home, it seems rather churlish to admonish her for raising her voice earlier. We are all humans, after all—all facing unseen suffering."

"Indeed," Branwell said, nodding enthusiastically. Charlotte predicted the composition of love poems on the homeward-bound omnibus.

"Show me what you have," Celia suggested, holding out her hand. "Let me see the notes, and I will tell you what, if any, conclusions I am able to draw from them."

"We indexed the drawings and the notes to sit side by side," Charlotte explained as she passed the ream of papers to Celia, "so that one directly relates to the other. Included are measurements, and each bone is labelled, though I can only hope accurately so. Emily had a book of anatomy, but it was more than a hundred years old, and Papa's medical dictionary is so heavily annotated it is rather hard to make out some of the information."

Celia took the papers from Charlotte and began to spread them out on her lap. Silence fell as she began to examine their contents. Charlotte watched her for any reaction, but her expression was steady, save for one moment when she bit down on her bottom lip, closing her eyes for a moment. As Celia read on, Charlotte let her thoughts drift away, listening to the crackle of the fire and the steady ticking of the longcase clock that stood in the corner. A life of purpose, a home of one's own: what greater contentment could there possibly be for either woman or man?

"Charlotte, dear," Celia asked when she looked up at last, "would you bring my writing desk so I may make a note of my conclusions while they are fresh in my mind? I must congratulate you and your sisters. This really is a first-rate record."

Charlotte obliged at once, holding a pot of ink for Celia, who spoke aloud as she wrote.

"The most obvious conclusion upon initial inspection is that this is indeed the skeleton of a child—one aged between eight and ten. However, further investigation of the evidence tells us a different story. The skeleton acts as an archive of experience, and these bones tell us that this individual had a life beset with poor health. See here how the bones are twisted and bowed: that's a sure sign of rickets caused by poor diet and lack of exposure to sunlight. You see it very often in the children who work in the mills. They go to work before the sun is up and finish after it sets. Also, here the bone has broken, more than likely after death, and probably because the bones themselves are weak and porous: a sign of scurvy, which comes from a very limited diet with virtually no fresh vegetables or fruit. This poor soul most likely subsisted on bread made with chalk or alum. Added to that, you can clearly see on these illustrations of the ribs that the child has woven-bone syndrome. I have seen this only rarely, but it is a recognised indicator of inflammation of the lungs. In all likelihood, the child had consumption."

"Poor little soul," Charlotte said.

"Little, but not so young as you might have thought. The child was suffering from malnutrition and was very small for their age, but though bones may deceive us, teeth don't lie. All the adult teeth have come, but not the wisdom teeth yet. That would age this person at between twelve and fourteen."

"The child must have been severely undernourished," Charlotte said.

"Which would suggest they lived in poverty. You can find many with the same ailments only a few streets away. Industry has brought great wealth to a few and great hardship to many. I would wager this was one such child."

"Can you tell if they were male or female?" Charlotte asked.

"Impossible to determine: even at this age there is no significant difference in the pelvic bones or skull. That would have to be determined by any other artefacts in the grave, if there were any."

"There was only a pendant and the sheet the bones were wrapped in, which was mostly rotted away," Charlotte said. "Are you able to determine the cause of death?"

Celia paused for a moment.

"I am very sorry to say that I am not." She indicated the drawings. "This person was very ill and would likely have died soon in any event, but if they were deliberately injured, there is no evidence of it on the body: no fractures, no cut marks, no signs of trauma. That doesn't rule out suffocation or poisoning, of course."

"But it is possible that the child might have died naturally and then been placed in the chimney breast for some reason?" Branwell asked.

"Possible," Celia confirmed, "though it is hard to fathom why. One works amongst such poverty and loss every day, and sometimes I fear my heart has become hardened to the daily cruelty of this modern age. And yet . . . what I see before me is evidence of a kind of murder, and the culprit is the cruel indifference of a society that values profit over people. Do you seek to find the true fate of this soul, Charlotte? For I will do all I can to help you."

"We are glad to be able to count on you, Celia," Charlotte said, taking her friend's hand. "You have thrown light onto the darkest corner, and I am sure your expertise will help us."

"This is a dark world we live in," Celia said. "It is our duty to burn as brightly and as fiercely as we are able that we may create a constellation of justice and truth to combat every evil."

"Indeed," Branwell said with nothing short of a heartfelt sigh. "What a magnificent lady you are, Mrs. Prescott."

So typical of her brother, Charlotte thought—always so quick to have his head turned. If only he could find a woman to fall in love with who wasn't married, then how very different things might be.

Then Charlotte considered Constantin Héger, and after a moment directed her thoughts elsewhere.

13

⚜

Emily

Emily and Anne were both pleased to note a slight easing in the severe cold—not so much that one could afford to lose one of the many layers they were bundled in, but enough to see that the great banks of icy snow that bordered the footpaths were softening a little, with water dripping off them in steady plops, and here and there to glimpse sodden, boggy mud beneath their feet. The sky was full of more snow yet to fall, and Emily was sure the worse wasn't over. As much as she loved the winter, it always cheered her to remember that before long there would be snowdrops nodding their drowsy heads as they awoke from winter slumber, and not so long after that, the whole countryside would burst into joyous, colourful, chaotic life. Death was never permanent: every part of nature revealed it. It was simply a moment of transition before living once again, Emily thought. The idea of never existing, never thinking, feeling, seeing or loving this earthly world again, was too much for her to bear, more so since she had spent such a very long time gazing upon the human remains of a life. Heaven might well be glorious, but how could it hold a candle to the moors that she loved? The only thing she could think of to do was not to die or, if she did, never to leave this land. She would live again within it, just as the snowdrops did, and just as the heather, reborn every year, was always there in the wind, the streams, the bend of the cotton grass. That would be her paradise.

"Emily?" Anne said from a few feet behind her. "Do you think about the poems and what it will be like if . . . *when* they are published?" Emily turned to look at Anne, one hand securing the hood of her cloak to her bonnet, the other holding her skirts above the mud and slush as she picked her way along the slippery path.

"I do not," Emily said. "I do not think of it at all. It was never my wish for my words to be put before other people. They may like them or they may not. I shall not care either way."

"Truly?" Anne queried, stopping for a moment to take a breath. "It must be very nice not to care at all for the opinions of others. I wish I knew how to armour myself so. Sometimes I can hardly sleep at night for worrying about it, not even so much for myself as for Charlotte. She is so very certain that the world will proclaim her a genius, Emily. Imagine the sulking that will set in if they do not."

"Hmm," Emily said. "She is resilient, our Charlotte. Look how quickly she's got over Monsieur Héger. Why, even if the reviews are bad, she will be right back at her writing desk within four years at the latest."

Anne laughed, then covered her mouth with her gloved hand, no doubt feeling a little guilty.

"Do not worry on Charlotte's account," Emily said. "Her work is rather good. Don't tell her I said that. It is not as good as mine, I'll admit, but it's passing fair."

"It's different for you and Charlotte," Anne said. "Both of you have a gift for creating worlds out of words—whole landscapes of emotion. I fear that all I have is myself, my own thoughts and feelings, regrets and hopes that are so very small and ordinary. How can that ever be considered to have any literary merit?"

Emily took her sister's hand as they picked their way across the slippery-boulder stepping-stones that stood unevenly in the still half-frozen stream.

"Why wouldn't your honest and true reflections have merit equal to any words ever written by anyone?" Emily asked. "What greater merit is there than the communication of the experience of one human soul to another? In this world of men, the literary types seek to elevate themselves above the ordinary. Their thoughts must be superior, their feelings more important than yours or mine. It's all artifice, Anne. Your thoughts, your feelings, your sentiment, as you put it, will ring true with those who read it. They will see honesty and integrity, and though you may never know their names, you and they will be connected somehow, not only now but for all of time. Besides, if I am honest, it is you who have the greatest courage of us all, you who speak the truth and will not flinch from it."

"Perhaps if that is so, it will be enough," Anne said modestly, but she squeezed Emily's fingers in thanks just before she let them go.

"Besides, we don't write for accolades." Emily thought for a moment. "We write because our souls demand it of us, and that is enough."

Conversation fell away into silent diligence as they walked that last mile up to Top Withens. The freezing air made every breath raw, and even within their gloves, their fingers were numb, their toes wet and icy. When the isolated moor-top house came into view at last, they paused for a moment, and the reason why they were there greeted them like a dark spectre waiting at the gates.

"I do not look forward to returning to this sad and terrible place," Anne said unhappily. "It feels as if misery has been cemented in between every stone that built it."

"Indeed," Emily said. "Still, let us warm ourselves with the thought of seeing fair Liston again, and that's a prospect to brighten any maid's day."

"Emily Jane!" Anne said, pretending to be scandalised. But she did not disagree.

The unhinged gate hung dormant now that the wind had dropped, and the dogs were silent and nowhere to be seen as Anne and Emily walked into the muddy yard. Emily shuddered, but not because of the cold. There was a sense of isolation here that seemed to have nothing to do with the location. It was as if the house itself were a half-mad hermit, pushing back intrusion with its own independent force of will.

"Miss Emily, Miss Anne." Liston appeared from within the barn, where he had clearly been working hard at something requiring a deal of physical effort, his curly dark hair and skin damp with perspiration, his shirt clinging to his work hardened torso. "I am very glad to see you both."

"We are glad to see you too, Liston," Emily said, suddenly greatly interested in the mud at her feet. "Very glad indeed."

"Mr. Bradshaw," Anne said, lowering her eyes and somewhat improbably bobbing a curtsey, her cheeks aflame, "have we happened upon you at an inconvenient moment?"

"No, please excuse me." Liston became acutely aware of his appearance, beckoning them after him as he hurried towards the house. "I bring the sheep in in this weather, but it involves a deal of mucking out, and as they are my enterprise and not Pa's, he says I may not use his employees. So needs must, and I've never been shy of hard work."

The moment they were within Top Withens, Liston grabbed an ancient-looking greatcoat flung over a chair and hastily shrugged it onto his shoulders, hugging it around himself as he closed the door behind them and bolted it shut.

"If we don't bolt it, the northeast wind will blow it in," he explained when Emily raised an eyebrow. At least there was no sight of old Bradshaw—only Molly the maid, who sat chopping onions at the table, and the elderly housekeeper Bess, ensconced silently by the fire, watching over a pot of something that smelt like mutton stew. If she registered their arrival at all, she did not see fit to remark upon it.

"Are you well, Liston?" Anne asked the young man, her sweet, serious face made grave with concern. "We've been so worried about you since you returned to Top Withens. Was your father's wrath very bad?"

"Not so bad, Miss Anne." Liston smiled stoically. "Pa has been powerful drunk since I returned—he ranted like a madman at me, though I couldn't say if the cause of his fury was my helping you remove the bones or inviting further scrutiny of his dealings, as he was hardly comprehensible and certainly in no state to attack me. He was barely able to raise his head off the table, in fact. So Bess and I put him abed, where he has been ever since and has shown no sign of stirring yet."

"Though it is a stay rather than a reprieve, I am glad to hear it." Anne smiled.

"It gladdens my heart to know of your concern, Miss Anne, but you have no need to worry on my account. When I was a child, my father was a man to be feared, but now I am a man grown, and he knows it. He will bluster and bully me, but he can beat me no longer without expecting such an attack to be returned in kind, though I would never willingly hurt him, and he knows that."

"You are indeed a very fine young man," Emily said, casting her younger sister a long sideways glance. "Liston, will it be well for us to look at the room once again and to ask you, and perhaps Bess, some other questions about that time? We are doing our best to try to identify the child in the hopes that we might be able to find a family to mourn them, or at least a name to add to the headstone."

"Of course, Miss Emily. I will do anything I can to help you and Miss Anne," Liston said eagerly. "I expect you remember the way to my mother's room, but let me guide you anyway. That way we may avoid the creaking board and stuck doors that may wake my father from his slumber, for though I have nothing to fear from him, I do not wish you to have to bear witness to his foul demeanour."

They followed Liston to that old disused part of the house, falling silently into step behind him as they navigated through shadows and dust-buried memories to find their way back to the shuttered room. Once outside Liston hesitated, suddenly looking very young and vulnerable, as a great sadness settled over him rather like a cloak. Emily supposed that he must have felt very alone in the world without even a sister or brother to lean on.

"Miss Emily, Miss Anne," he said, his voice low and quiet, "if it is well with you, I would rather not see that sad room again." He lowered his chin so that his shock of black hair fell over his eyes. "I'm sure you think me very foolish for taking on so, but I cannot face it."

"Of course we do not," Anne said before Emily could reply. "Everything you say makes perfect sense."

"Take this candle, and I will return shortly to collect you, then," Liston said, bowing rather awkwardly before leaving at the pace of a man who didn't want to be caught in a moment of emotion.

"I believe you are rather taken with young Mr. Bradshaw," Emily said, raising an eyebrow. "Have a care, Anne."

"Have a care over what?" Anne retorted. "Treating another human being with decency? Honestly, Emily, I should have thought you would be the last to get notions about attachments where no such notions are to be had. Now, shall we get on with the task in hand?"

"Very well, sister," Emily said, not wanting to distract Anne any further from their grim purpose, even though that rare flash of temper from her sister revealed exactly that which Anne denied.

14

Anne

The room was exactly as they had left it, and yet despite the bitter chill in the air and the pile of rubble in the fireplace, it felt markedly different, as if all the sorrowful shadows had left with the bones on that first day, leaving behind them simply an empty space. If that was true, then where had the anguish gone? Anne wondered. Had it taken up residence in another home? Was it now buried in the frozen earth forever, or did it roam as free as the howling wind?

It is all your imagination, Anne, she told herself sternly. *Your own fears haunting you—that is all.*

"I am glad that Liston didn't join us in here," she said to Emily as she went to the shattered window, soothing herself with a gust of freezing air and the rolling waves of icy white hills beyond. It was as if Top Withens were a ship that had sailed far north in search of Dr. Frankenstein's monster, unless, that is, the monster was already on board.

"Liston is a surprising young man," Emily said. Anne turned back to her sister to discover that she was already on her knees, examining every surface of the stones that had made up the interior of the chimney, the candle set down on the floor. "One would hardly expect to find such a gentle soul raised up here, where only the hardy can survive. I wonder if the Liston we meet is all the Liston there is, or if he hides a little of himself away."

"We all hide a little of our true natures away, Emily. Besides, what are you looking for?" Anne asked.

"I'm not sure," Emily said, turning each surface of a sizeable cut stone towards what little light the candle afforded, "except that there must be a reason why the bones were interred here in a room that had to be broken into."

"A good place to hide that which you do not wish to be discovered."

"True, but there are miles of moor out there that would do the job just as well, so why here? I can think of only two reasons: first that the place has a particular meaning for the person who concealed them here—a meaning that is somehow tied in with the bones."

"I see," Anne said, though in truth she wasn't entirely sure that she did. "And secondly?"

"That the culprit needed time, privacy and shelter to . . ."

"To what?" Anne asked.

"To do something that requires all those things," Emily said. "So I suppose I am looking for some trace, some physical remnant from the moment the bones were placed here that will tell us something."

"There are a great many dead birds here in the grate," Anne told Emily as she examined the chimney breast once again. "Five or six crow skulls, and the bones of smaller birds too."

"That would indicate that the birds were attracted to the chimney by the promise of carrion," Emily said, ever blunt. "Therefore we can assume the body was not skeletal when it was placed here."

"Excellent," Anne said, taking in another deep breath of cold air. Would that she could detach herself from the humanity and tragedy of the bones in the way that Emily could. It wasn't that her sister didn't care as much—Anne was certain that she did. It was just that Emily was able to unravel the most complicated weave into separate strands of colour, all the better to see how it had been made in the first place.

"Detecting does seem to involve a great deal of time looking for something that might not exist," Anne said, but Emily, absorbed as she was in studying every inch of every surface of a torn-out stone, did not reply.

Anne joined Emily on the filthy floor and, after several moments of silent work, stopped and stared for a long moment at what she had discovered, for it was almost certainly the strange and unusual thing that Emily had been looking for.

Clearly etched into the blackened surface of the stones were purposeful marks, not forming any letter or design Anne recognised, but rather something like the Egyptian hieroglyphs that had confounded historians until only a few decades earlier with the discovery of the Rosetta stone. As unlikely as it was that Egyptian writings should appear on the inside of a chimney breast in an isolated Yorkshire house, it was no more unlikely than any other explanation for the strange etchings.

"Emily," Anne said, offering forth her treasure, "these markings are unusual."

"Yes!" Emily said, taking the stone in her hand. "Yes, there is no mistaking that those are deliberate marks, is there? Well done, Anne—let us see if we may find any more and perhaps make sense of this fragment. It may well unlock the whole affair!"

After finding the first marked stone, other finds followed apace, perhaps because they had been placed side by side in the chimney breast wall, Anne considered, or perhaps because now Emily and she knew what they were looking for. As the morning dwindled away outside the shattered window, Anne and Emily sorted a small pile of similarly marked stones, thirteen in total.

"Look at what remains of the chimney breast," Emily said, gesturing at the ruin. "The stones are fitted together depending on their shape and size. If we follow the same principle with these fragments, we should be able to reassemble them and make whatever was intended whole once more."

So intent were the sisters on this work that they didn't notice how each stone dragged and thudded on the damp floorboards, reverberating throughout the timbers that connected the old house to the new, or how their eager voices rose a little more each time they successfully added another stone, gradually building up a picture of the strange relic that had been left as a kind of seal over the burial place.

"I feel certain that this will give us a path to follow in search of the individual who left the poor child here," Emily said, frowning at the strange design as it emerged. "We just need time to study it. I do not think we have it right yet; it seems disjointed and broken still. Anne, pass me my notebook and I—"

Before Emily could say more, they heard the sound of Clifton Bradshaw shouting below—such profane and ugly words that Anne felt her ears grow hot with horror.

"Bradshaw knows we are here," Anne said. "Come, Emily, we must leave."

"One moment more, if I can just find the piece that connects these two . . ."

"Emily, there is not another second to waste. We must go now!" Anne climbed to her feet, but her sister continued to move the stones as if they were pieces on a chessboard. Anne heard boots on the stairs, heavy footfalls approaching at speed.

"Emily!" Anne insisted. "Clifton Bradshaw is upon us! We do not have the time to make sense of this stone now. You are making enough racket to wake the dead, never mind old Bradshaw. If we are to reconstruct the hidden message, then we must take these stones away with us."

"How would such a thing be possible?" Emily scrambled up, casting around for an idea. "Curse the dressmaker who does not sew a pocket into every seam!"

"Pillowcases!" Anne exclaimed, flinging open the doors of the closeted bed, dragging two mouldy and damp such items from rotten pillows. "Put in only the most important stones, and I'm afraid we will have to ask Liston for his help once again, for we cannot carry these ourselves."

Just at that moment, the door exploded open, its frame filled with the furious bulk of Clifton Bradshaw, his fists balled, his face as red as blood as he thundered into the room surrounded by the strong stink of stale alcohol.

"Get out of my house, meddlers!" His roar filled the room, his eyes burning hot and spittle flecking his oily lips. "How dare you! You come in here, take what's mine without permission, spread lies and gossip about me, then have the nerve to come back to snoop again. Who do you think you are, you entitled little b—?"

"Close your mouth at once, Clifton Bradshaw," Anne said, taking three steps towards Bradshaw so rapidly that he stumbled backwards a little, startled. "I warn you, sir, if you speak one word of profanity in front of my sister and me, you will deeply regret it—do you hear me?"

And though it seemed unlikely that she—a rather slight woman of only average height—could make this hulk of a man, even given his age and state of sobriety, regret anything, Anne was deadly serious. She would not see herself or her sister threatened by anyone, least of all this unsavoury individual, this bully, this drunk. Indeed, the surge of rage that flooded through her seemed to double her in size. Her fists clenched, her eyes flashed as she squared up to their aggressor as boldly as a fighting man. For that moment, Anne felt as immovable and as powerful as the hills beneath their feet.

Even so, Clifton held his ground, his hand drawn back as if to land the first blow, and then, the next moment, it was as if his own bones crumbled away within his flesh, his shoulders stooping, his head dropping as he was overcome with sobs, raw and furious, the like of which Anne had never heard.

"Pa, in God's name!" Liston grabbed hold of his father's arm, dragging him out of the room. "You were not always this demon. I swear it. Once you were a decent man. What devil grabbed you hard enough that you would threaten a young lady? What would Mother think if she could see you now?"

"She'd be ashamed that her milksop son has become a milksop man." Clifton shook off Liston's hand, inhaling his anguish and straightening his shoulders. "Get these bloody women out of my house before I throw 'em out."

"Mr. Bradshaw, you will not be able to walk away from this matter forever!" Anne went after him. "The truth will find you out, sir."

Clifton stopped at the top of the old staircase, swaying precariously as he turned around to look at her, before lunging forward suddenly once more, grasping her by her arms and thrusting her back against the stone wall. Anne turned her face from his foul breath and spittle, aware of Liston doing his best to drag his father off of her.

"I will not be lectured by a girl who has never known anything of the world and the hardship it brings," he growled. "I know your family. Not as holy as you like to make out, are you, girl, hey?"

"Unhand my sister!" Emily looked around for a heavy object to batter Bradshaw with. Fortunately Liston dragged Clifton away.

"Let her go, Pa," Liston said as he battled with his father's iron grip on Anne's arms.

Anne felt the bruising bones of his fingers, the heat and weight of him on her, and could take not a moment more. She remembered something Branwell had told her once, and in one swift movement, she kneed Bradshaw hard in his unholies.

"There is no girl, sir," Anne told him as he released her, doubling over in pain. "I am a woman grown—a woman who works for her living and has endured as much loss and grief as you and your son— as much as any has hereabouts. It is clear that you know more about the bones hidden inside that room than you are willing to say. But mark my words. We shall reveal the all of it, and you shall answer for your sins."

"You're a witch," Bradshaw gasped, glaring at her as he struggled to catch his breath.

It was rare for Anne to be looked upon with such naked dislike— hatred, even—and yet she found it exhilarating and, yes, it was genuine, in a way so few of her interactions were.

"You are not the victim, Mr. Bradshaw," Anne added. "Your wife was a victim of disease, your son is a victim of your grief and anger, and the poor nameless child concealed within the walls of your house is the greatest victim of all. But *you* are not. *You* are a man grown, and unless you yourself hid a body in that room sometime after the death of your wife, then you should *want* to answer our questions, not evade them. After all, my sisters and I may be the only individuals who can help you and Liston clear the family name."

"I do not need your help, she wolf," Clifton said, turning and half staggering down the stairs, "but neither do I have anything to hide, and I'll show you that. You may ask me your questions, Miss Brontë, and then you will be on your way, and you shall not darken my doorstep again. For you will not best me twice. I promise you that."

15

Emily

Emily watched as her sister took a seat at the long table and waited for Clifton Bradshaw, who had excused himself to wash his face and to dress properly. Emily had never been prouder or more in awe of the woman who was little baby Anne no longer. Though she had known her all her life, and was familiar with Anne's steadfast determination and her iron will, she would never have guessed at the fire within if she had not just witnessed it with her own eyes. Here was a woman who would never let a tyrant or a bully win, a woman who would always stand up for those weaker than she, and today that person had been Emily.

Of course Emily was almost certain that if she had been the first in the path of Clifton Bradshaw's fury, she would have knocked him out flat with one of the big hearth stones. However, she had not been, and it was probably all to the good, since Anne's approach was just as impressive and slightly less likely to end in some kind of prosecution.

Anne had shown that, of the two of them, she was the one to talk to Clifton Bradshaw, and Emily was glad—content, even—to let her do so. Instead she stepped away from the table and joined Bess at the fire, taking a seat on a stool as Bess stirred and stirred away at something that had been cooking so long there must have been nothing recognisable left in the pot, while Molly, slight and silent, busied herself making a new batch of bread.

"They say the mistress is grievous poorly," Bess muttered to herself. "Won't see out the summer, they say. And I say it's a real shame, for it ain't the typhoid that killed her but him, and he knows it. He knows what he's done. For the Lord shall smite down the evil, Zerubabbel, son of Salathiel, stranger of Babylon, builder of temples, he who witnessed the night of my lady's passing. We'll all have tea."

"Be calm now, Bess," Molly said in a light singsong voice. "All is well with the world."

"Nothing's right with the mistress ailing, as you should know," Bess said sourly.

Emily leaned a little closer to Bess. It was clear that within her mind the old lady was far away, stirring her pot on another long-ago afternoon. To whom she thought she was talking could only be guessed at, but still Emily listened lest some nugget of truth be hidden in all that babble.

"My, but it's hot, ain't it?" Bess said. "If this drought don't break soon, the crops will be lost and folk'll starve. And that'll be him, bringing blight on us all with his curse."

"Don't fret, Bess," Molly said. "Look out of the window. Winter is here, and soon it will be Christmas."

"The mistress loves Christmas," Bess said. "She loves to sing carols while we cook, and we light extra candles all around the house to keep out the dark. I got something to tell you, madam—don't you think I don't know what you are up to."

"Now, then, Bess!" Molly did her best to distract the old lady, but she was not to be deterred.

Bess's beady black eyes sought out Emily's from under her frilled bonnet, and she nodded, beckoning Emily closer to her, then closer still. It was only when Emily's ear was but a few inches from Bess's toothless mouth that the old lady gripped Emily's shoulder hard and whispered another string of strange words before pushing her away.

"Bess!" Molly cried. "I am sorry, miss. She gets powerful angry sometimes over nothing at all."

"She means no harm," Emily said.

Taking in the words, she sat back and regarded Bess for a long time. Not for a moment did Bess stop stirring.

"What's the importance of those words, Bess?" Emily asked. "They make no sense."

"You know"—Bess looked at her darkly—"and just you remember that I know too."

Emily shuddered as if someone had just walked over her grave. Wherever Bess thought she was in that moment, her eyes had been as cold and hard as steel. As she looked at Emily, she had been seeing someone she truly abhorred, but who?

There were a few moments of silence during which Molly put new loaves in the oven, only looking up to watch Liston as he joined his father at the table.

"They say the mistress is grievous poorly," Bess said a few minutes later, her countenance altered once again. "They say she won't see out the summer." And she stirred and stirred and stirred.

16

∽∾∽

Anne

"You must remember very clearly the year your wife died," Anne said as Liston joined Clifton and her at the table. Clifton had seen fit to change into what Anne suspected was his best suit of clothes, and though it was a little worn and faded, he looked good in it, like a man not to be trifled with. Liston looked worried and sad, and Anne felt for him so, doing his best to be decent and respectable while his father ranted and railed at the world, as if none of his misfortune was his responsibility. It was a position she was somewhat familiar with from her dealings with her own brother, after all. Anne looked up to see Emily come to the table, frowning deeply.

"Were there many people working at Top Withens that summer, Mr. Bradshaw?" Anne asked Clifton.

Bradshaw shook his head, folding his heavy arms over the considerable bulge of his belly. At least his rage had ebbed away, and he seemed more sober than not.

"I do not remember," Clifton told her. "There are months after my wife's death that I recall hardly at all. She went away to stay with her sister, and in truth I was glad to see her go—at least I thought I was. We'd argued often, almost always about Liston. She wanted him educated, fancied up like a gentleman. I told her Top Withens is no place for a weakling, and it will never be a grand house, no matter how much you dress it up." He stopped talking for a moment, remembering. "I should have made her happy. I could have—I loved her enough. My sin is that I chose not to. I do not remember the summer after my wife died because I was lost—lost to drink and . . . other influences, Miss Brontë. I admit it."

"If you can't remember those months, then how can you be sure that you have nothing to do with the hidden bones?" Anne asked him frankly.

Clifton Bradshaw studied her face for a long moment. "I would know it, as I know all of my sins and name each one every day. In any case, I have something better than my memory."

Bradshaw got up, crossing the flags to a great dresser of dark oak that was bolted against the furthest wall. Removing an iron ring clanking with keys that he kept on his belt, he unlocked one of the cupboards, revealing shelves of what looked like bound ledgers, and it was indeed two of these volumes that he brought back to the table, dropping them onto the surface with a carefully measured bang.

"I have my records. My father taught me that not a penny goes in or out of this farm without it being accounted for. Everyone who has ever worked up here, be it for a week or for thirty years, like Bess, is recorded in these books. In fact, that year it was Bess who kept the books for me. I cannot know if those recorded in here were honest about their names and ages, and I do not care. The point is these two volumes are my memory for that year, more detailed and exact about the comings and goings than any human mind. And you are welcome to them."

Emily stood up as Anne drew one of the thick books towards her, standing at her sister's shoulder as she opened it and scanned the pages with her finger.

"Why didn't any of your workers stay for the whole season?" she asked after a few minutes of careful inspection. "Many seemed to move on after only a few days."

"Because I don't ask questions," he replied. "I don't want to know where they've been or what they've done or where they are going. That means I can pay less and they work harder. Even so, some of them can't work as hard as I need, and so I move them on until I find someone who can. That year, that was the last year that the farm was our main income. After that, it was the mill that made our fortunes."

"Mr. Bradshaw, do you keep your keys on you always?" Anne asked, nodding at the key ring that Clifton returned to his belt.

"I do," he said. "I am the only one who has them. If any door in this house is to be opened or locked, then it is to be by me."

"And was it so in eighteen thirty-two?"

"It was after Mary's passing," he told her. "After her death that summer, it was always so."

"And you never unlocked the room where the bones were discovered after your wife died?" Anne pressed on.

"No." Clifton shook his head. "Not until the screaming drew us towards it, and I could delay it no longer. At least since you took the bones that infernal noise has ceased."

Anne suspected that Bradshaw sought to distract her with his talk of supernatural occurrences, but she would not be diverted.

"Then can you suggest how someone might have concealed the body of a child within that room if it was not you?" Anne asked.

Clifton shifted in his seat and looked at Liston, who had been silent. Unable to meet his father's gaze, Liston stood up abruptly and walked away from the table. Anne couldn't help but notice that Molly followed him almost at once.

"The windowpane is broken in there," Clifton said. "They must have forced their way in."

"Climbed up, smashed through the glass of a small window, perhaps carrying a terrible load, then took apart the chimney breast and replaced it, all without the bark of a dog or the creak of a board? And yet you heard my sister and me as we talked in that room today. It seems unlikely, doesn't it, Mr. Bradshaw?"

"Perhaps it does, but there it is," Clifton said. "I suppose if I were in my cups, it's possible one of the men who passed through here could have lifted the keys from me for a while. Check the ledgers. We had all sorts that year: Travellers, former convicts and Irish. Perhaps it was one of them. Can't trust an Irishman."

"I believe you know my papa is an Irishman," Anne said coolly. "We do not stand such prejudice in our house."

"But you are in my house, Miss Brontë," Bradshaw said. "And there's a dead child that someone hid in my house. Now, you ask anyone round here who they think would be so low to do such a thing—Clifton Bradshaw or an Irish beggar—you see what they say."

Anne bit her lip, for it was true that the anger and fear felt against those fleeing starvation in Ireland seemed to mount weekly, increasing with every shrieking newspaper headline. Of course the recent influx of desperate people could have nothing to do with this event, which had taken place thirteen years earlier, yet for some the relevance of such facts didn't matter at all when they were searching for an excuse to hate and blame.

"So you believe a migrant committed the crime, stole your keys and went to great lengths to stow away their evil deed within your house—a theory that can never be proved either way."

"Can't help my bad luck, can I?" Clifton said with a shrug.

"Some say you have the luck of the devil himself," Emily said.

Anne wasn't sure what reaction she might have been expecting from Bradshaw, but it certainly wasn't the one she got: uproarious laughter, as the man tossed his head back, revealing his blackened teeth, and slapped his thigh hard until he wheezed for breath.

"Lass," he said, leaning across the table, "you should be careful saying his name too loud hereabouts. He might hear you and think you are calling on him. For let me promise you this: once you've invited the devil in, you'll never get rid of him, not even in death. Mark my words, for none knows this better than I."

17

⤜⤙⤚⤛

Anne

As it turned out, Clifton let them take the stones without further protest, his smug self-assurance that nothing could be found to incriminate him infuriating Anne.

In any event, it was well that when they met again after dinner, the process of fitting the stones back together took time, and that in itself it was rather diverting, as the report that Charlotte delivered from Celia Prescott was more than sobering. Each detail added humanity to the discovery, substance to their imaginations, hurt to their hearts. That the child had been so ill and malnourished that it had been prevented from growing to its proper size was a common enough plight, especially with the children who worked in the mills. And that Celia could find no remaining evidence of violence in the bones was something to hold on to.

"Could it be that the child simply died, a victim of circumstance, and that its parent, originating from another land, found a place to inter the child with ceremonies we aren't familiar with?" Anne suggested.

"It could be," Charlotte said. "The medallion seems Catholic, so that tells us that the Christian faith has some significance here, though it is hard to know what, when burial within the faith is possible nearby, if not in Haworth."

"I'm afraid I do not believe it," Emily said. "The child was gravely ill, certainly, but no one who loved their child as a mother or father does would hide their remains in that cold and lonely place. I believe the child was killed and concealed. That the burial place and markings hold the key to finding out who and why—that is why we must assemble this weird design and make sense of it somehow."

"Murder"—Anne spoke the awful word aloud—"if that's what it is. And that is what we all need to accept before we continue, sisters. There is infinite, careless cruelty in this word, and somehow one lives with it, side by side with inhumanity, as if it were a consequence of life. But this, this is a deliberate act, and we must all three of us understand the truth we are intent on. For at the end of our detections, if we are successful, we may face grave danger."

"I am not afraid of danger," Emily said at once.

"I know you believe that to be true, Emily," Anne said. "But perhaps that just means that you have yet to meet anything that scares you."

"That is true," Emily conceded, "though I cannot imagine such a thing."

"I am afraid," Charlotte admitted, her hands hovering over one of the stones as if she were loath to touch it. "I have been since we set foot in Top Withens Hall. Everything about that wretched place seems a bad omen. I wish to find the truth of this as much as you do, Anne, but aren't you afraid of what it may cost us all?"

Anne turned the stones this way and that until she fitted one more into the curious design. Her answer to Charlotte's question was that yes, she was afraid she would not find the courage to continue with what must be done. And yet a murderer could not be left loose in the world to roam unchecked—not if one decent person knew that they were free. They had to continue.

"Well, one thing is clear," she said, gesturing at the table rather than answering Charlotte. "Emily is right: there is a larger design here—one that can only have been made by taking out these stones, arranging them, then carefully replacing them in order. That means whoever hid the body had time; they had no fear of discovery or capture."

"Which can only strengthen the case against Clifton Bradshaw," Charlotte said. "Who else would be able to spend so much time alone in that room, certain they would be undisturbed? And it was he himself who told us he kept the only key on his person at all times. It seems likely the child's death was related directly to Mary Bradshaw's death—an unwitting victim of Bradshaw's grief and rage"—she looked at the design—"or some demonic ritual to restore her health?"

"We should consider Liston," Emily suggested. "He was grieving too, and if he attempted to emulate his father—then anything could be possible."

"But he was just a child at the time," Anne said, "barely twelve years old."

"There are plenty of that age who have lived a lifetime by then," Emily said. "Let us consider Old Bess, then. There is something very . . . unsettling about that woman. I believe she thought she was telling me secrets today, though I could make neither head nor tail of anything she said, rhymes and songs, biblical verses, all tangled up with all manner of nonsense. Molly was keen to quiet her down before she could say more, as if she had been told to do so. I had thought it was a show of Bradshaw's decency that he'd kept her on and not sent her to an asylum, but perhaps he is afraid that even as weak-minded as she is, she might yet reveal his secrets."

Anne watched as Emily slotted another stone into place. The strange and mysterious intentions of the creator were gradually becoming whole, if utterly unintelligible.

"It is also useful to note that another fire was never lit after these marks were made," Emily said. "Otherwise they would be obscured by soot. So we can assume that, as we suspected, the remains were placed in the wall, and this . . . whatever it is . . . was completed after Mrs. Bradshaw died and Clifton closed up that part of the house. That makes the mostly likely opportunity for the event itself to be that summer and harvest period up at Top Withens."

It was Charlotte who slotted home the last piece, and though she couldn't be certain, Anne wouldn't have been at all surprised if her sister hadn't kept that stone aside especially to gain that dubious honour. In any case, once the sisters looked at the whole picture carved into the rocks, a sense of deep unease swept through them in a single shuddering wave, and Keeper, who had been sleeping peacefully under the table, rose up all at once and howled a long plaintive cry that struck the sisters dumb.

"Shush, boy," Emily said, seeking to pull the dog into a hug, but he shook her off, scratching to get out at the door where Flossy was already barking, desperate to be free.

"Something has set the dogs off," Charlotte said anxiously.

"It will be the scent of something or a sound we cannot discern," Emily said, though her voice trembled a little. "The sooner we make sense of this, the sooner we can pack it away again."

"I hoped it would be about the child," Anne said, frowning at the pattern. "Something such as a memorial that might tell us who they were. This seems to be of another language entirely, almost of another world."

"I had hoped for a message of remorse," Charlotte said, "a confession."

"I had hope of neither," Emily said. "But equally I failed to imagine this, whatever it might be."

She climbed onto one of the rickety chairs that surrounded the dining room table to get a better view, spreading her arms like a bird to gain her balance. After a moment Anne followed suit, as did Charlotte. The three sisters standing upon their chairs gazed at the pattern while the dogs paced and whimpered below. A sense of disquiet wended its way between them, settling in the air and on their shoulders. Suddenly the little warm room ceased to be their soft grey haven, and from where they stood, it looked so small and long abandoned, damp and full of cobwebs. It felt to Anne as though they were looking on their own lives from very far away, and there was so very little of them left—nothing to prove they had ever lived at all.

Doing her best to swallow the sense of dread that infested her chest, Anne made herself examine the design. There was a circle enclosing a triangle. Several other smaller circles radiated around the latter, and within it appeared strange symbols and images the like of which Anne had never seen. There was something about it that felt malicious and—more than that—alive and knowing, as if it were watching them. Reaching for a piece of paper and a pencil, Emily began to draw what she saw.

After but a minute, the dogs began barking and howling again, Keeper catching at the hem of Emily's dress and tugging at it as if he wanted her to come away. A moment later the door opened and Tabby entered, mortified to see her girls standing on chairs. With a startled yelp, her gaze travelled from the sisters to the stones on the table, her expression turning from admonishment to ashen grey fear.

"Oh, dear Lord, save us!" Tabby cried, pulling first Emily, then Charlotte off their chairs with quite some force. Before she could be yanked down, Anne got off the chair on her own to find Tabby grabbing hold of Charlotte's face in her hands, pulling down her lower eyelids and examining the inside of her mouth. "Be there a devil in there? Get thee out of my children before I fetch the parson to drag thee out!"

"Tabby!" Anne said, pulling her off Charlotte once she realised Emily wasn't going to. "There is no devil in Charlotte or in any of us. We are all quite well. What is it that ails you so? Do you recognise this motif?"

"I know enough to know that no good can come of that devilment," Tabby said, lifting her apron to her mouth. "Get it out! Get it out right this instant—do you hear me? None of you is too big to feel the back of my hand."

Before Anne could react, Tabby elbowed them out of the way, and with far more strength than Anne would have imagined, the old woman scooped three large stones into her apron. At once Charlotte and Emily followed suit and so did Anne, taking as many as she could and returning at once with the others to gather the last few. Following Tabby's lead, they carried the stones a hundred yards or so up the icy track, dumping them on the edge of the moor.

Only when every single one of the stones had been deposited did Tabby strip off her apron, laying it over the pile. Then, with her face set with anger, she smartly clipped each one of them about the ear.

"Ouch!" Anne said, rubbing the side of her head.

"Such fools you are," Tabby said. "Such dim-witted fools, the whole lot of you. And you, God-fearing children of a parson and all! Do you, all three, believe in God?"

"Of course," Anne said at once.

"Yes," Charlotte replied.

"Almost certainly," Emily added.

"Then if you believe there is a God in heaven, why don't you believe that there is also a devil in hell, and just as the Lord wants to save your soul, so the devil wants to do his best to steal it? You can't have one without the other, children. This you should surely know."

"We are truly sorry," Anne said, rather hesitantly reaching for Tabby's hands. "We had no idea what we were constructing, only that it might help us find out more of what happened at Top Withens Hall."

"Top Withens?" Tabby shuddered. "I told you—I said Clifton Bradshaw sold his soul to the devil, and you thought I was a superstitious old woman. Well, look—there's your proof in that pile of rocks. That seals it. It does."

"Tabby, what does it seal?" Anne did her best to soothe Tabby, whom she couldn't ever recall seeing so agitated. "Why don't we return to the warmth of the house, and you can explain to us what you understood, for we could fathom nothing?"

"You may not step foot back in that house until I've cleaned out the filth you brought in," Tabby said, shaking herself loose from Anne.

"It is clean, Tabby," Emily said. "I helped you clean it just this morning."

"Cleaned it of evil, you fool," Tabby said. "I don't know what that abomination was meant for, but I know evil when I see it. That was the devil's work. And in your front dining room too. And I warrant that Clifton Bradshaw made that circle on the night he did his evil deal, and that the poor, killed bones they found up there were nothing short of human sacrifice. You foolish, silly girls, with all your books and learning, and yet you've brought a curse down on all our heads this night. No good will come from this. You mark my words. No good at all."

18

Emily

"Have we really stumbled on a *sacrifice* and unleashed a curse?" Charlotte asked, wide-eyed, her arm linked through Anne's, as Tabby went into the house to wake up the servant girl, Martha. "Oh, dear Lord, I think we must wake Papa and tell him what we have found."

"Be calm, Charlotte," Emily said. "We do not know anything more than that which Tabby has told us. And though she is very wise and very dearly loved, she also insists on greeting every single magpie she sees and enquiring after their family before turning three times anticlockwise to warn away bad luck—so let us take a moment to collect our thoughts and discover the meaning of the designs through establishing facts."

"Your words make sense, Emily"—Charlotte shuddered—"but rather less in the dead of night when your wretched dog won't stop howling and barking at nothing."

It was true that Keeper had followed them into the dark, where he, with little Flossy at his heels, continued to growl and fuss, pacing up and down the yard as if he perceived a threat that none of them could see.

"Pay no mind to Keeper—he is the best of dogs but not the cleverest. He's probably caught the scent of a fox, that's all. And as for Clifton Bradshaw, there is no conclusive proof that he made that design, aside from speculation and rumour. Should we lay these charges now, he will escape them as easily as he could have yesterday. The word of Tabby Aykroyd does not carry much weight with the law or the Church, and this world is not the same as it was when the Pendle witches were hung, when blind fear and superstition ruled all. Thank goodness. We must find evidence of a crime, not a bewitchment."

Charlotte shivered. "It is almost as if you can feel evil abroad in the land, and I am not sure that science and reason are much defence against it."

"It is the best defence," Emily reassured her. "That and the word of God. Stay here as Tabby wants and let me try to calm her a little so that she might let us back in the house before we all freeze to death."

Emily, far too curious to obey Tabby, found a very sleepy and rather baffled Martha being instructed by Tabby in the kitchen.

"Sage," Tabby said, brandishing a bunch of it at Emily. "Good luck I dried a good portion this summer. And salt—that's what we need. Fetch it all out. I'll burn the sage in the dining room, the hallway and the kitchen and anywhere else those demon stones went. Martha, you must make an unbroken line of salt on all the windowsills and doorways—every one—and make sure there is no gap; even the smallest is a weakness." Tabby thought for a moment. "Don't go mad, though. That's all the salt we've got until the snow melts."

"It's a difficult balance," Emily muttered to Martha, "between warding off evil and seasoning."

"I may be as old as the hills, Emily, but I am not as deaf as them," Tabby said. "As for you, you may go out and fetch me sprigs of rowan and yew to hang over the door. I'd keep them there all year round, but Mr. Brontë isn't keen on it."

"Is that truly an essential requirement at this hour, Tabby?" Emily pleaded. "It is almost midnight, and I'm not entirely sure I can tell what tree is what in the dark. I might accidentally bring home a sprig of may, and then who knows what chaos might ensue?"

"Take a lamp and get on with you," Tabby said, huffing her cheeks, rosy with indignation. "If your father should wake to see what we are about, he would think the world had gone mad and his daughters as wild as pixies. Let us just thank the Lord that his sight is not what it was. If he notices the salt at the windows tomorrow, Martha, it's for slugs."

"In December?" Martha yawned.

"Don't argue—just tell him."

"The thing is, dear Tabby," Emily said, as she called Keeper to her side, "that you are right, of course—we were very foolish to bring the—"

"Don't you speak of it aloud," Tabby warned her, brandishing a broom.

"—artefact into the house. But, as you say, we are Christian, God-fearing people, and so I can't help but wonder if the practices that you are currently engaged in to cleanse the house are perhaps a little . . . witchish."

"I swear, Miss Emily Jane, I shall beat you with this broom, I shall," Tabby said, flying at Emily, who dodged out of the way, leaping over a border of salt and out into the night.

"I was only asking," she called back once she was safely outside.

"This isn't witchery," Tabby went on. "These are the local ways: a shoe in the wall, a stone head on the gable and, to clean a house of any ill will or foul spirits, salt and sage. Once the evil is gone, we'll place the rowan and yew boughs at the door. Then none who are not invited will be able to enter."

"Does that include Mr. Nicholls?" Emily asked hopefully, earning another swipe from Tabby, even though it meant that particular salt border would have to be done again.

"This isn't instead of good Christian prayer and thought," Tabby told Emily. "It's as well as. My old ma always said belt and braces are best. God is the belt, and the old ways are the braces. Now, get on with you, and don't you return until you've done my bidding, or I'll send you to bed with no tea."

"Quite frankly, at this point, I'd take bed over anything," Emily muttered to Keeper as they disappeared into the dark.

It had taken only a moment for Emily to fetch some sprigs of rowan, though she was not sure if the bare twigs without a berry or a leaf on them would do as well. She knew there was a yew in the graveyard, as there often was. Tabby had told them when they were children that you would always find a yew where the dead rested: its roots grew deep in amongst the dead, wending their way through the eye sockets of their skulls to keep them from rising from the grave. It should take only a moment or two to locate the final item Tabby required, and then they could all go to bed at last.

There was nothing about the graveyard at night that alarmed Emily. To her it was a serene place—a place of rest. And though she had yet to meet a ghost here, she was fairly certain that if she did, it would be terribly interesting. Keeper, much calmer now, snuffled happily at her feet as they headed to the furthest corner of the graveyard, where a gnarly old yew stood guard. There was said to be a highwayman buried down here, and a poisoner. Once it would have been where they buried those who had not been christened, and there was a feeling of crossing as Emily approached the tree—a sensation of leaving all she understood far behind for the inky peace of the dark.

Placing her hand against the rough bark of the yew, she leaned her cheek against it for a moment, silently thanking the old creature, before smartly pulling off a branch.

It was when she turned back that she saw the figure standing between her and the parsonage. Keeper had seen it first; he stood perfectly still, growling softly, his ears flat against his large head. At first Emily thought it was a shadow, a trick of the fleetingly present moonlight, but though it remained motionless, the figure didn't vanish—it stood its ground in the gloom. From the shape of the skirt and bonnet, Emily could tell it was a woman, which only intrigued her further. What other woman was there in the world likely to be found in a graveyard at gone midnight on a winter's night?

"Charlotte?" Emily called out, her voice ringing like a bell in the crisp air. "Anne? Did you see fit to follow me?"

The figure did not move, nor did she reply, and in that moment, Emily had cause to remember her claim earlier in the evening that she was not afraid of anything. It was not precisely fear that she felt pricking at the back of her neck, raising the fine hairs on her forearms, but rather some kind of primal prescience that there was danger afoot. It was as close to fear as she had ever felt.

Taking the branch of yew in her grasp rather as though it were a broadsword, Emily moved a little closer to the figure, taking care not to step on the gravestones themselves. Keeper stayed exactly where he was, loyal protector indeed.

"Hello?" Emily called out again, dismayed by how thin and light the greeting sounded. "Are you alone? Or in need of assistance? Madam?"

It was hard to make out almost any detail in the dense night, but Emily thought that perhaps the woman was wearing mourning, for she seemed to be sheathed in a full-length veil. It was possible, though unlikely, that she had come to the graveyard at night to grieve alone, although if that were the case, Emily could not think who she might have been.

"I am sorry if I have disturbed you," Emily went on, taking one slow, deliberate step after the next, holding her lamp high. A little further and the figure would fall within her circle of illumination. "Please, do let me know if I may assist you."

All at once the figure started towards Emily with such speed she dropped the lantern, stumbling backwards and falling on a low stone. Sprawled on its damp surface, she was certain the person would be upon her at any second. Gripping the yew branch hard, she turned the splintered end towards where she thought her assailant might come from, yet, at the very moment Emily made herself ready, Keeper leapt over her, growling and barking ferociously as he charged towards the spot where the woman had been standing. Confused, fearful that the woman had merely been seeking help, Emily called to her dog to stop, and he dropped on to his haunches at once. Scrambling to her feet, Emily picked up the lantern, somehow still alight, and made her way to where she thought the woman was standing. There was no trace of her existence to be found.

19

～⌇⌇～

Charlotte

The day was grey, and snow fell like ash, heavy and suffocating. No matter how she tried to rally her spirits, Charlotte could not escape the great sense of unease that continued to follow her at every moment, as if disaster was looming around each corner. The renewed snowfall only added to the sensation that they were cut off from the world entirely, a little island of isolation far away from the world of logic and reason. Here the old spirits still walked the moors after dark.

Drawing her shawl a little tighter around her, Charlotte made herself search the graveyard that lay more or less right outside her bedroom window for any trace of the mysterious woman Emily had told them she had seen last night. But there was nothing or no one there now that Charlotte could see: just a shroud of morning mist, a palette of muted greys, as the weary sun struggled into the sky, and every footprint was covered anew. All seemed quiet.

Emily was at her writing desk scribbling away with what looked like alarming commitment, and Anne sat at the other end of the table turning over a small object again and again in her hand. As

Charlotte took a seat and prepared herself to try to write, she saw it was the medallion.

"I thought it was buried with the child," Charlotte said, eyeing the item.

"As did I," Anne said. "I found it caught in my clothes, and somehow it felt as if it was not wanted in the grave, so I put it in the evidence caddy. It might yet tell us something."

Charlotte fought the urge to snatch the thing from her sister and throw it on the fire. This was foolishness indeed—she had let Tabby and her tall tales insinuate their way into her head, whispering stories to her in the dead of night. What had *really* happened—a poor innocent killed—was bad enough, and that was what she must focus on.

"If we were able to find out where the medallion came from and the significance of the design, symbols and numbers," Anne said, "it might provide us with the evidence we need to identify the . . . individual."

"Certainly," Charlotte agreed, "though I cannot fathom how, save by showing it to every person we are acquainted with and seeing if it means anything to them."

Charlotte looked towards Emily, whose head was tipped to one side, her lips pressed into a thick line as she concentrated on the page.

"What are you doing, Emily?"

"Writing," Emily said, not looking up from the page.

"Writing now?" Charlotte asked her.

Emily stopped. "Yes, I had a vision of a story, and I wanted to write it all down before I forgot it. It is a marvellous, ferocious storm of a story. I shall set it at Top Withens, so neither of you may do the same—am I understood?"

"I don't know how you can write," Charlotte said. "I have been unable to think of anything else but the bones, Tabby's fear, the shadow woman in the graveyard. Emily, don't you need to know who or what that strange apparition was?"

"We will in due course, I am sure, and besides, all that has happened is precisely why I am writing," Emily muttered. "What a wealth of inspiration!"

"I sometimes wonder if she is entirely human," Charlotte said to Anne.

"I am sure she isn't and am glad of it," replied Anne.

Emily shot Anne a smile before putting down her pen. "I do own that I should put my thoughts aside for now and return to detecting. The medallion is almost certainly one that has significance in the Catholic faith. Aside from Charlotte's flirtation with Catholicism in Brussels—"

"Emily, it was hardly a flirtation," Charlotte said. "I simply made my confession out of curiosity."

"Well, you did not take the veil—that much is true," Emily replied. "Aside from that, I know of only two Catholic families close by: the Newells and the Riordans, the young family who moved in last spring to become loomers at Ponden. They are an Irish family but never seen at our church, so I believe they are likely to be Catholic and, if so, more likely to be able to read the symbols on the medallion. We can take it to them today and ask if they would be willing to teach us."

"And as for the stones that frightened Tabby so? It seems that we are at an impasse," Charlotte said. "How we may find out more I cannot fathom."

"There is more to discover yet. I am sure of it," Emily said. She drew out a folded sheet of paper from within her writing slope and pushed it towards Charlotte. It was a hasty sketch of the design that they had reconstructed last night, barely completed before Tabby had come upon them. "It is not as precise as I would like it to be, but I believe it is enough to try to identify the nature and the meaning of the symbols here."

"I suppose we could look for an anthropologist to converse with," Charlotte said thoughtfully. "Perhaps the Leylands might know of such a person? Or I could write to Monsieur Héger—he is bound to be acquainted with one. All his circle is so learned and intelligent."

"Perhaps—but I don't think we have six months to wait for a reply," Emily said. Her face instantly fell as she observed Charlotte's do the same, and though Charlotte turned away from her sister, Emily took her hand, sinking to her knees before her.

"Charlotte, forgive me. I did not mean to be so cruel. I am thoughtless and unkind, and you may slap me as hard as you like."

"I do not wish to slap you," Charlotte said, blinking away the tears that threatened. "After all, you speak only the truth."

"Well, perhaps, and yet I could have done so without hurting you. I am rarely wrong, Charlotte, but when I am, I own it, and I own it now. Will you forgive me?"

"How could I not?" Charlotte looked into Emily's grey eyes. "How could I not forgive the other half of me?"

The sisters embraced, and for a moment, Charlotte felt at ease, as if just for a few moments all her hurts and fears were salved by sisterly love.

"Well, while you two have been insulting each other," Anne said, "I have examined the ledgers Clifton gave us. They are rather haphazard and made up of more than one hand, but they do give us a fairly detailed picture of the comings and goings that summer at Top Withens."

"Any useful entries such as the name and residence of a killer?" Emily asked, climbing to her feet to peer over Anne's shoulder at the books.

"I'm afraid not." Anne shook her head. "So many passed through Top Withens from the beginning of that year to the end—almost a hundred. Hardly any were there for more than a week, and only one throughout that summer into the autumn—Annie Fielding, a kitchen maid. It is not a name I know, but even if it were, there must be scores of Annie Fieldings in Yorkshire alone, and she could be anywhere or most likely married by now."

The door opened to reveal their father peering into the room as if he was trying to make out their whereabouts. They all stood at once, and Charlotte went to him, guiding her father towards a seat at the table. Branwell entered behind him.

It was hard to see him so, their tall, proud, vigorous father, so blighted by the loss of his sight. But as hard as it was, Charlotte knew it was even worse for Papa. He hated to feel anything less than in charge of his life and the lives of his children, which was why it was rather concerning that he had chosen to bestow a visit upon them. Could it be that he sensed what they were about?

"Papa," Charlotte said, "how lovely! Shall I ask Martha for some tea?"

"No, Charlotte, I am soon to work," Papa replied, using the back of her chair to lean on. "But I was moved to come and talk with you all, for I had a most troubling night last night beset with bad dreams and ill feeling, a feeling that has persisted into daylight hours. I wanted to see all my children this morning and know for myself that you are all quite well. You've been out in this cold far too often and far too late for my liking."

"We are all well, Papa," Charlotte said gently, taking his hands, "are we not, sisters?"

"We are," Emily and Anne agreed at once.

"Quite the pictures of health," Emily added.

"I am faring well also, Papa," Branwell said, his voice a little husky. "Perhaps I sang rather too much and rather too loudly last night, but all in all—for a man whose heart is crushed into dust— my spirits are good."

"Papa, what disturbed you in the night?" Charlotte asked anxiously, a little worried about the salt that still lined every doorway and the scent of sage that still hung in the air.

"Dreams, dear, dreams," Patrick said. "I dreamt of your mama, that she came to visit me. I dreamt I saw her standing at the end of my bed, and she told me, 'Watch out for your children, Pat; be sure you keep them safe from harm.' It was the strangest dream—most wondrous to behold my love after all these years, but unsettling indeed."

"It was just a dream, Papa," Charlotte said. "And a dream of Mama cannot be so very terrible, can it?"

"And you are all quite well?" Papa asked again. His children gathered around him, kissing his hands and face.

"We are, Papa, we are," Anne said earnestly. "Please, do not fear for us."

The small room became crowded even further when, after a quick knock, Mr. Nicholls entered.

"You seem to have strewn salt about all over the place," he said with some confusion.

"Slugs," Emily and Charlotte said at once.

"In December?" Mr. Nicholls enquired.

"Why, yes, of course, sir," Emily said archly. "Where do you suppose slugs retreat to when the weather is harsh but indoors? It's a well-known problem in Haworth, sir, house slugs—they are a blight."

Wisely Mr. Nicholls decided not to pursue the matter further, instead placing his hand on Papa's shoulder.

"May I guide you, sir?" he asked, and Charlotte noted the deference in his tone and bearing with gratitude. Emily disliked Mr.

Nicholls with a great vigour, but at least he was a gentle man and decent—and always unfailingly kind to Papa, who could be cantankerous and difficult, especially now, when he felt so weakened. Charlotte helped her father find Mr. Nicholls's arm, meeting the younger man's eye as he took her father's hand. If Emily would allow him just a little grace, she would see that Arthur was not such a very dreary man after all.

"What are you up to?" Branwell asked his sisters as soon as Papa had departed the house. "Why is Tabby fortifying the house against an army of slugs?"

"We discovered this"—Emily handed her sketch to Branwell—"etched into the back of the fireplace where the child was interred—it must have been made at the same time. Do you recognise any of it or know of one who might?"

"I can only think of two experts in such matters, and one of them has quite recently surrounded our home in salt. The other is Robert Heaton."

"Robert! An expert in paganism?" Emily exclaimed. "I've always found him to be so very mild."

"Well, not an expert, perhaps, but the library at Ponden is the greatest for many miles, and as you know, Emily, there seems to be a book for everything within it."

"That is true! The answer is always to be found in a book," Emily said. "I shall go at once to Ponden. Why, Branwell, you are occasionally useful after all."

Branwell bowed his head before resting it on the table. "Then I shall endeavour to stay alive a little longer," he said, "just to serve my sisters."

"Then we shall all go to Ponden," Anne said. "And visit the Riordans on the way."

"Why on earth should we?" Charlotte asked her sister. "It is not an effective use of our time, Anne. Progress will be much quicker if we separate—we have learnt this before. Emily can go to Ponden, and you and I can visit the Riordans and see if we can find any Annie Fieldings around and about, which, though laborious, seems unavoidable."

"Charlotte is right," Emily confirmed. "And besides, the Ponden library is very much less enjoyable with other people in it. I will make faster progress by myself."

"Perhaps you are correct," Anne said. "You make a good case for reason and logic, but I am making a case of intuition and instinct— my intuition and instinct, to be exact."

"This is unlike you, Anne," Charlotte said. "You are always so pragmatic and sensible. Explain yourself."

"That is true"—Anne nodded—"and yet I can't help thinking about Papa coming into the dining room this morning. He seemed so fragile and weakened. Somehow the events of last night wended their way into Papa's dreams and frightened him. The truth is, we are adding to Papa's suffering because of the secrets we keep from him and because he is afraid for us. So the least we can do is to try our best to be safe."

"But the very worst that can happen to us at Ponden Hall is that Robert Heaton proposes to me again," Emily said.

"Besides, we are stronger together," Anne persisted. "Charlotte, you have a gift for reading people and drawing them out of themselves. Emily, you see connections and clues that a mind inferior to yours would simply not be able to fathom."

"When you say inferior, can you clarify the context?" Charlotte asked primly.

"As for myself, I keep our minds focused on the reasons behind it all: the human reasons why we must not let our detecting descend into petty squabbles." Anne looked pointedly at her sister. "And

Branwell—well, Branwell provides us access into rooms where lone women might not otherwise go and sometimes provides a fairly adequate distraction. When we are together, we are stronger and we are safer."

Her words seemed visibly to hearten her sisters, who smiled and nodded at each other, and even Branwell lifted his head from the table, glad to be part of their party. Linking hands, they formed a four-cornered coalition of wits, determination, cleverness and cunning.

"Very well, then, we may all go to Ponden. The Riordans will be at their looms anyway, so it seems sensible," Emily said with a magnanimous sigh, "so long as once we are in the library nobody talks unless I give them express permission."

"One moment, Emily," Charlotte said at once, following Emily out of the dining room. "I do not believe that we went through the proper channels deciding who should lead the expedition to the library. Surely we should each make a case and then draw a conclusion . . . ?"

"Has Robert Heaton ever proposed to you?" Emily asked.

"Emily Jane, why must you always be so . . . ?"

"There might well be greater safety in numbers," Anne said to Branwell as her sisters squabbled. "But there is certainly a great deal more peace and quiet in solitude."

20

Emily

Ponden Hall was a stout old house nestled in the crook of a gentle hill on the way up to Ponden Kirk, one of Emily's most favoured places in all the world. The last few hundred yards up to the hall were completed by traversing a fine broad avenue lined with chestnut trees that lent the house a sense of hard-earned grandeur.

It had been built to be a working house for a working family, and it was not aristocratic or ornate in the same way that Chester Grange and Oakhope Hall were. It had earned its status amongst the people of the area much in the same way that the name of the Heatons, the family who had always lived there, had: through endurance and consistency. The Heatons of Ponden had not always been strictly good, nor were they constantly respectable. They did, however, employ a large number of local people; sit on the parish council; donate to charitable works, including the school; and do their best to show the world that their more infamous days were behind them. There was some friction between Papa and Mr. Heaton these days, not least because the elder Heaton son was rather too much of a willing drinking partner for Branwell, but throughout their childhoods, all the Brontë children had always been welcome at the Heaton table, and of the four of them, it had always been Emily who visited the most, for held within Ponden Hall's sturdy walls lay one of the greatest loves of her life: the Heaton library, a most wondrous and curious array of books, some of which were centuries old, that included volumes on botany, poetry, philosophy and law and, it seemed to Emily, at least one book that concerned itself with every subject under the sun. Within this room she could travel through the ages without taking a single step.

"Branwell!" Robert Heaton greeted their brother first, hanging out of an upstairs window, waving cheerily. Robert Heaton was a nice young man, distinct from his rougher-hewn forebears in that he was sweet tempered and gentle. He was also, rather inconveniently, terribly in love with Emily and had been since he was about fourteen and she eighteen.

"Oh, Emily," he said the moment he saw her. "How very fine to see you! I was thinking only this morning how this damned snow had kept you apart from us for too long and that the house seems less bright without your presence in it. Come in—I'll meet you downstairs."

"And I suppose we are but the chaff blown along in her wake?" Charlotte said, affronted, as Robert disappeared within.

"Poor Robert," Anne said. "All these years and he has yet to give up hope on Emily returning his affections one day."

"I cannot help my natural attractiveness to the opposite sex, Anne," Emily said. "It's a curse to be this alluring."

It was not Robert who met them at the door, however, but Mr. Barraclough, master clockmaker.

"Mr. Barraclough!" Charlotte greeted him, a little startled by the sudden appearance of his tall figure in the hallway. Mr. Barraclough was a dour man, imposing, with a dark and sallow face that had always given Emily the impression of a malevolent cat poised to attack.

"Misses Brontë." He gave them a half bow before greeting their brother with a growl. "Branwell."

"Mr. Barraclough." Branwell hastily tipped his hat and hurried down the hall.

Emily could not help noticing that Mr. Barraclough's gaze followed her brother until he was out of sight, his eyes narrowing just enough to give her pause. Her brother had offended and enraged many local people in recent months, but what on earth could he have done to the clockmaker? Whatever it was, one got the sense that Mr. Barraclough was not a man to be trifled with, especially not when the motto he added to all of his clocks was so sinister: "Remember to Die."

"Is there to be a new clock for Ponden Hall?" Charlotte asked brightly.

"I am engaged with some business here," Mr. Barraclough replied, not exactly answering the question. "I trust your longcase is running well?"

"To perfection." Charlotte smiled. "Papa winds it every evening, and it is always perfectly on time."

"Good. Good day." Mr. Barraclough nodded. "I will see you soon."

"Odd fellow," Charlotte said, once the door to Ponden Hall was closed firmly behind him. "Such a skilled craftsman but so very . . . unprepossessing."

"I find him rather frightening," Anne said. "His voice creaks like an open coffin."

"Oh, that's good," Emily said. "I'm having that."

"Shall I call for tea?" Robert asked, eagerly greeting them in the hallway that wound down towards the great hall, as it was known and had once been, but which these days was a large sitting room with a huge inglenook fireplace, tall enough for a man to stand in.

"I do believe tea would be most welcome," Emily said, peeling off her gloves. "How is Moss? Is she delivered of her pups yet?"

"Not yet, but soon, I think," Robert said, ignoring all his other guests as he directed Emily to the great dark oak dresser that had stood against the far wall of the room for as long as anyone remembered. "See how she has made a nest under here? I think that is where her brood will be born any day now."

At once Emily plopped down onto the stone flags, sand and straw, her skirts billowing out around her as she let the mongrel hound sniff her hand, and gently stroked the ears of the expectant mother, who snoozled her in return. There was a considerable chance that the papa to the new arrivals was her very own Keeper, who had got out two months since, and had returned two days later after Robert had found him in the barn with Moss. As such, she felt a familial responsibility for their welfare.

"Robert, may we have a few moments in the library?" she asked, smiling for her admirer. "There may be a text in there that could help us settle a family argument. I am sure that I am correct, but as usual nothing but documentary evidence will do to seal the matter."

"Of course, Emily," Robert said eagerly. "Our library has a great attraction for many of our neighbours, but you know that you, especially, are always welcome at Ponden. Should I make a fire so that your favourite reading spot is nice and warm for you?"

"Regrettably I can't stay that long," Emily said, leaning in a little closer to the younger man, lowering her voice, "but if you can keep Branwell and Charlotte occupied for a few minutes, that would be wonderful. You know how Charlotte always likes to interfere. I do believe she was interested in seeing your weavers at work for an . . . essay she is writing . . . about . . . looms."

Emily turned to her sister. "Charlotte, did you not wish to see the skill of the Ponden weavers at work? Robert would be delighted to take you to them, he says."

"Wonderful." Charlotte smiled. "I do find it so fascinating. Branwell will come with me, I'm sure."

"Didn't someone mention tea?" Branwell asked.

"You are good to us Brontë folk," Emily told Robert.

"I am glad to be," Robert said at once. "As you know, I think of you almost as my own family."

"Yes," Emily said. "That is exactly it, Robert: you are like a little brother to me."

"Well, I . . . That's not exactly what I meant . . ." Robert replied as Emily climbed to her feet and beckoned for Anne to follow—before Robert could say what he meant and make it terribly awkward for all of them.

21

❧⁓❧

Charlotte

The weavers' room at Ponden was one of the things that kept the substantial house from being completely gentrified, despite the best efforts of the Heatons to make themselves gentlemen. The lofty room, lined on two sides by long windows, was made all the brighter by the light reflected off the snow that surrounded them. This room had been added along with the workshop and office below some forty years earlier to join the small farmhouse to the peat loft as a place of industry in the heart of their home. The wool was spun and carded down at the mill at the bottom of the hill, but it was here that the looms continued to click and clack in a regular percussion, and the best quality cloth was spun. Those great machines that could fill a building were on the rise, and as Charlotte stood by the door and watched the weavers work, she wondered how much longer such craftsmanship could withstand the emergence of the power loom—for a little while longer, at least, she hoped. The relentless march of the automated world frightened her as much as it thrilled her. So much more was possible now: so much more production, more trade, more investment. The tighter the globe was wound in cotton, the smaller it became, feeling as if even its furthest corners could be within reach for anyone with a mind to travel. And with that, the waste also increased—the by-products that were tossed away once they were all used up, amongst them the sickly impoverished children just like the Top Withens child.

"Mr. Riordan"—Charlotte smiled at the young man who worked one loom—"your work is very fine."

"Thank you, miss," he replied without taking his eyes off the work.

"Robert," Charlotte asked her host, "I wonder if it would be acceptable if I took a minute of Mr. Riordan's time to ask him for some information about my . . . er . . . interest?"

"As long as Pa doesn't catch him standing still and he meets his quota for the day, then a minute or so is yours entirely," Robert said, nodding to the other weavers. "Now, then, Branwell, let's see if we can locate that tea I promised you, shall we?"

"Marvellous," Branwell said, winking at Charlotte. "And perhaps a dash of brandy against the cold?"

"How may I help you, miss?" Eamon asked warily, stepping away from the loom, his large hands clasped anxiously.

"What part of Ireland are you from?" Charlotte asked him. He dropped his gaze, dismayed, no doubt fearing the scorn that followed his countrymen wherever they went. "My own father was born in Ireland, in Annaclone, County Down," Charlotte added.

"Really, miss?" Eamon smiled tentatively. "We come from Antrim, but have not been home for a long time. There was no work for me in Ireland after the British . . . Well, I was sent as apprentice to Paris, where I met my wife. We wanted fresh air and open country for our children, and. well, things are bad at home, so we took our chances and came to England. It's been a hard road. . . ." The shadow that crossed his face, careworn beyond his years, told a story of a little of that hardship. "But the Heatons are good to us. They pay us fair and give us a roof. My family is not hungry, and I am grateful every day for that, even if there are some hereabouts who would rather see us gone."

"I'm glad to hear it," Charlotte said, "and that you and your family have found a home here. My father has been parson some twenty-six years, and there are still some who see him as an outsider." Charlotte brought the medallion out from where she had kept it in her glove. "Mr. Riordan, I am wondering if I might ask you a question—about your faith."

"There's no law against my faith," he told her, worried. "Every man has been free to worship as his conscience dictates since eighteen twenty-nine. We worship at St. Anne's in Keighley, as is our right."

"So you *are* of the Catholic faith?" Charlotte asked rather tentatively. It felt so intrusive to enquire, yet who else could she ask? Certainly not the Tempests of Skipton or the Middletons of Ilkley: fine families of good standing, but Charlotte couldn't risk her questions escaping into polite society.

"Aye, we are. We don't want any trouble, though, miss. . . . I know some are against us, afraid of us even. . . ."

"Some, perhaps, sir, but not I nor my family," Charlotte promised him. "Rather, I was wondering if you might be able to tell me something about a Catholic medallion I have discovered. It seems covered in meaning, but I am blind to its symbolism."

"I will if I can." Eamon nodded, but it was clear that he was still suspicious of her interest.

Charlotte handed him the medal, and he seemed to recognise it at once, crossing himself and bringing it to his lips almost unconsciously. Somehow she found it comforting to see the medallion brought to its proper purpose, almost as if it had been restored to goodness by his simple gesture of faith.

"It's a miraculous medallion, miss," he said, smiling as if she'd shown him an old friend.

"What does that mean?" Charlotte asked. "Why is it miraculous?"

"I was a boy, apprenticed in Paris, miss, when it happened in eighteen thirty—that's the meaning of the date engraved here. A sister at the convent there, Catherine Labouré, was visited twice by Our Blessed Lady the Virgin Mary, and received a design for the medallion in a vision." He brought the medallion to the long windows so that Charlotte could see it in the light. "You see here how Our Lady is pictured radiant as the sun, crushing a serpent beneath her feet, offering the faithful protection in all her perfect beauty? And here the grace of Our Lady comes forth in celestial beams from her hands to those who invite it into their soul. The Holy Mother's arms are open wide to show us that she is the mother of God and of us all. The inscription is about her purity, her conception without sin. She is standing on a globe, which shows us she has ascended to heaven. And on the reverse stand twelve stars for the apostles, and also the crown of stars, as mentioned in the Book of Revelation."

"Book of Revelation," Charlotte repeated, under her breath. The mystery and symbolic mysticism of that book had long fascinated her; there was a rather beguiling magic to it that frightened her as much as it intrigued her, for the secrets to the end of time were held among its pages.

"The entwined cross and bar on the back show her closeness with Our Lord as his mother. The left heart is the Sacred Heart, Our Lord who died for the sins of all; on the right the Immaculate Heart, which intercedes for those who sin, and the flames—the burning love that Our Lord and Lady have for us. It is a powerful object of holy protection."

"Is it really?" Charlotte took the pendant back and looked at it, entranced by the idea that slipping the brass chain around her neck could protect her from sin, from evil. It made the circumstances under which the medallion had come to light seem all the more confounding.

"Are they very common?" Charlotte asked.

"Very," Eamon told her. "There was a great deal of cholera in Paris not long after, and millions of the medals were made, but those who wore them and who turned to the true faith were saved. There are those in Leeds and Bradford and closer who wear them for protection against disease, though I haven't seen so many here as I did in France."

"Thank you, Eamon," Charlotte said. "You have been most helpful. Only if Mr. Heaton should ask, would you mind telling him that I asked about looms? It's just a rather delicate matter that as the daughter of an Anglican parson I would rather keep to myself."

"Of course, miss," Eamon said. "There is one more thing. The second date, etched into the silver on the reverse? That has nothing to do with the miracles. It must have been added later, scratched on by hand, but I can't tell you of its meaning. I've never seen anything like that before."

"Thank you," Charlotte said, taking Eamon's hands in hers for a moment. "I do not yet know what it means either, but you have taken me a little closer to finding out, and if my family or I can ever help you in return, then be assured we will be your friends and allies."

22

Emily

Knowing the library's contents and the arrangement of its books a good deal better than Anne, Emily went straight to her most likely source of enlightenment: a two-hundred-year-old volume entitled, innocuously enough, *The Book of Magical Charms*, written, as far as she could divine, by two seventeenth-century witches. She had come across it before and had taken great pleasure in opening the thick vellum pages, stiff with age, and tracing her fingertip over the strange spidery print that was unlike anything else she had ever seen. But now, upon closer inspection, it seemed to contain nothing much more interesting than spells on how to cheat at dice and to curse your neighbour's cow and make a rather nice soup.

That had been her best hope. Now all she was left with was a rather dull volume on necromancy and something that claimed to ensure success in alchemy, which she was rather tempted to take home, as it would be so nice to turn lead into gold and never have to think about leaving Papa again.

"Oh!" Anne exclaimed, holding a large dusty book open in her arms. "Pass me your drawing, Emily, at once!"

"What have you found?" Emily asked her, incredulous. "You have not found the answer to a possible pagan sacrifice in *A Short Historie of Yorkshyre and Its Peoples*. I began to read that and then put it away when I realised that it was very much less interesting than looking out of the window. Family trees and such, isn't it?"

"Yes, but if you had looked a little closer, you'd see there is a book hidden within," Anne said, her eyes wide at her discovery. "By which I mean the pages of a second book have been bound into this one, presumably to keep it secret from prying eyes. After all, two hundred years ago a person could have been hung for having such material." Anne laid the book open on the floor. "Now, it seems as if most of the secret book has been torn out—only fragments remain. But one such fragment reminds me strongly of the mysterious design."

"Let me inspect the evidence." Emily knelt beside her sister, frowning deeply.

Anne was right. There were several inner pages, of a different size and quality of paper, that had been sewn into the original book and torn out at some unknown date by some unknown person.

However, when Anne laid out Emily's sketch of the mysterious markings next to the remaining corner of one torn page, it matched the fragment of design left behind almost exactly.

"How strange that you should choose this book amongst all the others on the shelves," Emily said warily. "It is indeed a very strange coincidence and far too convenient to be trusted."

"I did not choose it, though," Anne said. "I did not take it from the shelves. It was here on the window seat with a few others. But this one was on the top of the pile, as if it had just been left there a few moments ago, and so I picked it up, and beneath it is a very old prayer book and this, *A Botanical Study of English Trees*."

Emily looked at the disparate collection of books; she knew each one had been taken from opposite corners of the library and left here together with the very book they were seeking on top.

"These books have been left here for us to find," Emily said. "They all have meaning. I'm sure of it. It must have been known that we would call upon this library, though I suppose it is not all that surprising, given that no other library close by is open to women."

"Left by whom?" Anne's eyes widened. "And for what purpose?"

"Perhaps by someone who knows the truth about the Top Withens child and wants to aid our discovery," Emily said, frowning deeply as she tried to make the puzzle pieces fit. "Or by the fiend who made those marks upon the chimney! Who else would know what was hidden in this book and tear out the pages, perhaps for the purposes of some diabolical ritual?"

"And then," Anne said, "after the discovery of the bones, returned to Ponden to ensure they had left nothing behind that might incriminate them. Except they have. They have left two half pages in the book, one with enough ink remaining to match with your drawing. And left out clear as day, when it would have taken many hours of looking otherwise and we could have missed it altogether."

Emily sat back on her heels as the clouds thickened outside, dimming the late afternoon with the threat of more snow.

"Someone knows we took the stones," she said. "Someone knows we use the library at Ponden a great deal, and knew we would be likely to come here. Someone has devised a way to leave this book out for us to find as . . . as an invitation. No, not an invitation. A challenge."

"A challenge?" Anne asked. "A challenge to what?"

"Why, to catch them, of course," Emily said.

"Are you saying that the fiend is aware of us and seeks us out?" Anne glanced around as if she were a little afraid the suspect might still be hiding amongst the books.

"Whoever they are, I can't help but feel that they must either have observed us closely or know us very well," Emily said. "Somehow guessing our plans almost as soon as we make them. For only then could they know we'd come to Ponden library today."

"Throw the book away," Anne said unhappily. "Throw it on the fire, for it is evil."

"No book is evil, Anne," Emily told her sister, seeing Anne's unease. "Not even this one or the parts of it that have been torn out. The people who followed these ways were—are—no more dangerous to you and me than the ancient Celts or Romans. They had their beliefs, and we have ours, do we not? We have nothing to fear from words, Anne, only something to learn of our own human history."

"I would agree with you, Emily, if it weren't for the bones," Anne said unhappily, rubbing briskly at the tops of her arms as if she were suddenly very cold. "Even if these rites and spells are all a forgotten fiction, the bones of the child are not. And if the strange design is connected to the remains, and it seems impossible to imagine otherwise, then it is a book such as the one you hold in your hands at this moment, perhaps even that very copy, that incited murder."

Emily looked down at the book, feeling the reassuring weight of it in her hands. She could never think of any book as anything other than a friend.

"It is only ink and paper," she said. "It is Man who kills, Anne, as Man always has for his own cruel and distorted reasons. It is only that sometimes Man makes words his unwitting accomplices, and—oh—" Emily stopped talking as she made out the archaic description written along the margin of one of the torn fragments. "Oh dear."

"Emily?" Anne turned towards her, wringing her hands tightly. "What is it? What have you discovered?"

"The missing pages," Emily said, closing the book and returning it to the shelf. "It seems it is a charm to return the dead to life."

23

Charlotte

"Really, Robert, that is *so* interesting," Charlotte said, smiling intently at young Robert, who was earnestly regaling her with how the various Heaton business interests were performing. "How marvellous. I'm so pleased to hear it."

"Yes, we Heatons are quite a solid proposal, financially speaking," Robert said. "And speaking of proposals—"

"And who has visited you recently?" Emily asked.

Charlotte blinked at her sister. She had never known another individual who could turn the subject of a conversation with such a brazen disregard for manners as her sister.

"Visited us?" Robert blinked at Emily. "Well, not very many in these last weeks, though some have come to pay their respects. It is the season of goodwill, after all, Emily."

"Yes, and who has called on you, Robert, dear?" Emily persisted. "Perhaps last night or even today?"

Charlotte knew that Emily used the term of endearment in much the same way as she would have baited a fishing hook with a worm, to keep the poor young man in her thrall for as long as it was useful.

She didn't realise she was being cruel, of course—that was just her sister. The notion of falling in love was as strange an idea to Emily as walking on the moon might be—rather more so, in all probability.

"Oh." Robert looked nonplussed. "Oh, no one of note. We had the Barraclough brother over, for Father wants another clock, and . . . I was not here last night, but I believe that Bradshaw from Top Withens Hall came to discuss a business matter. We are to invest in a concern he is developing."

"I see," Emily said, looking at Anne, whose eyes widened.

It was really most infuriating to Charlotte. Here were her sisters making what seemed to be momentous discoveries, while she had been obliged to sit here and listen to the endless list of reasons that Robert Heaton thought he'd be a very excellent husband, and not even to her.

"Yes, Bradshaw has a good track record with turning a profit, and so it seems we may be partners in his latest endeavour—"

"I say, Robert, old fellow," Branwell interrupted his friend, looking rather disconsolately at his cup of tea. "As you Heatons are doing so marvellously, well, perhaps you and I could talk about a small loan between gentlemen? I have been too unwell to be sensibly employed for a while—poor Emily is quite beside herself with worry for me. And if you feed this brain, there is certain to be a return on your investment with my own good company."

"Oh," Robert said sweetly. "Well, of course, Branwell, anything for you . . ."

"Neither a borrower nor a lender be, our dear papa always says," Charlotte said primly.

"Besides, we must take our leave," Anne said. "We have a rather urgent matter to attend to."

And before Charlotte could take another breath, Anne had

dropped a curtsey and hurried out of the house with Emily in her wake.

"Well," Charlotte said. "Please do forgive my sisters, Robert. They rather forget themselves."

"It is allowable," Robert said wistfully, watching Anne and Emily march past the front window, "especially when one is so unforgettable to others."

It took Charlotte rather longer to catch up with her sisters than it took Branwell, who, although he was not particularly tall, had legs that were a good deal longer than hers. He caught them just as they were coming to Ponden Mill, the narrow, long, four-story structure that sat half a mile from the hall, well built with long windows designed to give as much light as possible to the industry within. The great clack and clatter of the spinning jenny at work could be heard from quite some distance away.

Charlotte could not be certain of what Branwell said to their sisters, but it was sufficient to persuade them to wait as Charlotte hurried to their side.

"What on earth did you discover that encouraged you to leave so abruptly?" Charlotte asked. "I am quite used to Emily being so wild, but you, Anne—I had thought better of you. And I have a great deal to tell you about the medallion, for many believe it has miraculous properties."

Charlotte told her sisters everything Eamon had told her. Then Anne relayed all that had happened in the library in hardly more than a whisper, as if she were afraid something other than themselves might be listening to their talk.

"Emily believes—and though it seems unlikely, I am bound to

concur—that the perpetrator must know of our detection and our lives most intimately." Anne shook her head. "And was it Clifton Bradshaw who visited Ponden and somehow—goodness only knows how—divined that we were bound there and left the book out for us? I am greatly troubled, Charlotte. I believe that we are in grave danger and that Bradshaw will harm us if he thinks his crime will be revealed."

"I would say more like strong peril," Emily said, her cheeks rosy from the cold. "Whoever it is, they want to engage us in a battle of wits, so it seems unlikely that they would harm us—where would be the entertainment in despatching your enemy before the battle had commenced?"

"Sisters," Branwell said, "I am concerned. If what you say is true, then as your brother, I order you to desist in the matter at once, tell all you know to the constable and go about your more ladylike endeavours."

"I think Emily is right," Charlotte said, ignoring her brother, as did her sisters. "I don't feel that there is immediate danger. But I do fear that danger to ourselves, and to our persons, is a prospect if we continue in this matter. Think of the figure that stalked Emily in the dead of night. We don't understand all of it yet, but it seems to me to be something larger than we can fathom, a storm of malice that we may be swept away by. It would not be dishonourable to step away from this matter now. In many ways I should prefer it."

"No," Emily objected. "If we do not accept this challenge, then these people go on unchecked and perhaps more dangerous than ever. If we can discover the name of that poor child, that is the very least we can do. To return the child to memory, even if it is only ours."

"I wish we did not know any of it," Anne said. "I wish the bones had remained hidden, for I would like to put away all of our knowledge of this terrible business and go back to our safe and orderly lives, writing, thinking and walking as we always have."

"Or drinking," Branwell offered up. "Drinking is a marvellous way to divert oneself."

"I don't believe you really mean that, Anne," Charlotte said, drawing her cloak tighter around her shoulders as the chill wind buffeted them, the icy water that oozed out of the mud seeping into her boots. "You are one of the bravest and most remarkable human beings ever created. And yet you do not have to continue on this path if you feel it is taking too great a toll on your gentle nature."

Anne walked on a few steps, Emily silent at her side, leaning on the drystone wall to look out across the gentle valley. It felt as if the sun had been up only an hour or two before it sought shelter from the winter, and already the sky was pinkened by its demure departure, as the first signs of frost began prickling along the stones and branches of the stark landscape. Charlotte looked on as Anne unlaced her bonnet, tipping her face up towards the gentle snowfall settling on her long lashes.

"If only you weren't such meddlers," Branwell said gently, offering Charlotte his arm as they strolled on. "Most people are perfectly content to go through life thinking only of themselves, their families, where the next crust is coming from and whether or not they have done enough to earn a place in heaven. Not so my sisters. You are so concerned with the magnitude of life and all its complexities. It's as if all existence flows through you, and you feel every moment of it most keenly. I know you consider my opinion worthless, but I fear for you, Charlotte—for all of you. I fear for how much you care for it all; so much caring can only bring harm to you."

"Are you made of the same stuff, Branwell, dear?" Charlotte asked. "Is not all that you do to yourself an attempt to block out so much caring?"

"Well, of course it is," Branwell said. "I am nothing if not obvious. Except . . . except that Lydia has been writing to me, Charlotte—well, not exactly letters. I expect the risk of such a note being discovered is too great, but she sends money. And it gives me hope. For she must care for me still, must she not? And sometimes it is as if I can hear her voice in the wind calling out for me, as if her soul is speaking directly to mine, promising me our time will come. As long as I believe that, I can continue to live, though each hour pains me."

Charlotte touched her gloved hand to her brother's cheek, wishing dearly that she believed such hope was merited, as much as she wished it for herself and Constantin.

"Just hold fast a little longer, dear brother," Charlotte said. "And face this storm with your heart unguarded. Your sisters may need you yet."

"At your service."

Branwell bowed ostentatiously, and Charlotte smiled to see the purpose in his expression. Oh, hope was a cruel mistress; she lured you on towards the cliff edge, knowing full well you were likely to fall, but there was nothing to be done, save follow her anyway.

"I am resolved to continue," Anne said as she and Emily returned to Charlotte and Branwell. "This matter gives me a greater sense of unease and discomfort than I have ever known. But we shall persist, shall we not? For that is what we Brontës do. And besides, I have remembered something that might be of great significance."

"Tell us, Anne," Charlotte pressed her.

"There is a Barraclough clock standing silent at Top Withens Hall, where it was locked away until recently with all that part of the house."

"And?" Emily said. "How does that relate to our mystery?"

"Because we met its maker leaving Ponden Hall just as we

arrived, and"—Anne looked at each of them in turn—"there is a Barraclough clock in the library where the books were left out for us to find."

"Mr. Barraclough—" Emily stopped dead. "His Christian name is so unusual that I wonder I didn't make the connection earlier."

"What connection?" Anne pressed her.

"Mr. Zerubabbel Barraclough, that's his name. And in the midst of her raving, Bess said Zerubabbel was there the night Mary Bradshaw died."

24

Anne

As soon as the four of them were home, Branwell found a letter waiting for him in the hallway, and excused himself to his room at once. Anne watched him take the stairs two at a time, and felt a stab of anxiety for her brother. Surely whatever could raise his spirits so abruptly could lower them just as brutally. As for Anne and her sisters, they crowded into the warm kitchen gingerly, stripping off their soaking boots and stockings, and warming their bare toes before the stove, while Tabby served them a freshly baked batch of havercakes and hard cheese on their laps, as if they were little children once again.

Indeed there was a tangible kind of comfort to be found in the kitchen—in the smell of freshly made oatcakes and the condensation that ran down the inside window. It reminded Anne of simpler times, when Tabby would gather them around her faithful old chair in the corner and tell them tales of the countryside, as they listened wide-eyed, munching on seedcakes or custard tarts. There were often mystery and mischief in Tabby's stories of great black demon dogs or children taken away by the fairies, a changeling left in their place, but though they were always fascinated, they were never afraid. All was well when they were within the walls of their little house and Tabby's stout frame was between them and the dark. And though they did not speak aloud, Anne was sure that Charlotte and Emily were just as hungry for that feeling of secure familiarity— despite their brave words—as they were for the warm, buttered oatcakes.

"Do we think Mr. Barraclough, a man of excellent standing and reputation, can really have something to do with the bones?" Charlotte asked, keeping her voice low for fear that Tabby would hear her.

"We only know that he has a connection to both Top Withens and Ponden, and that he was at the house just before we found the strange collection of books Emily believes was waiting for us."

"And that Bess mentioned his name and that he was the witness of her lady's passing," Emily said.

"But we cannot know what Bess means. You said yourself she speaks in riddles."

"Barraclough is a strange fellow though. Unmarried, still living with his mother . . ." Emily looked around at her spinster sisters. "Well, perhaps not all that odd, but even so. He makes a good living. It is strange that he hasn't taken a wife."

"Is he not a Freemason?" Anne asked. "We should ask Branwell what he knows of him, for even though it has been some years since he last visited the chapter, he was very closely involved once. A Freemason might have ways to cover up a crime, if he has friends in high places."

"If we could only find a way to definitively place him at Top Withens that summer," Charlotte said. "But even so, I cannot imagine it. He is a quiet man, a man often seen in church. Compare him to Clifton Bradshaw and all that his name evokes. It seems impossible that the devil could be any other than he."

"I believe our best chance of finding the answers we need is to locate Annie Fielding, as listed in the ledger," Emily said thoughtfully as she ate. "To be able to speak to someone who was at Top Withens Hall at the time—someone who was not a child then or who is not now so old and addled that they can barely remember their own name—would be extremely helpful. Though where one begins to find that particular person, I do not know. I know of no Annie Fieldings at all. Do you, Martha?"

"I do not," Martha said as she collected up the dishes. "I do know four Fieldings, miss."

"I was thinking of Annie as we returned from Ponden," Anne said. "It seems to me that if a young woman had the determination to stay up at Top Withens Hall for almost a full year, when hardly any did, then she might well have reason to want to stay close: family in Haworth or another nearby village—or a sweetheart, perhaps. And if that was the case, then there is a chance she might still be nearby and living under a married name by now."

"Do you know of any married Fieldings, Tabby?" Anne asked as Tabby returned from the back kitchen—after all, she seemed intimately acquainted with the lives of every individual within a twenty-mile radius.

"I know five Fieldings," Tabby said shortly. As kindly as she had been to them on their return, plying them with warmth and comfort, she was still cold and stiff. Anne knew that Tabby was withholding her full love as punishment for their insistence at continuing to explore all that she considered to be most dangerous and foolish. And Anne loved her all the more for it.

"There's Harriet Fielding who goes to the school, just turned eight," said Martha. "Or Susan Fielding from Oxenhope—she's as old as the hills, older than Tabby even. Or Sarah Fielding, whose pa caught her with Leonard Ackley in the back pasture, taking—"

"I believe she's known as Sarah Ackley now," Anne said hastily before Martha could add any more detail. "But none of those sounds the right sort of age."

"If it were *Agnes* Fielding you were looking for, that would be another matter," Tabby remarked.

"Why do you say that, Tabby?" Anne asked, already on her feet ready to fetch the ledger.

"Well, she keeps house just down the hill," Tabby said. "Never married."

"It *could* be Agnes," Anne said, examining the ledger by lamplight as her sisters gathered round. "See, here, how the letter I presumed to be the first 'n' has a tail, as a 'g' would. And that 'e' could just as easily be an 's,' or any letter of the alphabet for that matter. If it were hastily written, or drunkenly, it could very well be Agnes after all."

"Where does Agnes keep house?" Charlotte asked Tabby.

"At Mr. Barraclough's, of course," Tabby said. "How do you not know that household when you have one of his own clocks standing in your hallway?"

The sisters exchanged glances.

"Surely this cannot be a coincidence," Anne said. "Detectors do not believe in coincidences."

"It is but a few steps to Barraclough's shop," Emily said, peering into the hallway, where she was checking the time of the very same clock. "I do not believe it is too late to call."

"We should not draw conclusions until we have made a careful appraisal," Charlotte cautioned. "We can make observations from a distance, gather what intelligence we may covertly, until we are able to reach an informed judgement."

"Where's the fun in that?" Emily said. "If we are to win the game, we have to play."

Anne felt a surge of fear at Emily's assertion; even so, she was not about to let Emily make this call alone, and neither, it seemed, was Charlotte.

"Where are ye going now when you've only just got in?" Tabby asked as the three women hastily grabbed half-dried stockings from the back of a chair. But just as they were about to exit there was a knock at the front door.

"You stop where you are," Tabby ordered them. "If that's fancy people at the door, you can deal with them. I can't be doing with fancy people on a Wednesday."

"Isn't it a Thursday?" Emily muttered.

"Martha," Anne said, "please see who it is."

Anne tapped her foot impatiently as Martha opened the door, but her agitation slowed to acute curiosity as she heard the well-spoken voice of a lady and Martha showing her into the dining room.

"There's a lady to see Miss Charlotte," Martha said with wide eyes.

"Oh, how dreary," Charlotte huffed. "Is she the wife of a curate?"

"No, miss, an actual lady: Lady Hartley. Here is her card. She said to please forgive her intrusion, but she had a most important matter she wished to discuss with you, Miss Charlotte."

"With me specifically?" Charlotte asked, delighted for a brief moment before the reality of having a fine lady awaiting her in their humble dining room sank in. "Oh dear." She smoothed down her tangled hair. "Having spent all day with my sisters, I am in no fit state for a lady!"

"Well, luckily for Anne and me, she doesn't want to talk to us—after all, we had nothing to do with bringing the bones down from

Top Withens, so as the inconsequential personages that we are, we are free to go and visit with the Barracloughs without her." Emily gave Charlotte one last look up and down as she repinned her hair and straightened her collar. "As for you, Charlotte Brontë, you'd better put your stockings on."

25

Charlotte

Charlotte took a moment to compose herself before she opened the dining room door to find Lady Hartley seated at the table wearing a rather magnificent berry red cloak and hat. Feeling the blood in her veins wash cold with panic, Charlotte closed the door again and hurried back to the kitchen.

"Martha, please go and take Lady Hartley's cloak and tell her I will be in directly," Charlotte told the girl sharply as she began to repin her hair for the third time, trying hard not to notice her frayed cuffs.

"But . . ." Martha looked perplexed. "But you were just in there. You just went in, miss, and then came out again."

"No, I did *not*," Charlotte insisted, so overwhelmed with fluster that it seemed the only solution to her discomfort was to wind back the last few moments as if they had never happened at all. "I peeped in, and can you imagine my horror when I saw that no one had properly attended to Lady Hartley? Do you expect me, the mistress of this house, to do your work for you, Martha?"

"No, miss," Martha said, her bottom lip quivering.

Charlotte knew she was being waspish and unfair to the poor

girl, yet she went on, finding herself unable to turn back from the path she had set out on. And the fault was not Martha's but her own heightened sense of inadequacy when confronted with a person of such quality.

"This is a respectable house," she went on, "not the sort of house where we leave titled ladies sitting in damp cloaks, Martha. Now, go and do your duty, please, and try your best not to shame me any further."

Martha sighed with the very particular melancholy that only a girl of her age possessed, and slumped off to do as she was told, even though it seemed she might have been on the verge of breaking into heartfelt sobs at any moment. Charlotte felt terrible.

"You've no need to be nervous of a fine lady simply because she is fine," Tabby told her from the sink without turning around.

"I'm not nervous," Charlotte said, the lie plain for all to hear in the tension in her voice. "Not for myself, at least. I just want our household to reflect well on Papa. It is not often we receive visitors of such note. I would hate for word to get out that we live in a ramshackle hodgepodge of chaos and clutter, Tabitha Aykroyd!"

Though Tabby's back remained firm, Charlotte didn't need to see the old woman's face to know she had grievously upset her, for it was plain in the set of her shoulders and the angle of her head.

"Oh, Tabby, I'm so sorry," she cried, rushing to wrap her arms around Tabby's waist and resting her head on her shoulder. "I *am* nervous—I'm terrified. I so wanted to make Lady Hartley's acquaintance, but now she is here, in our shabby little house, I am quite overcome. You know how I am with great people, people of breeding. I am always so afraid that they will see me, small and plain and inconsequential as I am, and laugh in my face."

Tabby turned towards her at last and held her close, just as she had used to when Charlotte was a child.

"Now, you listen to me, Charlotte Brontë," she said. "You are not small—not in any sense, excepting the obvious. You have a giant's heart and a giant's intellect, and I daresay that even the writing that you are constantly wittering on about is very decent too, for how could it not be when you learnt your storytelling at my knee?"

Tabby took Charlotte's face in her hands and planted a kiss on her forehead. "This Lady Whatever-her-name-is may have fine clothes and fine ways and a carriage with *six* horses waiting in the lane—as if anyone ever needed six horses to pull one person!—but she is still just flesh and blood, not better nor worse than you and me under the eyes of God. So you remember that, and you go in there with your head held high, and if that don't work, throw a few of them long words you are so fond of into the conversation—that shuts most folk up."

"Thank you, Tabby," Charlotte said. "Thank you, and I am sorry."

"Here's a cloak and bonnet." Martha held both items up. "What am I to do with them?"

"Hang them up, you foolish child," Tabby said. "What else are you going to do with them—bake them into a pie?"

"Oh, Martha, I am sorry I was so sharp," Charlotte said.

"S'all right, miss," Martha said. "I know you are feeling nervous about the lady, but you needn't be. Fine people like her are used to dealing with ordinary and plain folk like you and me."

And it was with that rousing cheer ringing in her ears that Charlotte opened the door to the dining room for a second time.

Lady Hartley looked perfectly comfortable as she sat, Flossy installed at her side, as though they were old and dear friends. Though this did a little to ease Charlotte's nerves, still she found she was holding her breath. Suddenly she saw their humble little dining room anew, crowded as it was with aged furniture. How very paltry it must have seemed to this woman, who occupied not one great house but three.

For a moment Charlotte thought about shutting the dining room door again, so very ill at ease was she. All she could think of was her irregular teeth and less-than-refined accent. However, there could be no third opening of the door. Now was the time to walk through or never, and Charlotte had made up her mind long ago that she was not a "never" kind of person.

"Lady Hartley," she said, dropping a small curtsey and bowing her head, "I am so very pleased to make your acquaintance."

"Miss Brontë, you are so kind to entertain me uninvited, but the truth is that ever since that poor dear soul was laid to rest, I have been unable to think of anything else," Lady Hartley explained with earnest distress. Somehow ageless, she was a very well-made woman. Her day dress was tailored to suit her every curve, and her pleasant demeanour made her naturally attractive, as was often the way with a woman who thrived on contentment and a life well lived. On this day, though, it was clear to Charlotte that she had been weeping, such was her strength of feeling over the matter of the bones.

"Lady Hartley," Charlotte repeated, curtseying again and wishing with all her might that the boards beneath her feet would open up and swallow her whole. She might well have the intellect of a giant, but at that precise moment, she felt that she had the social graces of a dumbstruck fool or, even worse, Emily. "Please do not distress yourself further. I would be glad to help you in any way that I can."

With gargantuan effort Charlotte forced herself into the room and shut the door behind her, praying silently that she would not say another foolish word aloud.

"We are so honoured that you have graced us with a visit," Charlotte said. "I only wish that we had suitable refreshments especially prepared. As it is, Tabby is making us some tea, and we have a little cake, which, though it was made yesterday, is very nice."

"You are too kind," Lady Hartley said warmly. "I do find that life is always improved by a little cake. Don't you?" Her expression sobered, her eyebrows drawing together in concern as she came to the point of her visit. "I cannot stop myself thinking about the matter of the Top Withens bones, Miss Brontë, and this afternoon I realised at once that I could not wait another minute to come to you and lend you my support. Please, tell me more about the awful discovery at the Hall."

Charlotte hesitated, unsure of whether a woman as fine as Lady Hartley would have the stomach for such horrors, but then again wasn't this the campaigner who walked the slums of Bradford and Leeds, shedding light on the terrible conditions there? And it was this woman who had persuaded her husband to fund orphanages and poor schools throughout the region. Lady Hartley was not a sheltered woman; rather, she was a beacon of hope for many.

"Clifton Bradshaw, the master of Top Withens, claims he discovered the bones when he was tearing down a wall, looking for . . . Well, he says he was searching for the ghost of his wife when he came upon them."

"The ghost of his wife?" Lady Hartley's expression was unreadable. A person such as Lady Hartley was used to much more sophisticated company than Charlotte's, and though in this house they might talk of ghosts as commonly as the weather, Lady Hartley would not be used to such country philosophies.

"Nonsense, of course," Charlotte went on. "I believe he was not fully possessed of his faculties at the time. He claims not to know how the bones came to be hidden there—that he thought they must have been there for scores of years. However, the moment we heard of his scheme to rebury the bones on his land, we were resolved that they must be brought down from Top Withens Hall at once and given a Christian burial, as you know."

"It troubles me so to think of any being so isolated and alone, even in death," Lady Hartley said, and Charlotte was moved to see there were tears in her eyes. "Dear Miss Brontë, I must commend you for your swift and decisive action in recovering the unfortunate remains."

"You are very kind," Charlotte said. "But it is all any decent, upstanding person would do."

"Well, before I visited you, I talked to Lord Hartley, and we resolved to provide the funds for a proper headstone for the child," Lady Hartley said. "Do you have a name for them that we may instruct the mason?"

"We do not," Charlotte conceded, wondering for a moment how much she might tell Lady Hartley. Everything about her was drawn to the other woman. From her neat and gentle manner to her clear green eyes and corn gold hair, she had an air of decency about her that was rather comforting, like a lantern in the dark. It would feel like a burden lifted to confide her thoughts to such a woman. "The skeleton was small in stature, and we thought it a child of about ten, but it seems it was more likely to be between twelve and fourteen."

"Oh, my dear," said Lady Hartley, reaching for Charlotte's hand, tears brimming in her soft green eyes once more. "Oh dear, I am so distressed to hear that. If you know anything of my work, Miss Brontë, then you will know that my husband and I invest a great deal of our charitable efforts in improving the lives of impoverished children. Leonard and I were not blessed with children ourselves, and so we have made it our mission to try to provide safe haven, education and comfort for as many children in need as we are able, setting up our own establishments and funding those that already exist. Do you know how the child died?"

"No," Charlotte admitted. "There are no signs of violence on the bones, but we are able to determine that the child was sickly and malnourished."

"Poor dear." Lady Hartley bent her head in sorrow. "Poor, dear soul." Her hand tightened on Charlotte's as she drifted into silence.

"It is indeed very troubling," Charlotte said. "All of us at the parsonage have not been quite the same since the bones were found. It is as if a great sadness and . . . well, a kind of darkness were released along with the bones."

"Yes, that makes perfect sense," Lady Hartley said. "You do have a wonderful way with words, Miss Brontë. I suppose that the poor child may have lain there decades. There are houses round these parts that are hundreds of years old, and past times were so barbaric and cruel."

"They were," Charlotte said hesitantly. "However, it seems that it was probably as little as thirteen years ago that the child was placed there."

"Thirteen years only?" Lady Hartley's hand rose to her chest. "How can you be sure?"

Charlotte knew that she should temporise, that she should say something vague and uncertain so as not to shock the lady or draw her further in, but she seemed so very moved by the plight of the lost child, and she was looking at Charlotte with such an open and benevolent expression, that Charlotte found she wanted to impress her very much.

"Well, you see, Clifton Bradshaw's wife died thirteen years ago, and at that time he locked up that part of the house. We know that a fire has not been set in that room since the bones were interred there because. . . . well, there were no traces of soot or blackening about them. And it could not really have been more recent, because . . . well, because they are bones and not flesh."

"How very astute of the constable to make such deductions," Lady Hartley said.

"In fact," Charlotte replied before she could check herself, "it was I who made the deductions, or rather my sisters and I, and not the constable. I'm afraid to say, Lady Hartley, that our local law enforcement, such as it is, leaves rather a lot to be desired."

"I see." Their hands still joined, Lady Hartley leant a little closer, her gentle eyes searching out Charlotte's and holding her gaze for a moment. "You really are quite a remarkable young woman, Miss Brontë. It is rare to find such a talented and driven young person these days. Most of the girls I know are so taken up with marriage and children, which is perfectly right for some, but when I look at you, I am reminded of myself. Your mind is free to think and wonder and expand. You are a woman who not only attains knowledge but who acts upon it. I know that we shall have a most stimulating friendship."

"I should like that." Charlotte flushed with pleasure.

"So then in all likelihood there is a murderer at large," Lady Hartley said thoughtfully, "who is mostly likely to be this Clifton Bradshaw, I should think."

"That would seem the most likely conclusion, but there is no proof to that end," Charlotte said. "He maintains his innocence very steadily. Short of a confession, there is not much we can do, unless we can discover the name of the poor child, perhaps, and in so doing discover how they were connected to Top Withens Hall."

"Indeed, that is what we must do."

At that moment there was a banging at the door, then the window.

Charlotte smiled tightly. "Our maid will see to it," she said, and indeed, after a moment, they heard the door open and close, and Martha appeared in the doorway.

"It's Joseph Earnshaw, miss. He says he has post for you."

"Well, as you can see, I am entertaining, Martha," Charlotte said. "Have Joseph leave the correspondence on the side table."

"But you said you'd give me a hiding if I didn't put these Mr. Bell letters into your very own hand, Miss Brontë!" Joseph called from the hallway.

"I said to him," Martha said. "I said, what would Miss Brontë be wanting with a letter addressed for some Mr. Bells!"

"Let him in," Charlotte said, standing, only knowing that she had to get the letters—and Joseph and Martha—out of the room as quickly as possible before Lady Hartley retracted her offer of friendship.

"Miss." Joseph came in, bundled up in what looked a coat cast off from his father and great boots that had certainly seen better days. And yet his eyes were bright, his smile broad and he had an air about him of a boy who had not been caught red-handed in the dead of night, trying to catch a glimpse of the bones. Charlotte couldn't help but admire him for it. "Here is your correspondence."

"Thank you," Charlotte said, slipping the letters out of sight behind the mantel clock. "Martha will give you a farthing on your way out."

"Not a ha'penny, miss?" Joseph asked. "For there are four letters there, miss, each of them addressed to the Messieurs—"

"A ha'penny it is." Charlotte waved him away. "Now, be off home, back to your mother."

"Thank you, miss," Joseph said in his poshest voice, bowing first to Charlotte and then to Lady Hartley. "I look forward to doing business once again."

Charlotte repressed a smile as she resumed her place beside Lady Hartley. Though Joseph seemed always to appear at exactly the worst possible moment, he took a certain joy in life that was very heartening to see.

"I have come up with a plan of action," Lady Hartley said without mentioning Joseph, or the Mr. Bell letters, for which Charlotte was eternally grateful. "In the course of my charity work, I have met with the great and the good, prime ministers and princes, and I speak to all as plainly as I speak to you, for I resolved when I was very young that all should know my mind whether they liked it or not. By conducting myself in this way, I have found that very soon I have the measure of whomever I am conversing with. And just as I have found you to be an intelligent and resourceful lady of exceptional character, so shall I divine the true nature of Clifton Bradshaw. You and I shall visit him, and he will open up his very soul to me, Miss Brontë—you wait and see."

"Lady Hartley, you are so very kind," Charlotte said, "but I couldn't possibly ask you to visit Top Withens Hall—not in this weather. It is a rough, cold and isolated place, more so in this snow. And Clifton Bradshaw is an unpleasant, coarse man whom someone as fine and as gentle as you should never meet."

"Nonsense, Charlotte." Lady Hartley seemed adamant. "He is no match for me. I shall return tomorrow after breakfast. My carriage shall take us up to Top Withens, and Clifton Bradshaw will find he has met his match."

"I'm sure he will, Lady Hartley." Charlotte thrilled with admiration. "I am certain of it."

"You and I are cut from the same cloth, I can see, Miss Brontë—or Charlotte, if you will allow it?"

"I will, madam," Charlotte said, quite overcome. "I should be delighted if you would call me Charlotte."

"Excellent—then you shall call me Catherine, and we shall be the firmest of friends," Lady Hartley said. "On this day begins a lifelong acquaintance, Charlotte. You mark my words, for I am determined to be your great friend until the day you die."

Especially now, after the last few days of distress and darkness, Charlotte could think of nothing more pleasing.

26

Emily

What there had been of the December sun had set while they had been warming their toes by the fire. The latest fall of snow had abated, and the village was muffled in a fresh winter coat that covered its regular dirty facade with one of picture-perfect charm.

After stopping for a good few minutes to converse with Lady Hartley's six fine black mares, Emily and Anne walked past the church to find a rather enchanting sight at the top of Main Street, as an array of lanterns and candles in windows twinkled amongst the snow-softened buildings that tottered down the hill. Haworth was a working village, full to the brim of the filth of industry, but now, for a moment at least, it was as if the last century had been swept away and here they were, standing in one of those Christmas cards that everyone seemed so keen on these days. *What a very pretty illustration they would make*, Emily thought.

Dear Keeper could not contain his happiness, inhaling everything he encountered with joyful snorts, diving into the deep drifts that gathered at the side of the lane with yelps of puppyish delight, a four-pawed comet of joy that did much to ward off the shadows that had seemed to gather around them since the discovery of the bones.

Zerubabbel Barraclough was not the only clockmaker in the area, but he was the best, his work sought after across the country and even on the Continent. Due to their fine workmanship, and the resulting price, it was considered a mark of prestige to own a Barraclough longcase; their own dear papa was inordinately proud of theirs, as there were only a handful of such clocks to be found within twenty miles or more.

The Barraclough establishment was a tall, narrow building at the top of the hill, with a small shop front where in the morning Zerubabbel would lay out his less expensive wares. With the shop front firmly shut, Emily and Anne made their way down the narrow alley that led to the back, Keeper leading the way, perhaps in the hope that they were to visit one of the five butchers who flourished in Haworth, though on this occasion he was to be disappointed. Even so, Emily was certain that Keeper had made a nasal note of the establishments where he was most likely to acquire precious treasures of bones and old hide. Keeper was not the brightest dog that Emily had ever encountered, but when it came to getting fed, he was extraordinarily resourceful and devoted. With that in mind, she tied him to the gatepost in the alley that ran along the back of the butchers, patting his broad head as he looked plaintively up at her.

"I promise we won't be long, O fierce one," Emily said. "Keep an eye out for lions and ghostly ladies who don't leave footprints."

Anne knocked at the door.

"We're closed!" came a brusque shout from within. Widow Barraclough, though elderly, was not a woman to be trifled with; indeed, she was known in the village for her sharp tongue and fierce temper, which could reduce many a good man to a puddle, should they happen to stray into her path at the wrong moment. Perhaps that was why Zerubabbel was not one for opening his mouth all that much—perhaps his mother had taught him it was safer not to.

"Knock again," Emily urged Anne.

"You knock again," Anne said unhappily. "I'll stand behind you this time."

"But she is much more likely to be nice to you," Emily told her, pushing her forward a few steps. "You are by far the nicest of us—everyone says so."

Anne sighed. "Shall that be my epitaph, 'the nicest of the Brontës'?"

Nevertheless she knocked again, a little firmer this time.

"Good afternoon?" Anne called. "Mrs. Barraclough? It is Anne Brontë from the parsonage." Anne paused. "And my sister Emily."

"And do you suppose that because you are Anne from the parsonage that we are any less closed for you?" Widow Barraclough said, opening the door and looking at each of them in turn, her lips pursed most sourly.

Anne looked at Emily for help and Emily helpfully remained silent.

"We have not come to try to make purchases from you," Anne said. "We simply wanted a moment to talk with your housekeeper, Agnes Fielding."

"Talk with my housekeeper?" Widow Barraclough snapped. "And how is that going to get my house cleaned and my dinner made if Agnes is talking to you? You will wait until she has her half day off, which is two weeks tomorrow."

"But we don't have two weeks, madam," Anne said. "We must talk to Agnes now; it may well be a matter of life and death."

"You Brontës with your dramas," Widow Barraclough said. "Everything is a matter of life and death with you lot. Well, if it is so important, then you may explain it to me and let me judge how much life and how much death are weighed in the balance."

"You will know of the bones found at Top Withens Hall," Anne said. "The bones are of a child, hidden in that room most likely in eighteen thirty-two. We think that Agnes was working there at that time. We are hoping she might be able to tell us something that will lead us to discovering the name of that poor soul so that a headstone may be engraved and perhaps a family traced."

The door slammed in their faces.

"Well, that went well," Emily said.

"What else was to be done?" Anne said, turning to her sister. "Do you think that we Brontës are always having dramas?"

"Not at all," Emily said. "Well, at least not *we* two Brontës—I can't speak for the other lot."

Just as they were about to leave, the door opened again, and this time it was another, younger woman who opened it. Though Emily was not familiar with her, she supposed that she had to be Agnes Fielding.

"You'd best come in," Agnes said in a low voice, standing aside for the sisters.

They stepped straight into a small kitchen and living room, which was at the back of the house, because the shop front faced onto Main Street. The Barracloughs were a respected family and affluent by Haworth standards. Nevertheless their home was not large or luxuriously appointed, but in marked contrast to Widow Barraclough's reputation, it was warm and welcoming.

"So Zerubbabel is not at home?" Emily asked, partly because she enjoyed saying Zerubbabel out loud, and partly mindful that Agnes might well speak more freely if she were not overheard by her employers.

"He's out," Agnes said, glancing at the clock on the mantel, which was flanked by a collection of animal skulls ranging from a fox and a badger all the way down to a tiny field mouse, each one boiled clean so that they glowed white in the candlelight. Emily thought once more of the Barraclough motto, "Remember to die," and wondered if all those animals had met natural ends. "We expect him home soon, mind, and he is very punctual, so you'd best say what you must. Mr. Barraclough does not enjoy society."

"I agree; it is very tiresome." Emily took the direct route. "We wanted to ask you what you remember about your time working at Top Withens Hall."

The look on Agnes's face was more than enough to confirm that she was the Agnes Fielding they had been looking for, for it was one that was shocked, dismayed and guarded in turn. Once again her gaze turned nervously to the clock.

"Why should you wish to know about that?" she asked. "It is no business of yours."

"No," Emily agreed. "And ordinarily I should find such reminiscences very tedious indeed, but the widow will have told you why we are here."

"She did." Agnes nodded. "I cannot help you, for I saw nothing during my time there other than the floor I was scrubbing or the veg I was peeling."

"There may be something, no matter how small or inconsequential, that you remember that might help us find the next path to take," Anne said. "Please, Agnes. If you could share with us anything that you might remember?"

"It's a lifetime ago," Agnes said. "I was barely more than a child, and now my days are preoccupied with the missus and her son. I am sure I can't remember anything of use to you."

"May we at least ask you some questions that might prompt a recollection?"

"As long as you're quick," Agnes said. "Mr. Barraclough will be wanting to be fed. He's a right old mither when he is hungry."

"You worked alongside Bess for the best part of that year," Emily began at once. "You must have seen the comings and goings. Was there anything . . . strange?" Emily asked. "Were children common-place amongst them?"

"Not that I recall," Agnes said, knitting and unknitting her restless fingers as she spoke. "But I was mostly in the house and didn't have much to do with those who came to work the land—they were housed and fed in the barn."

"What was it like up there in those days?" Anne asked.

"Like any farm, perhaps a little colder, a little more remote. Bradshaw didn't pay me much mind, and I did my best to keep out of his way."

"Were you afraid of him?" Anne asked.

"Afraid? No." Agnes's forehead wrinkled at the very thought. "When you are in service in a place like that, there are worlds that don't touch, hardly at all. The world of the house and the world of the farm. He was sometimes in my world, but he wasn't a part of it. The most I'd have to do with him would be to clear up his muddy boot prints from the flags, and that was it." She glanced at the clock. "Does that help you?"

There was something amiss here—Emily could sense it—in Agnes's benign smile, her calm and measured responses. It simply wasn't . . . Well, it wasn't like Haworth for someone to be given an opportunity to gossip freely and to refrain. Talking about one another was about the only source of entertainment outside of a rare treat like a concert or a good book. And as many of the villagers couldn't read as well as their children, then hearsay was at the very top of their list of leisure activities. Agnes was doing her very best not to tell them something. If Charlotte were here, she would have drawn the truth out slowly and carefully with such a care that Agnes might not even notice that she was being beguiled. But Charlotte was not here, which meant Emily would have to do it her way, and there was nothing subtle about that.

"You are holding something back from us," Emily said. "Not lying, not that, but not telling the truth, not all of it. The question is, why? Whom do you want to protect, Agnes? Is it yourself? Are you trying to hide your own transgression?"

"What? No!" Agnes was horrified. "How dare you!"

"Emily," Anne interjected calmly, "you cannot make assumptions like that about this good woman's character, especially not in a village where one word out of turn can become a rumour before you know it, and then suddenly the whole village is poking its nose in."

"There is nothing for the village to know here," Agnes said urgently. "I do my work and live a quiet life, and that is all."

"I'm sure it is," Anne said gently. "And I'm sure you aren't hiding anything. After all, nothing can be kept secret for very long in Haworth, can it? Please, tell us, do you remember if Top Withens ever felt like a dangerous place—a place where something so terrible could happen?"

Agnes looked deeply into the fire, and it seemed to Emily that she was seeing those long-ago summer days there in the flames.

"Dangerous, no. Odd . . . unfamiliar . . . disjointed and strange, yes."

"Can you try to explain to us what you mean?" Anne asked. "Help us get a picture of the farm back then?"

Agnes sighed heavily, her eyes on the clock once again, but nevertheless she began to talk, to truly talk this time.

"Work were scarce that year—I know that much. So when I heard they were looking for a housemaid, I didn't think twice about it. I went up in the spring, and I was happy. It was a warm spring and so pretty up there—blue sky and meadow flowers. It was a decent house at that time. Mrs. Bradshaw was a good woman from a good family, and she'd made that draughty old house a comfortable and elegant home, at least as best as she could. You could see how Bradshaw wanted to please her—he wanted to make her happy, and that were nice to see."

Emily and Anne exchanged a glance; it seemed impossible to marry that portrait of Clifton Bradshaw with the man they had recently encountered. Could the death of his wife really have altered him so very much, or had something else—something darker and more sinister—influenced him that summer?

"Bess directed my work," Agnes went on, "cooking, cleaning, setting fires, laundry—I liked the routine of it. You could let your mind wander elsewhere without any great trouble. Liston were a young boy who loved his mother, but he loved Bess and me too— so sweet he was, so good-tempered and helpful. Every morning he'd sit with the mistress and learn his letters and numbers, and in the afternoon he'd work with his father. I was content enough until . . ."

"Until?" Emily pressed her, taking a seat on a small three-legged stool that sat in the corner.

"I don't know how any of this can help," Agnes said unhappily. "How can dredging up memories of that summer produce a name for a child I never set eyes upon?"

"It may not," Anne said, "but you are the only other person still in the area who was at Top Withens at the time, apart from Bess, who is not clear in her own mind anymore."

"Well," Agnes sighed, "two instances I do remember, though I wish I didn't."

"Tell us," Emily urged.

"There was one afternoon—couldn't have been more than a day or two after Mrs. Bradshaw passed—that Liston . . . well, he went into a rage the like of which I never seen. I expect that he was mad

with grief, lost and confused, but even so . . . what he did was . . ."
Agnes looked up at them, her eyes triangles of worry. "It was awful."

"What did Liston do?" Anne asked.

"He took up one of the butcher knives and flew at Bess, holding
it so hard to her throat that he drew blood. He demanded she tell
him every detail of his mother's death. Bess told him what we all
knew. That his father had been out of the house that night and that
Mary had passed in her sleep. She said if he expected her to know
more, then he was wrong and he'd have to cut her, for she had no
more to say. Still Liston held the knife there, and for a moment, I
thought he would draw it across her neck. And then he broke down,
and Bess, she took the knife from him and held him in her arms. But
Bess, she was always different after that—distant and cold somehow.
She told me that she hadn't known until Mary Bradshaw died that
she could kill another if she wished it. I don't know what she meant,
and I never asked her, for I was always afraid to find out."

"Liston"—Anne looked at Emily, who shook her head in
return—"wielded a knife?"

"Never saw such violence from him before nor since," Agnes said.

"And the other incident?" Emily asked.

Agnes could not tear her eyes away from the clock, as if she could
feel her master drawing ever nearer.

"Clifton Bradshaw was a hard man, but I'd never seen him be
unkind to his wife until the weeks before she died, and suddenly it
was as if she could do no right. Every word she spoke provoked a
cruelty. And then as she lay dying, he began to entertain"—she
shifted uncomfortably in her chair—"*guests.*"

"Guests?" Emily glanced at Anne. Agnes had said the word with
such distaste that for a moment, Emily wondered if she had mis-
heard her.

"Yes." Agnes nodded. "There was different celebrations of sorts, night after night. Crates of wine and kegs of ale arrived, and great quantities of fine foods were delivered almost daily. I asked Bess about it, and she told me to mind my business—ever so sharp she was, which weren't like her at all. And then one morning, I found her asleep over a pile of potatoes she was supposed to be peeling. I woke her up, and she told me she'd been up all night serving the master and his guests, and she'd be doing it again that night, as he trusted only her. Well, they hadn't been in the house—I knew that much. So that night, after the house slept, I crept out. All was still at first, but soon enough I could hear the sound of revelry carried on the wind, so I followed it."

Agnes looked up at the sisters, pulling herself back into the room.

"I don't like to talk about what I saw there, but I was mightily glad that I met Mr. Barraclough up there that summer, bringing in a new clock. He told me he was seeking a housemaid, should I require a new situation. I had been uncertain, but that night I made my mind up. Even now, when I have been out of that place for thirteen years—and as a God-fearing woman I don't like to talk about it—all I will say is that it were pagan, unnatural . . . devilish. If you were wise, you'd leave this all well alone. Sometimes the past can hear you, you know. It can hear you say its name, and it comes stalking after you to catch you up and drag you back."

"Agnes," Anne said, "is Mr. Barraclough a good man? Would you ever have reason to suspect him?"

"No." The clock chimed five, and with it, Agnes's lips were sealed. "No, I will say no more. You came to ask me if I remembered a child, and I do not. If you want to know what I saw that night, then you can go and look for yourselves."

"Look at what?" Emily asked her.

"When you come out of the front door of Top Withens, you will see about a half mile away a small, tight copse of trees," Agnes said.

"Dead Man's Copse, they call it. You won't see what I saw that night, pray God, but there may be some trace of it remaining there. You go there and see what you may. I will tell you one thing more, and one thing only. What I saw there that night, it returns sometimes in my nightmares, and it still wakes me in a cold sweat until this very day."

"What's this?" Zerubbabel Barraclough came in through the door, stopping dead to take in the scene. "Misses Brontë, we meet again—twice in one day. Have you come to see me?"

"We—" Anne began.

"We did," Emily cut across her. "Papa is afraid that our clock is running slow and wondered if you might service it."

"Your sister told me only this morning that it was running perfectly."

"And it was," Emily said. "And then it went quite mad this afternoon. Agnes was just taking our message to relay to you."

Emily met the gaze of Widow Barraclough, who had appeared from the other room as she completed her story, and her heart sank as she realised how very quickly it would unravel under further questioning. And yet Widow Barraclough said nothing. Perhaps she too sensed the worry that came off Agnes in waves, as if it were she who had just been caught in a lie and not Emily. In any event it seemed that Zerubbabel's mother did not wish to concern her son with the true nature of their business either.

"I'll attend to your clock tomorrow," Mr. Barraclough said. "Good night, and watch your footing on the cobbles—they are treacherous this evening."

"Thank you," Emily said, wondering how such a concerned warning could sound so much like a threat.

27

Anne

There was something that Charlotte wasn't telling them—that much was clear to Anne from the moment they arrived home. Anne found her sister skittish and excitable, unable to settle in one place or, what was more, to listen to what Agnes Fielding had told them. That Charlotte was keeping her interview with Lady Hartley to herself was highly irregular. Under normal circumstances she would have regaled them with every detail of the meeting at once, whether they wished for them or not. But even as Emily was describing with great dramatic emphasis the look on Agnes Fielding's face as she had spoken of the evil she had seen, Charlotte's thoughts were clearly elsewhere.

Charlotte was, as Aunt Branwell used to say, "quite taken" with Lady Hartley or, as Tabby would have said, she had had her head turned. Anne could only hope it wouldn't be turned away from the matter in hand for very long, for Charlotte so distracted was of use to neither beast nor man.

In any event, their conversation with Agnes Fielding had left them none the wiser exactly, though her refusal to discuss her master was intriguing. At least she had given them another path to follow, and one that had taken them a little further in their detecting, even if she was unable or unwilling clearly to point the way. It *was* frustrating that she wouldn't say what she had seen that summer night, but Anne understood why perfectly well, and so did Emily, which was why neither had sought to press her further.

Haworth and all the countryside around it were places where superstition had purpose and meaning. It was an armour against ill fortune, which no one who grew up there ever believed was down to something as arbitrary as luck. The belief held firm that speaking of darkness was enough to bring it down upon your head, and heaven knew, Anne felt the very same way. Though she had been brought up under the protection of a Christian god whom she loved dearly, she would always bid good day to a magpie, and you would never find her leaving a new pair of shoes on the table (even though she could not remember the last time she had had a new pair of shoes). Heaven forbid she should accidentally look at a crescent moon through glass, for that would result in throwing salt over her left shoulder and a good deal of spitting. So, though Anne was well-read, educated, informed and as devoted to her faith as any Christian woman should be, she understood how the old ways were still ever present, living alongside the good people of the village, even walking with them on their way to Sunday service. It was, as Tabby said, a belt-and-braces approach, and one that served them well.

"And how did you fare with Lady Hartley?" Anne asked the moment she could find a way in between Emily's words.

"Well." Charlotte's smile was guarded, just as it had been when she was a child protecting a new book from her sisters' grasp. "Very well indeed. I like Lady Hartley enormously, especially now that we have become more friends than acquaintances. She is very bright and vital, and so very interested and moved by the Top Withens bones. Indeed, Lord and Lady Hartley have resolved to pay for a headstone for the grave, which I thought was so enormously reflective of her and Lord Hartley's reputation for being truly decent and charitable people. I found her to be exactly the kind of lady I myself aspire to be, the kind who uses her influence to remake the world. You know, I was thinking of how she became instrumental in welfare reform, and—"

"What did you tell her about the bones?" Emily asked Charlotte suspiciously. "Charlotte, you didn't tell her everything we have discovered, did you? Please say you did not tell her that we were detectors?"

"No, of course not!" Charlotte protested before glancing away. "Well, not *exactly*."

"Charlotte!" Anne shook her head in disbelief. "What *did* you say exactly? For I hardly need to remind you that our interest in detecting is not one that we wish to be made public knowledge—you above all are aware of this. As far as all outside the three of us are concerned, we are simply seeking to name the child; that is all."

"Indeed, yes," Charlotte said. "I am no fool, Anne."

"Are you not?" Emily muttered under her breath.

"Of course I did not reveal that we were attempting to solve the mystery of the bones, only that we had between us worked out an approximate time when the bones had been put there—something that impressed Lady Hartley very much. It was entirely independently that she surmised that Clifton Bradshaw was the most likely perpetrator, which I may have mentioned we agreed with, though we had found no evidence strong enough to convict him. Being a woman of high principle, Lady Hartley declared that she would like to speak to Bradshaw herself, and so we are going to pay him a visit tomorrow to see how he responds to her questioning. Anyway, do tell me more about this infamous copse."

"You are going up to Top Withens with Lady Hartley!" Anne exclaimed. "You are detecting with another!"

"This is typical Charlotte," Emily said, propelled to her feet by an explosion of temper. "She is always so keen to improve her lot that no sooner does she make the acquaintance of a fine lady than she has dropped us, Anne. For we are no use to her social ambitions. Charlotte is a high-society detector now!"

"That is not it at all," Charlotte said, blushing furiously. "It was only that she was so interested and engaging. And she had filled her life with such purpose that it made me consider how very little I have done with mine. Catherine—"

"Oh, it's *Catherine* now, is it?" Emily scoffed.

"*Catherine* has made herself someone important and influential— someone men of power listen and defer to—purely by her force of intellect and personality," Charlotte went on. "She is admirable in so many ways, and yes, I suppose I am guilty of wanting to impress her. Indeed, I suppose that I thought it could not hurt us as we embark upon our creative endeavours to have a patron in high places who might champion our works."

"Our works, Charlotte?" Emily asked her. "Or yours?"

"Ours, of course!" Charlotte looked hurt, and Anne was worried to see her sister so overwrought and highly strung, her colour high and her eyes glittering.

"Charlotte sharing confidences with Lady Hartley might not sit easily with us, Emily," Anne intervened, "but she is our sister, and we must trust that she has only the best intentions for us all and this mystery. In fact it seems to me that to shock Clifton Bradshaw with a visit from Lady Hartley is a good idea—it is always useful to see how a suspect behaves in unexpected circumstances. We might have preferred it if Charlotte had revealed her strategy to us before implementing it, but I can see that she has, in fact, been very shrewd."

Emily was not persuaded, but at least she said nothing more, simply drawing her writing slope towards her as an announcement that she would not be conversing any further this evening.

"Well, then," Anne said, hoping to settle Charlotte's fevered state and draw her mind back to the matter in hand, away from the plans and dreams she was no doubt already building on the back of this brief acquaintance. "Taking all into account, I have devised a plan of action."

"Do go on." Charlotte made sure to look very interested.

"We believe ourselves to be great detectors," Anne said. "And it is true that we have uncovered and resolved more than our fair share of conundrums. But this, I believe, is the most difficult mystery we have ever faced, and to solve it we must take paths we have not yet conceived of. Tomorrow we shall all three head to the moors: Charlotte and Lady Hartley to visit Top Withens; Emily and I to look at the copse that Agnes spoke of so darkly, then on to the Wage of Crow Hill, for I believe we must seek out the appropriate expert who will help us translate those runes once and for all."

"What sort of expert would that be?" Charlotte asked.

"I believe we must engage the services of a witch."

28

Emily

Having drawn the short straw when it came to who would bring up the matter of witches to Tabby, Emily rose at dawn and went down to the kitchen to ask Tabby how to find the witch of the Wage of Crow Hill, for though everyone knew of her, very few knew exactly how to find her.

It was a matter that had to be handled with tact, Anne had said, and everyone knew how gentle and sensitive Emily was in conversation, and how she might coax information out of a person so subtly that it would not even be noticed. Emily had never heard herself described in such a manner before.

And it should be the one of them Tabby favoured the most, Charlotte had added. Since it had always been clear since they were tiny children that it was Emily who bore that crown, whom Tabby loved the most, then it should be Emily who approached the dear, sweet old lady. Though Emily had pretended to be flattered and coddled into being the one to ask Tabby about the very subject that most vexed her, she knew as well as her sisters did that the true reason they had chosen her to talk to Tabby was because they themselves were too afraid to. And so, while Charlotte was still preening for Lady Hartley, Emily went to ask.

"As if I'd know the address of a witch!" Tabby exclaimed furiously. "Me, a good, God-fearing woman, as pious and proper as any. And anyway, what would you want with a witch? Did I circle this house with salt and dress the doors with rowan boughs in vain? Are you so determined to end your days as a toad or a goat that you are prepared to ignore my warnings and not stay away from such unholy ways?"

"No, dear Tabby," Emily assured her. "It is only that we require the expertise of a person acquainted with charms, runes and spells to help us decipher that"—almost too late Emily remembered that they had promised Tabby the mysterious design had been destroyed and no record of it kept—"that which we cannot. Charms and runes that we discovered in a . . . book, yes, a book we found at Ponden Hall."

"A book, you say?" Tabby seemed a little comforted. "I don't suppose any true harm can ever come from a book. However, though you may think me a pagan, I am afraid to tell you, Miss Emily Jane, that your Tabby Aykroyd, loyal servant of this house for more than twenty years who has loved you as if you were her own child and hoped you might return even a scrap of such understanding and affection for her, does not know the witch of the Wage of Crow Hill."

"Oh." Emily was disheartened.

"I do, however," Tabby said, "know the visionary of the Wage of Crow Hill. And I suppose she might be able to help you, as a scholar of all things. Listen good now, for she lives a solitary life and makes it her business to be hard to find, and I will not tell you the way twice."

"I will," Emily promised, smiling at the prospect of a most interesting day.

"Oh, and there's one other thing," Tabby said.

"What's that, dearest Tabby?" Emily asked, hugging the old lady.

"You'll have to cross the border into Lancashire," Tabby said. "For she's all that's left of the Pendle wit . . . wisewomen now."

"Lancashire, hey? Oh well," Emily said. "Needs must."

29

Charlotte

Charlotte had risen with the dawn, encouraged by the prospect of the day ahead and looking forward to spending a morning with Lady Catherine Hartley. So she took great care over her hair and wardrobe, choosing the rings that best accentuated her fine fingers, and fastening around her neck a little string of garnets that was once her mother's.

Just as she considered herself ready, she heard the sound of horses and Lady Hartley's carriage was outside, though it came as something of a surprise to Charlotte to find her sisters and Branwell waiting ready to accompany her.

"Oh," Charlotte said, looking at them with some dismay.

"What do you mean, 'Oh'?" Anne asked her.

"Well, it's just that Catherine—Lady Hartley—asked *me* to accompany her up to Top Withens, not all of us."

"I am happy not to come," Branwell said, attempting to turn on his heel but failing when Emily pinned him to the spot. "But if I must, I own it would be preferable to do so in a carriage."

"We are travelling more or less to the same place," Anne said. "If you are to ride up there, it seems unkind to make us walk when there will space enough in such a fine carriage."

"It's not a question of what is fair, Anne," Charlotte said, "rather of what is proper. I am not in a position to extend Lady Hartley's invitation, and I certainly don't want to impose upon her good nature."

"Oh, good Lord," Emily said. "The sun is up, and I can smell spring in the air. I'd much rather walk anyhow. Come on, Anne, Branwell. Let us leave Charlotte to her airs and graces."

They were all taken aback as Keeper, who a moment before had been sleeping in the kitchen, leapt up with a furious bark and hurled himself at the front door, snarling and growling as if the devil himself had come to call. Bemused, Emily opened the door, and the dog flew out of the house, bounding and leaping over the gravestones with quite some speed, disappearing into the distance.

"How very strange," Emily wondered. "I rarely see him so vexed and toothy."

"I imagine that it is just too fine a day for any self-respecting dog to want to be inside," Lady Hartley said, appearing on the doorstep with a beaming smile. "I always say you must let the beast be free or pay the consequence. Don't you agree, Emily?"

"I suppose I do," Emily said, offering a rather begrudging curtsey, as if she were suddenly a surly child being forced into study.

"We are of an accord." Lady Hartley smiled warmly. "I hope you don't mind my taking your sister away from you for a few hours this morning, Emily, Anne, Branwell? We are rather keen to try between us to get to the bottom of this matter with the bones, rather like lady constables—can you imagine?" Her laugh was very merry.

"I cannot!" Emily replied. "It seems inconceivable. As it happens, Anne, Branwell and I are also heading up the moor this morning. Please do not run us down when you pass us by."

"We shall do better than that," Lady Hartley said at once. "Join us in my carriage. It will be rather a tight fit, but we five can scheme and plot, and the journey will go all the faster."

"Thank you, Catherine," Charlotte said, smiling encouragingly at her siblings.

"It would be very pleasant," Anne said, stepping out into the bright morning.

Emily followed the small party out into the lane, walking to the horses, resting her hands on their necks as she looked at them.

"These are very fine animals," she told Lady Hartley, "maybe too fine for the rough roads up to Top Withens. Take it gently. As for me, I will walk and ease their burden a little. Besides, I must keep an eye out for my dog."

"Then I will accompany Emily, and so shall Branwell," Anne said at once. "We need him for our journey today."

"Well, hang on," Branwell began, but Anne had already secured her arm through his.

Charlotte felt a little pang of uncertainty as she saw her three siblings walk away without her, as if she was losing them somehow. And then Catherine opened her carriage door, and all such misgivings evaporated with the morning mist.

30

Charlotte

Though the sisters seldom used it, there was a broad track that led up and across the moors all the way to Top Withens and beyond. Charlotte did her very best to enjoy the slow and rather sedate journey, as the carriage trundled back down to the bottom of Main Street, then picked up the lane that took a gentle incline following the spine of the hills, rather than the steep and rocky paths that Branwell, Emily and Anne would take. Framed by a carriage window, the scenery seemed tamed somehow, as if she were viewing it framed and hanging on the wall of a fine house. And then there was the whole business of trying to think of interesting things to say. Making friends came so much more easily to her than it did to her sisters, but even so, the casual chatter of a fond acquaintance was not one that Charlotte was practised at. It wasn't until she had found true common ground with either Ellen Nussey or Mary Taylor that Charlotte had really felt able to share her deepest thoughts and feelings with them. She hoped that such a bond might grow between her and Catherine. There was certainly early promise in their interactions. Nevertheless, without her family flanking her, she felt desperately shy and inadequate.

"Oh, please don't be shy of me, Charlotte, dear," Catherine said, as if she were somehow able to read Charlotte's mind. "For I myself feel leaden of tongue and vacant of thought, and if neither one of us can begin a conversation, we shall be in a pretty pickle."

"Forgive me," Charlotte said with a small smile. "But I refuse to believe that you have been vacant of thought in your whole existence."

"Then you know me better than I could have hoped for," Catherine replied, laughing as the carriage rattled on. "Whether or not one should speak one's thoughts is another matter. My dear husband is always imploring me to keep mine to myself, but I ask you, Charlotte, what good has ever come of silence?"

"I suppose sometimes silence can protect others from hurt," Charlotte said. "For example, I wouldn't have minded Branwell keeping silent about some of his adventures. And I rather like it, as a state of being. But when it comes to the inner workings of my mind, it is full of noisome thoughts and ideas, each demanding to be heard. Fortunately for me, my papa has never been of the mind that a young woman should be raised to be quiet and insignificant— rather the opposite, in fact."

Catherine nodded, her eyes drifting towards the view of the rolling countryside. "Would that I'd had a papa more like yours. Most assume my childhood was very grand, but I began life in a lowly position and have come to be a person of consequence only through the machinations of fate, rather than breeding."

"Oh?" Charlotte enquired, doing her best not to look too intrigued. "Was your father strict?"

Catherine winced, telling Charlotte that the word "strict" might have been something of an understatement.

"Papa was the younger brother of his family and the headmaster of a small school for boys. My mama died soon after my birth, and I was brought up his only child, the only girl at the school, where I was regarded as a curiosity or a pest much of the time. Papa was not a warm man, so when he died just after I turned ten, I found it hard to mourn him, though everyone expected me to. Then I was transported to live with my uncle, Papa's older brother, at Oakhope Hall close by to Haworth, as you know, and—well, I expect you are familiar with the family history thereafter."

"I knew that there had been more tragedy than seemed fair at Oakhope," Charlotte said, not wishing to elaborate. "I've always thought what a fascinating house it is. Is it true that it is built upon a network of man-made caves?"

"It is." Lady Hartley nodded. "My ancestor was a strange man with a passion for follies and grottoes. There are at least two temples on the grounds and all manner of passageways and secret rooms."

"Your childhood there must have been wonderful," Charlotte said, "so much opportunity for adventure."

"My life there was more comfortable than it had been at school, but sadly not wonderful—rather unhappier still. My aunt looked upon me as a burden, and my adopted older brothers hated me at sight; they tormented me daily. It was quite a dreadful time. Even so, when my adopted brothers both died within a few months of each other, I was very sorry. Suddenly I was fourteen years old and something of an heiress. It was quite an adjustment to make, to rise up to expectations. That others had suffered and lost their loved ones and lives for me to find myself in such a fortunate situation has never escaped me. I decided on my eighteenth birthday that what wealth and privilege I had would be put to good use. God smiled at me when, soon after that, I met my dear husband, and within the year we were married and honeymooning in Paris. What gloriously happy months those were. You know, the cruelty I grew up amongst had hardened my heart so much that I believed it would be better to marry for status and fortune than for love. That was until Leonard brought me all three. I do believe that my husband's love healed me of all my hurt." Lady Hartley patted Charlotte on the back of her hand. "What I am trying rather inexpertly to say, Charlotte, my dear, is that I recognise a little of my younger self in you—only a little, because you have far greater potential than I ever did, and it will not be an accident of circumstances that brings you to the fore, but your own very great talents and abilities. So please do not be shy of me, and I will do my best not to be shy of you. Is that agreeable? And please don't forget to call me Catherine. I can only hope that somehow I might be able to guide you towards the same happiness I have found for myself."

"Thank you, Catherine," Charlotte said warmly. "I count myself very fortunate to have met you."

"Good," Lady Hartley said, just as the coach drew to a stop outside the gate at Top Withens. "Now, let us see what Clifton Bradshaw makes of me, shall we?"

31

⤜❧⤐

Anne

In truth it did seem a little strange to Anne that in all their countless long walks across the moors, they had never, not once, ventured into this tight-knit thicket of woodland before. It had not been a conscious choice. It simply had never been attempted or even thought of. Indeed, so used was she to walking around the circumference of the woodland that she'd forgotten it was there, almost as if it were invisible.

Anne had read that when the Romans had first come to Britain, they had believed it to be the island of the dead. The local tribes they encountered were so strange and superstitious that it seemed to those invaders that this was a land of ghosts, already half lost to the underworld, with whole realms existing out of sight. It was something like that she felt as she crossed the border from the snowy moor into the quiet decay of the wooded area.

Here the evergreen cover of the conifers was so dense that only a little snow had settled on the ground, leaving a blackened carpet of fallen needles to form a sucking pulp with the sodden peat. There was no birdsong, no noise at all except for their own footsteps.

"What *are* we doing here exactly?" Branwell asked, drawing his muffler tighter around his neck. "I thought we were going to see a witch, not drown in freezing mud, which, if I am honest, is not my favoured method of death. I'd rather be turned into a toad. At least a toad knows where he stands with other toads. Toads are much less likely to be deceived and ignored."

Anne could only surmise that Branwell's last letter from Mrs. Robinson had not been to his liking.

"Agnes Fielding told us to come and see for ourselves if we wanted to know what events she witnessed here the summer that the Top Withens child was hidden in the chimney," Anne said as they trudged on. "Though now we are here, I must admit I cannot conceive of what could possibly remain of an event that took place so long ago."

Though they took but a short time to walk around the little copse, it seemed to be taking them twice as long to walk through it and out the other side. It was so difficult, so boggy and damp, that for a little while Anne fancied that they really had wandered into one of those hidden lands the ancient Romans had written of, when the weather and the locals had proved too unpalatable for them to bother conquering on their first attempt: the lands of the hidden folk, always there and always out of sight.

"Perhaps we might see something that would link these woods to the markings from the fireplace," Emily suggested as she looked around. "Look for carvings in the trunks of the trees or a great sacrificial altar in a clearing . . . ?"

"I'm fairly sure we won't find anything like that . . . Oh." Anne stopped in her tracks just behind her sister, with Branwell at her shoulder. For sure enough, just ahead was a small circular clearing made luminous by the snowfall that had covered it. At its centre there stood a formation of three huge stones. One great flat flag lay across two others on a slight tilt, rather like a giant's table.

It was Anne who broke ranks first, walking into the clearing to inspect the unexpected sight.

"There are boot prints still visible here," she said, pointing to the indentations in the snow, "softened by the last snowfall, but still present. Someone has visited here recently—last night or perhaps early this morning."

Emily looked at the prints as she walked around the stone to the other side. The horizontal stone was set so high that it met Emily between her breastbone and her waist.

"I was half expecting them to be the same as the ones I saw in the graveyard, but they are much bigger," she said. "And these are the prints of a man's boots, I suspect. What's on the table?"

"Food," Anne said, brushing a layer of powdery snow off a loaf of bread, some apples and a bottle of cider. "Left by the owner of those boot prints, I'd wager, for they are not rotten or spoiled."

"Perhaps an offering." Emily picked up an apple and took a bite out of it. "Usually when a child is born, or someone has died, folk still leave out gifts to the old gods, just as they would never forget to talk to the bees and tell them their news for fear of offending them."

"Who would have thought it important enough to leave this here in weather like this?" Anne wondered, running her gloved hand along the surface to clear off more snow. In truth she had been expecting to find more strange markings, but there were none that she could see, just the smooth limestone she was so familiar with. "Not even Tabby would come all the way up here in this weather to honour the hidden folk."

"Top Withens is the closest house," Emily said. "Even so, there is nothing here to suggest what it might have been that shook Agnes Fielding so badly."

"Who do you think made this altar?" Anne asked.

"No one, most likely," Emily said. "It looks strange, I grant you, but this formation is hardly any different from those at Alcomden Stones—it is just that it is on its own and hidden away by trees. It most likely has always been here, or at least since a great wall of ice left it this way thousands of years ago."

"Another thing to note," Branwell said, "is the trees themselves. Scandinavian pines are not indigenous to these parts, but have most likely been deliberately cultivated. I would suggest that the trees were planted around these stones some forty or fifty years ago, with an aim to keeping them from public view, perhaps for some kind of ritual."

Anne and Emily looked at Branwell.

"Branwell, what an intelligent suggestion!" Emily said.

"There is no need to sound quite so surprised," Branwell said. "I do have my uses still."

"See how it benefits you, not to be inebriated?" Anne said.

"Well, let me see. I'm freezing cold, wet through and not entirely sure what we are looking for or, indeed, if I even really know my sisters anymore, so frankly, no, I do not."

"If Branwell is right, this was treated as a secret sacred place for years before the bones were hidden," Anne said, a thought striking her. "Do you remember—one of the books in the pile we found at Ponden Hall was on the symbolism of trees? Could it have been a pointer towards this woodland as a part of the mystery of the child?"

"Pine trees are considered symbols of wisdom, fertility and life never-ending," Branwell told them. "I cannot tell you why I have that knowledge, since it comes from my days as a Mason, and our secrets are not for the ears of mere women."

"Well, the trees were full-grown when Agnes came here," Emily said, noting Branwell's contribution, but ignoring his barb, "following the sounds of something she did not wish to describe. Could she have witnessed a murder? Could the child, already weak and sickly, have been sacrificed here?"

"I do not believe so," Anne said. "Agnes didn't want to talk of the evil, but if she had seen something so terrible, she would have spoken of it, I am sure. She is a God-fearing woman, and it would be a great sin to hide such knowledge."

"Unless she was too afraid to speak up," Emily said. "Perhaps she feared that if she did, she would be in danger. Perhaps it was Zerubabbel Barraclough himself she saw that night, and he has had her in his thrall ever since, unable to escape his clutches."

"Zerubabbel Barraclough?" Branwell questioned them. "You suspect him of nefarious deeds?"

"He is of interest to us," Anne said. "He had access to Top Withens that summer, his housekeeper worked there that very same year, and he was at Ponden just before we found the books. He certainly doesn't want anyone to know his business, and he doesn't seem too fond of you, Branwell."

"Ah, well, there was a slight discrepancy in the lodge accounts when I left, but it had nothing to do with me," Branwell said. "Barraclough has never really accepted that to be the case and never fails to remind me of that. You truly suspect him to be the culprit?"

"We have no clear suspicions as yet," Emily said. "After talking to Agnes, I have even wondered about Liston. . . ."

"It cannot be Liston," Anne said at once. "Every interaction we have had with him has shown him to be decent and good. One cruel deed does not make a monster, Emily—you should know that. Besides, he was only a boy at the time, grieving his mother."

"Liston is a fine fellow," Branwell added. "A jolly good man."

"Perhaps," Emily said, keeping any further thoughts to herself.

"There was *talk* back when I was in the Masons," Branwell said with a rather oblique waggling of his eyebrows. "Nothing to do with the lodge—that was entirely respectable—but there was a cohort of local gentlemen who formed a sort of Hellfire Club and engaged in rather hedonistic activities."

His sisters looked at him blankly.

"You surely know what I am implying without my having to soil your tender ears with more detail."

"Please do," Emily said with an entirely straight face.

"Well, one heard of very . . . loose behaviour at immoral gatherings . . ." he stumbled on. "Individuals disrobing and engaging in—"

"Oh, Branwell! Stop soiling my innocent ears!" Emily cried, pulling down her bonnet with her hands and making Anne burst out laughing.

"You are a pair of hoydens," Branwell said, smiling begrudgingly at his sisters' merriment. "However, it is possible that a decent young woman like Agnes Fielding would have been very shocked to see such events."

"But we cannot know or guess at what she saw, whether it be violence or seduction," Anne said. "All we know is that this seems to be a sacred place for those who still follow the old ways. If the bones and the markings on the fireplace have something to do with a pagan ritual of some kind, then perhaps the gatherings Agnes spoke of—the feasts of food and wine—were held here. Perhaps the Hellfire Club you mentioned, Branwell, was a sort of version of ancient ritual used as an excuse for debauchery."

"Well, they never invited me," Branwell sighed.

"We do know Clifton Bradshaw was a changed man just before and after his wife's death," Emily said thoughtfully. "And we know that whatever is written on the torn-out pages of the book is a charm that claims to raise the dead. Rumours have persisted that Clifton Bradshaw sold his soul to the devil. But perhaps he was so crazed by grief that it wasn't his soul he was trying to sell; perhaps he was trying to buy back another—his wife's. And perhaps the poor child whose bones we found paid the price of that transaction."

"I know that I stand to lose the feeling in the lower half of my body if we stay here a moment longer," Branwell said. "If you are determined to drag me around from place to place, can we at least go and visit the witch now, and give me something to look forward to?"

"It is an hour's walk, Branwell," Anne said. "Do you wish to go home?"

"I do not," Branwell said with some determination. "For I miss the time when my sisters and I shared every thought and every secret, and we were always a four-cornered house. I miss the times when we told one another everything and never kept secrets from one another."

He looked pointedly from Anne to Emily.

"Well, we do too, brother dear," Anne replied tentatively. "Is there something you wish to tell us now?"

"Is there something *I* wish to tell *you*?" Branwell said. "For heaven's sake, let us go and see this witch, and perhaps she can magic me a new set of feet."

32

❧❧❧

Charlotte

Liston was already in the yard as they arrived, perhaps having glimpsed the team of horses coming into view when they were still some way down the track. It was, after all, a very unusual sight to see such a very fine carriage progressing up and over the moors, and Charlotte imagined that the stark black of the horses must have been visible against the white-blanketed hills from some distance away.

Someone certainly had alerted the occupants of the hall, for as the carriage came to a halt, Bess, Molly and Clifton Bradshaw himself all emerged from within, standing in the frozen mud, bundled in an assortment of mufflers and blankets. At the sight of Clifton Bradshaw, Charlotte shuddered as if a shadow had passed over her and with it, a terrible, fleeting sense of danger, like a warning borne upon the wind.

Charlotte waited for Lady Hartley to make her exit as the coachman, a tall, silent gentleman called Hemming, came around to hand them down. As she waited, her gaze sought out Clifton Bradshaw's face, intrigued to see how he reacted to the unexpected arrival of such a great lady. Charlotte wasn't sure what sort of expression she might have expected to find on his face—perhaps one of disdain or contempt at the prospect of yet more interference—but it was neither of those. Clifton Bradshaw looked utterly stunned at the sight of Lady Hartley, as if he had just received a powerful clout about the head and had yet to come to his senses. His gaze followed Lady Hartley in disbelief; his jaw fell open. He was aghast and, yes, afraid to see such an eminent person.

Such was the power of wealth and status, Charlotte thought to herself, the ability to knock flat any beneath you. Even one as proud and unruly as Clifton Bradshaw was cowed by Lady Hartley's regal presence. How wonderful it must have been to believe that wherever you trod upon this earth, the very seas would defer to your superiority. And yet Catherine had come from a place lower than her own. Perhaps it was possible, even now, that Charlotte might learn to occupy the world as if she were entitled to it, just as Lady Catherine Hartley did. She would watch very closely and learn.

"You must be Mr. Clifton Bradshaw?" Lady Hartley held out her hand to him and Charlotte watched as he simply nodded, almost as if he were in a trance.

"I am, for my sins," he said. Taking her gloved hand, he bowed over it, refraining—only just—from kissing the back of her hand.

"Mr. Bradshaw, Liston"—Charlotte realised rather belatedly that Catherine would not expect to introduce herself—"may I present Lady Hartley of London, Leeds and Oakhope Hall. I'm sure you are familiar with her name and good works."

"I am honoured, madam," Bradshaw said, gesturing towards Liston and his servants as he straightened his shoulders. "We all are honoured by your presence. How may I serve you?"

"I rather think the question is how I may serve *you*, sir," Lady Hartley said with a lightness that surprised Charlotte. "Sir, I come to relieve you of your terrible burden."

"And what burden is that, Lady Hartley?" Clifton Bradshaw asked her, his eyes still wide as he observed her, who in the meantime became all the more intimidating because of her poise.

"Why, your burden of guilt as a murderer, of course." Her voice was as soft as the promise of summer, her words as devastating as a thunderstorm, and indeed Bradshaw looked as if he had been struck hard by lightning, dazed and dazzled. "Now perhaps you will invite us into your home for some refreshments?"

"Molly, tea," Clifton barked at the young woman, who curtseyed and began herding Bess inside. "Liston, I don't know why you are standing around like you've nothing to do. You'd best see to these horses—make sure they are fed and watered."

"Yes, Pa." But Liston too seemed to have fallen under Lady Hartley's spell, standing perfectly still as he watched her and frowning slightly, as if he couldn't quite believe she was there.

Charlotte followed behind Lady Hartley, as did Clifton, as she made her way into Top Withens Hall as confidently as if it were her own. Once inside the hall, she peeled off her gloves, laid them on the refectory table and removed her cloak, handing it to Clifton to hang up without once looking at him directly. Charlotte watched as Catherine, without a moment of hesitation, sat at the head of the table, indicating to Bradshaw that he should come and sit in the chair to her right. After a moment Bradshaw did as he was told.

It was an object lesson in power and class—in becoming something greater than you were born to be. And yet at what cost? Charlotte wondered. Would she find it a great loss not to be part of the swirling currents of the world, but rather to rise above it and sail upon its tide? Charlotte thought not; rather she imagined what great good she could do if only the world would acknowledge her existence as important.

"Charlotte, dear, will you hasten the tea?" Lady Hartley asked her, without taking her eyes off Clifton. "I'm terribly thirsty, and the young lady seems rather preoccupied."

Charlotte did as she was bid, and found Molly removing one of two sharp-looking knives from Bess's clenched fists, as she stood transfixed by the oven, gazing at Lady Hartley.

"Can you manage, Molly?" Charlotte asked her, rather concerned.

"Oh yes, miss," Molly said sweetly. "Sometimes Bess gets terrible afraid for no reason and clutches onto a blade, but I shall have them loose in no time, and before you know it, she will be sweet as honey once again."

"Be sure your sins will find you out," Bess muttered as Molly carefully prised open her fingers. "Be sure they will hunt you down."

Liston came in from outside, then crossed at once to take the other knife from Bess and guide the old lady into a chair.

"Where do you keep your good china?" Charlotte asked Molly, who could not take her eyes off Liston.

"I'll fetch it down, Miss Charlotte," Liston said, gesturing at the top shelf of the dresser. "Molly, bring the tea directly."

Charlotte noted how Liston kept his head bowed, making a concerted effort not to look at Catherine, which led her to believe that he too was feeling desperate.

"Polly, put the kettle on," Bess sang as she watched Liston arrange the cups on the tray. "Polly, put the kettle on. We all fall down."

"Now, then, Bess," Molly said, "you've got yourself in a muddle again."

Charlotte and Liston took seats at the table.

"Mr. Bradshaw," Lady Hartley said, "please, tell me everything you know about the discovery of human remains within this building."

Bradshaw shook his head, bewildered.

"There's nothing I can tell you that I haven't already told Miss Brontë here more than once. Nothing more than all must know, the way folk gossip round here. We found the bones—that was the first I knew of them. I was in error not reporting them to the law or the parson. At first I assumed they were at least a century old. But the boy found a medallion that dates them to but a few years since. And that is all I know. Lady Hartley, you must believe that it was not me who hid the bones in my house, nor took the life of the one who once owned them."

"I do not believe it, sir," Lady Hartley said. "In short, I think the opposite is true, and it would be for your own good to admit it to all now. Do you agree?"

At last Clifton Bradshaw looked up from his hands into Lady Hartley's eyes. Charlotte was shocked to see them brim with unshed tears. "Why do you wish me to, madam?"

"Because it is the truth. Because it is your doing," Lady Hartley replied evenly.

Bradshaw frowned deeply, his fingers knitted together in distress as he shook his head once.

"I have sinned, madam," he said. "I have sinned against my wife, my son; I have sinned against my employees—even Old Bess there; I have sinned against God, but I did not murder that child."

Charlotte sat back in her chair, amazed to discover that in that moment she believed him.

"Pa, you must tell them what you told me," Liston said. "You must speak the truth."

"Liston!" Bradshaw hissed at his son, swearing under his breath.

"The truth?" Lady Hartley directed her gaze to Liston, her expression softening a little. "What truth, young man?"

"My father is no murderer, but he has done wrong. Pa, tell them, for it might explain it all."

Clifton shifted uncomfortably in his seat, fascinating Charlotte as she watched him. Here was a man quite different from the one she had met on previous visits. It seemed that Lady Hartley disarmed him a little further with every word and look she directed at him, in a way that neither the law nor Charlotte herself had been able to. It was really quite incredible to witness; though she did not know it, Lady Catherine Hartley would make an excellent detector.

"Nothing will be gained from it, boy," he growled.

"And yet now all must be laid bare," Lady Hartley said with velvet-clad determination.

Bradshaw rubbed his rough hands over his face and shrugged like a man who had agreed to put a noose around his own neck.

"Liston was not the only child here that summer," Bradshaw said, looking at his son. "Times were hard—I needed my labour cheap. As usual I chose as my workers single men and maids, those who didn't have family or other such commitments: bodies that were strong and willing to work for less if no questions were asked. But still, I needed more hands on the land."

Lady Hartley was silent, but her eyes did not waver from Bradshaw's face. Clifton held her gaze for as long as he could, and then it was as if all the energy within him drained away in an instant. His shoulders slumped, his eyes closed, his chin dipped as he turned his face away from her, unable to bear her scrutiny a moment more.

"Mr. Bradshaw, you told me you long for peace, and that you cannot confess to what you haven't done," Lady Hartley said. "So why don't you confess to what you have done?"

"I made an arrangement," Bradshaw said heavily. "A private one. I heard of a woman offering cheap labour, and I went to meet her. She was the headmistress of an orphanage school in Halifax. We struck a deal; I paid her the price of two grown men's wages, and she allowed me use of twenty or so orphan boys for the summer." He lifted his chin in a faint gesture of defiance. "If you ask me, being up here under the sun and in the fresh air with good food in their bellies was the happiest most of them had ever been, but for some of them . . . well, they were too young and too sickly to be here, yet I kept on working them—I had to. Some of them . . . perished . . . and were taken to the orphanage to be buried. When the season was finished, she came and took the rest of them down again, back to the orphanage. She offered me the same deal the next year, but I didn't take it again."

"Why not speak of this before?" Charlotte asked him. "It is not the practice of a good man, but neither were you alone in the exploitation of impoverished children, Mr. Bradshaw. I don't even believe you to have broken a law."

"Because now I have a shame that I did not then," Bradshaw told Charlotte. "Those boys were younger than my own son, and I treated them worse than dogs. I did not take one aside and kill him and brick him away behind my walls, but I might as well have done, for those who died did so because of my greed. That inhuman abhorrence I will confess to—I will wear it on my chest like a brand—but the death of that hidden child, that was not my doing."

"Mr. Bradshaw," Lady Hartley said, standing up abruptly, gesturing at Charlotte to fetch her cloak, "perhaps you are not as familiar with my life and my work as you should be, for I work tirelessly for improved conditions, education and justice for all children—for the many and the one. I *will* name the killer of that lost child for all to hear. Do you believe me?"

"I do," Clifton Bradshaw said, standing to meet her gaze. "And do you believe me?"

"That remains to be seen," Lady Hartley said. "Your fate remains in your own hands . . . for now. You should do what you know to be right, sir."

As the carriage pulled away, Charlotte kept her eyes fixed on Clifton Bradshaw's face for as long as she was able, trying to interpret what emotion she saw imprinted there, but Top Withens was already far behind them before she was able to draw a conclusion.

"Well, wasn't that fascinating?" Lady Hartley said. "He is guilty—I'm sure of it—and we almost had him, Charlotte. We almost had him. But he is a practised liar."

"Though it seems hardly likely, given all the circumstances surrounding the discovery, I find . . ." Charlotte hesitated to speak, lest she displease Lady Catherine. "I find that I am inclined to believe he did not harm the child or hide the bones within his house."

"Why, Charlotte?" Lady Hartley asked her. "Because he was humble, racked with guilt and wore his tears like pearls?"

"I suppose so," Charlotte confessed. "His regret seemed plausible."

"Oh, my dear"—Lady Hartley patted Charlotte's hand—"you live a sheltered life, whereas I have made it my vocation to look into the shadows and shine the brightest light I can on the horrors I find there. A dear young lady like you can have no idea of the depth and depravity of true evil, nor the tricks and disguises it will employ to hide itself in plain sight. But I will reveal it to you, my dear. And when you truly understand it, it will quite take your breath away."

33

❦

Emily

The journey to find the visionary of the Wage of Crow Hill had been a surprisingly pleasant one, given the weather and the remoteness of the visionary's address. Indeed, it took less than an hour, and best of all, Emily thought cheerfully, no one talked to her for the whole of the walk. Keeper had yet to make an appearance: a minor concern that gnawed at her a little, as usually if they were both out of the house and separated, he would somehow come to her side eventually. Still, perhaps in this weather, he'd chosen an oven-warmed flagstone in the kitchen over being with her, and Emily couldn't blame him if he had, as much as she missed his great foolish head constantly butting at her for attention.

At last a dwelling came into sight, so well covered by snow that, even though a thin reed of smoke wended its way upwards directly out of the roof, it would have been easy to discount the concealed mound as another bend of the hillside, had you not been looking for it.

"Well, as this is the only home for several miles in any direction,

I believe we have arrived," Emily said. "Do you suppose she might lure us into an oven and have us for her dinner?"

"I think we have long since been far too old and tough to be appealing to child-eating witches," Anne said. "And besides, I am fairly certain such a humble abode could not house a full-sized oven."

"I, for one, would be quite happy to be thrown on a fire," Branwell said. "I shall offer myself up at once."

As they approached, Emily could see that the structure was more of a hut than anything resembling a house. It was made of drystone walling that seemed to have been gathered from the moor, every irregular shape fitted together in a lovingly crafted puzzle and formed into a circular construction. It was not thatch that showed through the snow where the warmth escaped, but the grasses and heathers of the moor itself, draped over the humble abode like a rather magnificent cloak.

Even then its location was supremely discreet, situated as it was halfway down one of the steeper slopes of Crow Hill, facing towards Pendle. Perhaps, Emily thought, that was so that the visionary could better keep an eye out for approaching witch-hunters.

A makeshift door made of old timber fitted a low entranceway quite neatly, and Emily found herself rather taken with the little dwelling, for it looked as if it might have stood here for a thousand years or just been thrown up yesterday, and she was drawn to the notion that a person couldn't tell which. Its solitude and remoteness, and the way that it was enfolded so gently into the arms of the landscape, appealed greatly. Indeed, if it had been on the Yorkshire side of the border, it would have been perfect.

"Miss Visionary, are you in?" Emily called out before knocking on the door as Tabby had instructed her to do. "My name is Emily

Brontë. I am visiting with my sister Anne—our friend Tabby Aykroyd sent us and sends with us the message that when the crow speaks the truth, the very hills rumble."

Emily had questioned Tabby closely on the meaning of the nonsensical phrase, but Tabby had simply made her repeat it over and over again until she was certain Emily had remembered it correctly.

"You don't want to end up as a puff of smoke, do you?" Tabby had said, and Emily could not be sure that she was teasing.

A low growl came from the other side of the door, but there was no sound or movement within. The growl turned into barks that sounded strangely familiar to her, which was explained when the door was dragged open and Keeper burst out of the hut and into Emily's arms, planting her flat on her back and covering her in drool.

"Calm yourself!" she laughed, struggling into a sitting position with the great hound nestled on her lap as if he were Flossy. Emily was rather surprised to find a very pleasant-looking, rosy-cheeked young woman standing over her, holding on to the collar of another great thickheaded black dog.

"How did my dog get here before me?" Emily asked her.

"Dogs know things," the young woman told her. "Your dog saw fit to tell me that you were coming visiting today, and that is just as well, as I do not like to be startled by company."

"I understand exactly," Emily said, taking Branwell's hand and climbing to her feet. "What a fine fellow," she said enthusiastically to the visionary's dog. "I was always rather put off the idea of being a witch by the thought that their familiars were felines, birds or toads and the like. If anyone had told me dogs were allowed, I should have taken a different path, for certain."

"I'm not a witch," the young woman said. "I am Elizabeth Goode, visionary, so if you've come all this way for a love potion in the hopes that you may avoid the lives of old maids and ne'er-do-wells, then you've come in vain." She gave all three of them a swift appraisal. "You shall all die unmarried. Good day to you."

"That is not why we have come, Miss Goode," Anne said crossly, her cheeks flushing. "And though you may be a wild woman of the moors, there is no excuse for rudeness, madam. We have been sent to you by your friend Tabby Aykroyd, and we have said the secret words, or whatever they are, and as it happens we are here on a very serious matter. One might expect that, as a visionary, you would already have perceived that."

The young woman pursed her lips and shrugged, standing aside to let the three siblings in. "Very well, come in if you must, and please, if you are to address me, call me Lizzy. Miss Goode makes me sound as old as the hills."

"We were rather led to believe that you *were* as old as the hills," Anne said as they stepped inside the dwelling. Once the door was shut, the only light came from the central hearth and a tiny beam of daylight that shone in through the opening in the ceiling. The hut was warm, though, and smelt pleasantly of herbs, smoke and dog. There was a warm bed covered in furs in one half, and everything else a lone person and their dog required to survive in comfort stored in and around the little home, including a decent collection of books and a variety of meats and fish drying and curing on hooks over the fire. "For our Tabby is so old, and she said she had last come to you when we were but small children."

"I must own the fact that I do not know your Tabby Aykroyd, though she surely knows me," Lizzy said.

"But how can that be?" Anne asked her.

"The visionary of the Wage of Crow Hill is a hereditary role," Lizzy told them. "It passes from grandmother to granddaughter. Tabby must have known my granny, who was also called Lizzy Goode. In time, when I find a man who pleases me sufficiently, I shall bear a daughter, and her daughter will be named Lizzy Goode. Then she will take over this place when I am returned to the earth. For that is how it has always been and how it will always be."

"And have you yet found a gentleman to please you?" Branwell asked her.

Lizzy looked him up and down. "No," she said.

It seemed unlikely that a life as perfect as this one could continue for very long, not when the mills and machines of industry were cutting ever further into the wild land, but Emily hoped that Lizzy's certainty was well-founded.

"I have never met a visionary before," Emily said happily as she took a seat on a low wooden stool, with both her Keeper and the great black dog leaning against her as if they had always been the best of friends. "What does such a life entail?"

Lizzy shrugged, throwing some herbs and berries into a pot of simmering water that hung over the fire.

"I keep my own counsel, live my life simply and in harmony with Mother Nature and all her animals. And from time to time, when I am blessed with a vision, I see into the future and make a prophecy," Miss Goode told her. "But I don't bother telling people my prophecies much these days—they are never grateful for the warnings, and in truth sometimes it is kinder just to let fate take its path unseen."

"Well," Anne said, "we have not come for a prophecy, but for your expert advice, if you will give it to us. We have some coin to pay you for your time."

"As you have not come for love potions, I shall help you," Lizzy said affably. "I cannot tell you how very bored I am with silly girls coming up here, thinking I can conjure up a husband for them out of thin air."

"We promise not to tell our sister Charlotte where you live," Emily said.

Emily took the stoneware mug of heather tea that Lizzy handed each of them, grateful to wrap her frozen fingers around its gentle warmth, as the great beast of a dog laid his head on her lap.

"You are so very young to be living such a life of solitude," Anne said. "Did you never think that you might want something different for your life than that which had been decided even before you were born?"

"No," Lizzy Goode told her, and that was the end of that conversation. "So, if you have not come for a love potion or a prophecy, then tell me what have you come for."

"It might be that we journeyed in vain, as you are not precisely a witch," Emily said, producing from her pocket the drawing she had made of the strange design. "We recently came across these symbols inscribed within the hidden burial place of a child we suspect might have been murdered. We are trying to find out the names of the child and of the one who would commit such a crime. The only further information we have is a drawing of part of a similar design found in a two-hundred-year-old book of charms. And we believe it might have some link to the stones in the copse near Top Withens."

"I see," Lizzy said, eyeing each of them in turn. "Well, then, I shall reveal to you a great and closely guarded secret, and if you ever reveal it, I will hunt you down and cast a thousand curses on your heads. Do you wish to continue?"

"We wish to continue," Emily said.

"We swear to keep your secrets." Anne nodded.

"I could wait outside?" Branwell offered.

"Too late now," Lizzy told him. "Your fate is already sealed. I am a witch, not a wisewoman or a silly girl who fancies herself good with herbs and charms. I am a Pendle witch born into the old magic that has been practised and protected by them like me since those ancient times when they would call us Druid. And if you ask for a wisdom of dark magic, then you must be prepared to pay that price. Are you prepared?"

"Yes," Emily said at once.

"Then we shall continue. Let me see what you have brought me."

"Here." Emily handed Lizzy her drawing.

Lizzy held the paper under the shaft of smoky daylight, her eyes squinting as they first adjusted to the light, then widening. Before Emily could say anything, Lizzy had thrown the drawing onto the fire and leapt to her feet, then begun tossing various leaves and powders into the flames to make them spark and briefly change colour as she murmured some kind of incantation.

"Lizzy, what did you see on the paper?" Emily asked her, also taking to her feet so that Keeper fell over onto his side midsnore. "Why did you burn it when we are not sure we are done with it?"

"I burnt it for your sakes and for mine," Lizzy told her with genuine fear in her voice. "That you have been travelling abroad with such an abomination in your pocket is very concerning indeed and deeply dangerous. What you had in your palm was the worst kind of ill-used witchery, stitching together your God and the rituals of men, along with a summoning spell and a trap. It's an abomination. You are very fortunate as it is that you have not had the worst kind of evil turn up at your doorstep and invite itself in. Spells like that made out of anger and desperation are a beacon—an invitation to darkness and danger to gather round."

"Oh dear," Anne said, looking at Emily. "It looks as though we might need some more salt."

"The one saving grace is that whoever made that foul charm is not a witch, nor have they held counsel with any real witch or anyone who truly knows the old ways, and as such I believe it is not as powerful as it could have been. What they have done is to make a monstrosity—a sacrilege—out of ancient practices long since buried in the ground and forgotten, and tangled it up with such hate and ill will that it can only have been made by the worst kind of soul."

"You called it a summoning spell?" Emily asked her. "To summon forth the devil?"

"No." Lizzy shook her head. "No, though it might be hidden under that false promise. The person who made that spell believes themself to be the devil already. What you discovered is a trap—a trap set to capture innocent souls and in doing so make them captive forever."

"Souls?" Anne asked her. "You use the plural, and yet only one set of remains has been discovered."

"Only one set that *you* have discovered," Lizzy added. "This madman believes himself to be under the influence of the dark moon— the new moon, you might call it, when the moon is cloaked fully by the night, unseen and invisible, but still there, wielding its power over all who walk the earth. It's on the nights of the dark moon, when his hunger demands to be fed, that this creature seeks satisfaction."

"But then . . . there could be scores of hidden bones?" Anne asked, sceptical. "One child might go missing unnoticed, but surely not hundreds?"

"Not hundreds, no," Lizzy said. "The dark moon is only one of the conditions they seek to carry out their ritual. There is another circumstance that must be aligned in order for him to act."

"What is it?" Emily asked her. "Could you tell it from the drawing?"

"I cannot, but I can tell you what I feel if you will stand it."

Emily and Anne exchanged a worried look.

"Tell us," Anne said.

"That somehow it is you who have awakened the monster—you who have set him to kill again."

"Us?" Emily said. "Because he knows us, and he knows that we are looking for him?"

"You didn't come here for a prophecy," Lizzy said very gravely, "but you are going to receive one anyway, it seems, so listen and listen well. The one who made this mark is seeking a terrible kind of peace, the kind that is only found after the acquisition of a new soul. There will be more to come. The next dark moon is tomorrow night."

34

Anne

"If Clifton Bradshaw killed that child," Anne told Charlotte the moment she returned to the parsonage, almost before she set foot through the door, "then it is likely that there are more victims, Charlotte—and that there may be another soon."

"What do you mean?" Charlotte asked, taking off her bonnet.

Anne had expected her to look as bright and as vivid as she had yesterday when she had spent time with the vivacious Lady Hartley, but today the opposite was true. Her sister looked pale and drawn, depleted by the day. There were shadows beneath her eyes, and as little as she was, she seemed even smaller somehow, as if a piece of her had been stolen away by the hours that had passed since last they met. Perhaps, Anne thought, she should have insisted on them all staying together after all, especially when there was so much danger abroad.

Anne took Charlotte's cloak and led her into the kitchen, where Emily was making bread for the morning. Tabby, having prepared that night's supper, had already taken to her bed, and Martha had gone home to her pa's house. Emily was alert, as on edge and keen as Keeper at the scent of a rabbit, and since both her sisters were out of sorts, Anne took it as a sign that what they needed more than anything now was each other.

"Branwell!" she called up the stairs, forgetting for a moment that she was likely to disturb Tabby. "Do stop brooding over whatever was in your last post, and come and be with your sisters, for we need you."

"He's been strange all the day," Emily said, thumping down the dough on the flour-covered tabletop with quite some clout. "Kept asking us if we had anything to confess. Anne and I? We never have anything to confess—it's always you older two who are piling up secrets and scandals."

"I have no secrets," Charlotte said wearily, taking a seat by the range. "I cannot claim that my misplaced affections for a certain gentleman are a secret to anyone who loves me. Indeed, Emily, you and Anne know me better than I know myself. Look at me and tell me what scandals I might be harbouring, for at this moment, I feel quite undone and tired of feeling at all."

Emily stopped kneading the bread and looked at her sister.

"What did you discover at Top Withens?" she asked Charlotte, wiping her hands on her apron, and she and Anne gathered round.

"That though Lady Hartley is adamant, I am wavering in my belief that Clifton Bradshaw is guilty of cold-blooded murder. I have no evidence for this belief other than that I sat at his table and saw him speak with what I took to be true honesty for the first time since this matter began. Lady Hartley insists otherwise, however, and she is a far more worldly person than I. Her work on behalf of the poor has taken her into circumstances so terrible that we could hardly imagine them, sheltered as we are."

"Worldly does not always equal wise, Charlotte," Anne said. "And you have the wisest heart I know. What you are able to divine through your feeling and intuition is almost as formidable as your mind."

"I thought that was so, but"—Charlotte shook her head—"what do we really know of the world, Anne?"

"As much and more than any lady who rides in a carriage and lives in three houses," Anne said. "We who see children die, wives beaten, men of God drunk and lecherous—we are not sheltered from reality, Charlotte; we *are* it. Lady Hartley is very admirable, I'm sure—her philanthropy is much admired in well-appointed drawing rooms—but do not doubt yourself on her account, not now when we need your mind more than ever."

"Then tell me what you discovered when you visited the witch of the Wage of Crow Hill," Charlotte said.

"She's not a witch—she's a visionary," Anne and Emily replied in unison.

"Lizzy Goode was able to interpret the marks that Emily sketched, and she was very vexed by them," Anne said. "She told us that it wasn't a witch who made such a ghastly design, but that they were made by someone more like a madman: a lunatic who has twisted ancient lore and Christian beliefs to suit his own hateful vision. The inclusion of the medallion must be part of that strange mix."

"Gracious." Charlotte sat forward a little, her waxen complexion drawing colour from the warmth of the range.

"And what's more, she believed that the death of the Top Withens child was not a lone offence, but that there would be more, Charlotte: that when a collection of events, or signs, as she believes the monster sees them, combines, he will strike again. Miss Goode thought the discovery of the bones, and our detection, combined with the forthcoming night of the dark moon, a phase when the moon doesn't shine at all, might make that strike . . . imminent."

"I find this theory quite terrifying," Charlotte said. "All my courage has flown away, and I wish we had never become involved in the matter of these diabolical bones. If by trying to solve this mystery, we have caused harm to another, then . . . we are just as guilty as the monster!"

"I do not disagree, Charlotte," Emily said, letting down her damp hair and spreading it over her shoulders to dry, "but I don't believe we may turn back now, much as we might wish it. We know the monster is aware of our efforts, and our only source of protection is to reveal his identity. So hold fast a little longer—if we can stay safe until after the dark moon, then at least the danger will have passed for a little while. Did you discover anything new at Top Withens?"

"Indeed I did." Charlotte's sigh was heavy of heart.

Anne settled on a stool at her sister's feet as Charlotte told them about Bradshaw's confession to using child slave labour. "It may be that though it was many years since, there might be someone there who would remember the names of the children who didn't return from Top Withens. So tomorrow I believe we must travel to Crossed Keys Orphanage and its school."

"I shall come with you," Branwell said, appearing at last, his shirt loose, his hair tousled as if he had been sleeping, his eyes red and swollen as if he had been weeping. "For goodness only knows what endeavours you get up to when you are out of my sight."

"We should be glad to have you, brother," Anne said, "though I am afraid that if we are being hunted by the very creature we seek, there is the possibility of danger abroad for us all."

"The only thing I fear," Branwell said with neither artifice nor flourish, "is isolation and solitude from those I hold dear."

"Did your letter make you very sad?" Anne asked Branwell.

"Perhaps you should tell me that, Anne," Branwell said. "Perhaps you should all tell me if the letter I received made me very sad. In the meantime, I am going out—I will see you on the morrow."

"Our brother is very strange," Anne said after Branwell left.

"Well, he is awake," Emily said. "The two states seem to go hand in hand."

35

Emily

They scarcely talked for the rest of the evening, each lost in her own thoughts. Again and again Emily ran through her mind the possibilities of who the nameless monster could be, for it had to be someone near to them, someone privy to their movements if not their thoughts. If it was not Clifton, could it be Barraclough or perhaps a Heaton? For a moment Emily narrowed her eyes at Mr. Nicholls, who had joined them for dinner, and then at once dismissed him as a potential suspect. Thirteen years ago, he had still been in Ireland, and besides, he was not nearly interesting enough to be hiding a secret devotion to an ancient demonic witchcraft cult. As it was, he had given up conversing with Charlotte on the second attempt, engaging Papa in a low, droning conversation about liturgy.

Emily had thought she understood the extremes of the human soul—that she had witnessed every insane and awful impulse that could possess a heart and drive it mad—but this monster, whoever he was, was something worse than she had ever imagined, and that disturbed her greatly. It could be that Lizzy Goode was wrong, of course. That she was an interesting and compelling woman was not in doubt, but they had no proof that she was right in her supposition other than her word. And so Emily clung to the thought that such abhorrence simply could not be true if she had yet to imagine it.

After supper the sisters convened around the table.

"Then tomorrow we shall take the coach to Halifax—agreed?" Emily suggested.

"Yes," Charlotte said, "I believe Halifax is our next best hope of discovering more information. Perhaps the matron Bradshaw schemed with is still in their employ, and if she is, then at least we will be able to alert its trustees to her misdeeds. Lady Hartley is particularly keen to find a way to press Bradshaw further—"

"Is Lady Hartley added to our ranks now?" Emily asked Charlotte. "Will we ride to Halifax in her fine carriage tomorrow?"

"No," Charlotte said. "She told me she has another important engagement to attend to, but that she will continue to pursue the truth. I am sure she thought Clifton Bradshaw would simply bend to her will, and he did, more than a little. It was quite astonishing to see, and we would never have known about the orphanage if it was not for Catherine. In the meantime, she will ask her husband to make some enquiries with suppliers and merchants Bradshaw deals with in the hope it might bring more pressure to bear on him."

"A forced confession is not a safe one." Emily frowned. "I suppose we all might admit to something we didn't do if our livelihoods were at stake. It doesn't seem like the tactic of a principled and fair person."

"And who was there to stand up for fairness when it came to the fate of that child?" Charlotte asked her.

"That is true, I suppose," Emily admitted grudgingly. "But has *Catherine* lost her taste for detecting already?"

"Catherine is not detecting," Charlotte replied, treading carefully. "That is not an occupation I would ever undertake with any

214 &ep; *Bella Ellis*

but you, my sisters. She thought she could bring her influence to bear on Bradshaw, and she did. Tomorrow it will be just we three at Halifax. And I am fearful that we may not be match enough to stop this creature."

"Not so," Anne said at once, taking Emily's and Charlotte's hands in hers. "We are a match for it, sisters—more than a match, fearful as we may be. Let us resolve that this demon in human form shall not pass wherever we stand guard."

But before they could make such a resolution, there came a furious knocking at the front door, and terrified shouts and cries from without.

"Goodness me!" Charlotte cried, going to the window. "It's the Earnshaws at the door, terribly distressed. Whatever can the matter be?"

The sisters tumbled into the hallway to discover a scene of chaos and confusion. Tabby, her long silver hair plaited down her back, was brandishing a brass candlestick, and Papa was behind her, his pistol cocked and loaded, though owing to his poor eyesight, it was not pointed in the right direction.

"Begone, villains!" he threatened the longcase clock on the stairs.

"Wait, Papa." Anne stepped in front of him, gently removing the gun from his hands. "It is not villains—it is our neighbours, and they are in great distress."

The moment Charlotte opened the door, Sarah Earnshaw collapsed across the threshold, weeping with such anguish that any word she tried to utter was incoherent; all that could be seen was that she was terribly upset. Her husband, Martin Earnshaw, knelt at her side, holding his wife close to him, his own face streaked with tears.

"We need help," he told the Brontës. "We need help, and you are the nearest people we could think of to go to."

"Of course, Martin," Patrick said, walking towards the sound of Martin's voice. "Tell us at once what has happened."

"It's our boy, our Joseph. He's gone—he's been taken from his bed, we think. His clothes and boots are left behind. There is a smear of blood on his pillow and in his place this strange thing—a thing we have never set eyes on before."

Kneeling down beside Martin and his wife, Anne held out her hand, knowing exactly what Martin placed in her palm the moment her fingers closed around it. Her hands were trembling as she lifted them aloft for her sisters to see what lay within.

It was a miraculous medallion exactly like the one that had been found with the bones, with the same image of the Virgin Mary on one side. Reaching out, Emily turned over the medallion and drew in a sharp breath, for on the other side of the locket was a date etched into the back just as there had been on the other medallion, but with one crucial difference.

The year inscribed was the present year, eighteen forty-five.

The meaning was clear to Anne and her sisters: Joseph Earnshaw's life was in grave danger, for whoever had killed the child at Top Withens thirteen years earlier meant to kill him too, at the next dark moon. Lizzy Goode was proved right after all. They had awoken a monster.

36

❦

Emily

There had been a grim urgency to their journey that morning, every stage of it seeming to take too long. The freezing rain soaked them through as they waited for the omnibus, none of them able to bring themselves to set foot in the Bull, not when the search parties that had been out all night looking for Joseph were returning home desperately cold and empty-handed.

As soon as he had heard the terrible news the Earnshaws brought to his door, Papa had sent for the constable, who immediately proceeded to Top Withens Hall with some local men, making a thorough search of the house and the Bradshaw properties. Nothing was discovered, to the disgruntlement of the villagers. Emily and Keeper had been amongst their number as most of them had set out across the moor, despite the late hour and the snow, searching every barn, every outhouse, ditch and cave for any sign of Joseph. Emily had heard them muttering to one another in the dark, catching snatches of names and suspects carried on the wind, all of which belonged to outsiders: folks who were a little strange or simply strange to Haworth. It seemed to make no difference that most of those mentioned had been nowhere near Haworth thirteen years earlier, when the Top Withens child had died. All those cold and frightened people wanted as they searched in the dark was someone to blame, someone real, made of flesh and blood, who could chase away the nightmare vision that each of them held in their minds. Someone they could hang.

From without, the Crossed Keys Orphanage looked a well-appointed establishment.

It was an elegant building, situated on the outskirts of town, that had been built as a home for a wealthy gentleman. Upon his death some thirty years earlier, and having no living descendants, he had bequeathed it to be used in perpetuity for the benefit of the impoverished and unfortunate children of Halifax and its environs. His financial legacy had expired some years earlier, and the orphanage now survived on the patronage of local wealthy families.

A redbrick house, it presented as pleasingly symmetrical, enclosed by sweeping lawns and mature trees that gave it an air of gentility and refinement promising a child a nurturing and secure foundation on which to build a life. In Emily's experience, however, outward appearance was often a veneer, carefully pressed down in order to hide the secrets that lay beneath. The Crossed Keys Orphanage was no different.

Charlotte rang the bell. It tolled with sombre resonance that spoke more of funerals than of young and tender lives.

"Imagine arriving here, a child all alone in the world, to the sound of that bell," Anne said unhappily. "It must feel like stepping off the edge of the world."

"But better than life on the street, Anne," Charlotte reminded her, "or in the workhouse or debtors' prison. I pray God we will soon see an age when man no longer cages children for the sins of their fathers. We must be grateful to the great and good who fund such institutions as this one, for though it may be hard here, at least the children receive an education. It is a good deal better than scratching out a life in the gutter or working to death in the mills."

At last the grand door opened, and a waft of warm, pungent air escaped from within: air that smelt of sweat and grime, boiled cabbage and—yes—desolation.

They were appraised by a tall, slender woman dressed in a mourning gown that was nevertheless embellished with a great deal more black ribbons, crêpe and lace than one might have expected from one in her position. As fine as her gown was, her expression and demeanour seemed to be made up of entirely vertical lines; even her main features were downward slashes of dour expression, her thin brown hair pomaded tight against her narrow skull, leaving a pale line of scalp running down the middle of her head.

"Yes?" she asked, imperious and dismissive.

"We are here on an urgent matter that requires your immediate attention," Emily said at once, causing her sisters some astonishment, for Emily was not normally one to take the lead when it came to conversing with strangers. On this occasion, however, there was no time to lose—certainly no time for Charlotte's niceties and manners, and all the rest of that time-consuming waffle. "You must show us your records of all inmates for the year eighteen thirty-two and allow us to interview any within who were present in this establishment during that year."

"Must I indeed?" The woman regarded Emily through hooded lids that made her eyes appear almost entirely black. "For what purpose?"

"We work on behalf of Bell Brothers, a firm of solicitors," Emily told her. "A great fortune has been bequeathed to a person we believe to have been at this establishment in that year, whether inmate or employee we are not yet sure, but we must ask a great deal of questions before we can say more. And it must be now, before the fortune is returned to the treasury unclaimed."

There was not a flicker of expression on the woman's narrow face, and yet something moved her, and Emily was certain it was the mention of money. Even before they stepped over the threshold, she had the measure of the woman.

"Then you'd better come in. I am Mrs. Poole," she said, her voice as thin as a reed. "I am headmistress here, and have been these twenty years. Please follow me."

They followed Mrs. Poole into what had once been an elegant and lofty entrance hall, now painted in shades of grey and draped in shadows. Mrs. Poole, who seemed to glide over the stone flags like an apparition, led them into an office that smelt of carbolic, and was as neat as a pin and as bare as a dead man's house.

"I was here in 'thirty-two," she told them, taking a seat at her desk. There was only one other chair in the room, so all of the Brontë siblings stood, with Branwell, who had been sullen and near silent, leaning casually against the bare wall as if any contact with something resembling authority inspired instant rebellion. Mrs. Poole observed them all in turn for several seconds each.

"I have had many dealings with solicitors, and never have I seen any such as you. Three spinsters and a . . . gentleman." She spoke the last word slowly as if it were not really pertinent when it came to Branwell.

"That you have never met any like us before does not mean we do not exist," Emily said. "So please hasten to answer our questions. As I mentioned, this is a matter of urgency."

"Well, I have been here since my dear husband, Mr. Poole, died, and a kindly benefactor saved me from ruin by finding me this position. This place and its occupants have been my life ever since. My calling, you could say, for I do believe that all children—even the lice-infested, ignorant, ungrateful little . . . persons who occupy this place—deserve a chance at bettering themselves as I have bettered myself. When I was born—"

"Please forgive me for interrupting you, Mrs. Poole," Emily said, "but you see the truth is, we do not care about your personal philosophies. Restrict yourself to the matter in hand."

Mrs. Poole visibly seethed. It seemed she was a woman used to extolling her own virtues a great deal. Even so, the prospect of money kept her civil and, more important, to the point.

"Other than myself only our cook, Mrs. Seed, and one of our tutors, Mr. Markham, were at Crossed Keys in the year you speak of. He was an inmate here as a boy and returned to us last year to tutor the boys after making a great account of himself at school and university, thanks to this establishment."

"That is most inspirational," Emily said. "I believe it would suit us to talk to Mr. Markham first, and then to Mrs. Seed. We shall find them ourselves and return to question you last, by which time you will have all the records we require ready for us."

"That is out of the question. I shall accompany you at all times," Mrs. Poole said, affronted, her death mask of composure slipping a little more as she stood up with a scrape of her chair. "I cannot allow strangers to wander about amongst the children, speaking to anyone, saying anything they like. I cannot allow the boys to be frightened and surprised. Why, they might say anything, for they are always lying. And then where would we be?"

"You may not come, Mrs. Poole," Emily told her with a tone of authority that surprised even her. "We cannot do our work properly or thoroughly unless we can talk to those concerned separately and in confidence. You will know our findings soon. As for your children, they have nothing to fear from me or my junior assistants."

Emily turned to her siblings. "Come along, staff. We have much to do, and time is running out."

37

Anne

"Junior assistants?" Charlotte questioned once they were a few yards safely down a corridor, heading towards the sound of children chanting their times tables.

"Inspired, I thought," Emily said. "And now we have free run of the place. Do try not to get into trouble, Branwell."

Uncharacteristically, Branwell simply ignored Emily, too lost in melancholy to respond—which only begged the question of why he was here with them. Usually when this kind of mood descended on him, he was straight to the apothecary or the pub, but on this day, he had risen early and been ready for the trip even before Anne. There was something brewing, a storm gathering behind his eyes, but for now they did not have time for one of their brother's tantrums. Whatever it was that was currently breaking his heart would have to wait.

"Why question her last, though, Emily," Anne asked, "when she is almost certainly the woman who sold child labourers to Clifton Bradshaw that fateful summer? I, for one, did not like her at all."

"That is exactly why, Anne," Emily explained. "We can be

certain that she will lie to save her neck and then continue to deceive if she thinks she might profit from it. And I am certain that if she accompanied us, she would do everything in her power to frustrate and interfere. In short, I believe the most useful and interesting person we can talk to here is this Mr. Markham, for he may have known the Top Withens child himself."

The further they ventured into the building, the colder it became. Indeed, it rather seemed that Mrs. Poole kept only her own quarters properly heated, and somehow it felt colder in this neglected former home than it had outside.

"I am reminded of Cowan Bridge," Charlotte said, shuddering. "The cold and heartless régime seems always to follow me wherever I go. Even worse, we appear to have happened upon an establishment just like it: cruelty cast as charity."

They paused outside the schoolroom, peering in through the open door of a large, high-ceilinged room with long windows that must once have been very grand and fine. There were perhaps fifty boys in the class, ranging from the older boys at the back, who looked as though they wouldn't be kept on at the orphanage for much longer, to little children at the front, whose faces retained the soft malleability of babyhood, their serious and solemn expressions pulling at Anne's heart. Surely all such little children needed was kindness and play, yet there they sat at their slates, huddling together on the benches for warmth, as this Mr. Markham talked over their heads. The once magnificent fireplace remained unlit, though whether through prudence or design Anne could not be sure. Charlotte was right: a place like this afforded much greater opportunity than a life on the street, or even within a poor family in which poverty and hard work would wear a body to dust before it reached the age of ten. Even so, if she could, Anne would rip it all down and begin again—build a world that was equal and fair where a human soul was prized above profit—but in this modern age of machinery and progress, it seemed an impossible fantasy, stranger and more exotic than the childhood worlds she used to build with Emily.

Anne knocked briefly before entering to the sound of benches scraped backwards as all the boys stood.

"Please be seated," she told them kindly, before addressing Mr. Markham, who observed her and her party with quite some astonishment.

"Please do accept my apologies, Mr. Markham," Anne told the fair, slender young man who was nervous and earnest in his demeanour, "but the matter is urgent. Indeed it is one of life and death." She nodded towards the hall. "May we have a moment of your time?"

"You have me at a disadvantage, Madam . . . ?"

"Miss Brontë." Anne took his hand and shook it, putting Mr. Markham at an even greater disadvantage, as he was taken somewhat off guard by her businesslike demeanour. "My colleagues and I are making enquiries on behalf of our employers . . . Bell Brothers, solicitors—you have heard of them?"

Mr. Markham blinked, uncertain of how to reply. "Certainly the name does ring a . . . bell," he replied, blushing furiously.

"Excellent. We simply require a few minutes of your time to talk in private." Anne smiled slightly as she fixed him with her implacable gaze. "For though you may not know it, you might hold the key to saving a young boy's life."

Mr. Markham held Anne's gaze for a moment longer before nodding decisively.

"James Cranton!" Markham called to one of the older boys at the back of the classroom. "Please take over leading the recitation of our exercises. I will be but a few minutes. If I hear anything but the sound of earnest learning coming from within, there will be consequences—am I understood?"

"Yes, sir," the boys droned in response, but none seemed overly concerned by this threat. Though he must have been twenty-five at least, Mr. Markham looked barely older than his charges, his cheek still as smooth as a child's. Even so, his serious expression endeared him to Anne, who did so prefer people who were sensible to moments of gravitas.

"The classroom is terribly cold," Anne mentioned to Mr. Markham the moment they were out of the door. "I imagine it is very hard to learn well when one's fingers and toes are blocks of ice." She had not meant to comment, but her words revealed themselves upon her lips before she was aware she had thought them.

"Yes, we are all very cold," Mr. Markham agreed, dropping his head as he led the sisters into another classroom that looked as if it had been used quite recently. A number of times tables were still written out on the board in a feminine hand that did not match Mr. Markham's, Anne observed. Perhaps Mrs. Poole also taught the children, though for some reason Anne couldn't imagine that such a severe and angular woman could have such a delicate hand.

"Mrs. Poole allows us a small amount of coal a day, but it barely lasts an hour. We are a charitable institution—we must spend our funds wisely." He recited a phrase he heard often, no doubt. "When I am paid, I buy extra coal for the classroom, but I am afraid to do it too often. Otherwise I suspect Mrs. Poole would withhold even that allowance."

"It is a shame when such kindness is taken advantage of," Charlotte said, taking a seat at one of the benches Mr. Markham pulled out for the sisters. "The children are lucky to have such a kind tutor, Mr. Markham. Having experienced, if only for a short time, the great discomfort and unhappiness of a similar place, I know that your generosity will mean the world to these boys."

Mr. Markham nodded, blushing deeply once again.

It was time to bring the conversation to the point.

"Mr. Markham, you grew up within these very walls, did you not?" Anne asked, dismayed to see how the question unsettled the young man, putting him ill at ease.

"If you mean to say that because of my unfortunate start in life, I am not worthy of a teaching position here, Miss Brontë, then I regret we must end this conversation at once, for though I have come from the gutter, with no family to speak of, I have worked every day of my life to improve not only my lot, but the lot of the children here."

"Sir, you misjudge me," Anne said, leaning towards him, her gaze intense. The gesture only made his cheeks all the hotter. "Our own father came from a farmer's hut and took himself to Cambridge, then into the church. We don't condemn you, sir—we applaud you. We are here to ask you about your life here in the year eighteen thirty-two."

Mr. Markham nodded, straightening his collar and his shoulders in one move.

"I was eleven, and looking for a situation to go to, as my shelter at Crossed Keys was about to come to an end. If you believe this to be a grim establishment today, it was far worse thirteen years since. There was no staff, save for Mrs. Poole and Cook, and twice as many boys. Poole gave lessons, but they were poor and ill managed. Boys were beaten every day, starved and put out in the cold as chastisement, sent to the mill most days. Many died—consumption and typhoid were the main causes, but I believe some were also simply too weak or too harshly treated to survive. Indeed, it was in that year that Crossed Keys gained a new benefactor, and the boys' situation improved a little—they were no longer sent out to work, or at least they were not supposed to be. It was an unkind childhood: one where I lost so many friends that I soon saw fit not to make any more. But I was educated and fed, and I am grateful even for the cruelty that brought this place into my life. I'm not sure what else I can tell you, Miss Brontë."

Anne's expression had softened as she listened to Mr. Markham. He was one of those rarest of creatures, a thoroughly decent human being.

"Mr. Markham, were you one of a number of boys employed out of Halifax the summer of that year up at Top Withens Hall?"

"I was." Mr. Markham smiled faintly. "Though it would hardly be described as a happy time, at least it took me away from this place for a summer, and I was grateful of that."

Anne glanced at her sisters before continuing. "And do you remember any children who vanished from Crossed Keys or Top Withens that summer? Presumed runaways, perhaps?"

"I cannot say precisely," Mr. Markham said, dropping his gaze and turning away from them, a distinct posture of unease threading its way through his stance.

"What do you mean by 'precisely'?" Charlotte asked him—she had been sitting quietly, content to observe, but now she rose to her feet, walking to where Mr. Markham was standing. Though he was not a tall man, she was obliged to turn her face up to meet his gaze.

"To run away, even from Crossed Keys, was to run into the arms of death," Mr. Markham said. "Every boy here knows the truth of that, both now and then. We knew that on the street we'd most likely have to thieve or worse in order to survive. In here we had a chance—a small one, but it was a chance. There was a boy they said ran away, but . . . I could never make sense of such a story."

"Please, Mr. Markham, tell us about this boy," Anne said, glancing at Emily. Could it be that they were about to discover the name of the Top Withens child? The thought filled Anne with a swirl of conflicting emotions, bringing to mind the images of those poor, forlorn, abandoned bones and, worse still, of Joseph Earnshaw at the mercy of a madman.

"My friend John—John Rafferty." Mr. Markham smiled faintly. "He was an Irish boy, came over with his mother to look for work. John was small for his age, like so many of us, and often ill, but his sense of fun and mischief never wavered, and he was never one to give up hope, despite his own frailty. The rest of us would be sickly and frozen, and he'd take care of us, bringing in extra sticks to heat the dormitory and swiping bits of food from under Cook's nose. He was different from most of us because his mother still lived. She had found work living in and, unable to take a child with her, left him at Crossed Keys until she found a better position. How we all envied the letters she wrote him, though his reading was not good. I'd read them for him. The last letter spoke of a new job with a cottage that would suit them both, and that is why it is difficult to countenance that, knowing he was so close to a home with his ma, he ran away before we left our work at Top Withens, leaving even his boots behind. But that's what Mrs. Poole said, and her word was . . . *is* . . . law in this establishment."

"John Rafferty." Anne whispered the name, turning to her sisters, who were very quiet and very grave. It seemed likely that this was their child, anonymous no more: a boy with a name and a spirit, a mother and the hope of a better life.

"Can you be sure that, unable to wait, he didn't run to his mother?" Charlotte asked.

"I'm afraid not." Mr. Markham shook his head gravely. "Mrs. Rafferty never heard from him again as far as I know. I visited her once, after I was compelled to leave the orphanage upon turning twelve. I think perhaps I hoped for a little motherly comfort, but there was none to be found. I met a woman so out of sorts and vexed with worry that it was terribly sad to see. She told me she had to take in a lodger to make ends meet but was terrified that she would be found out and thrown out of her master's cottage—she made me promise her not to speak of it, and I swore I wouldn't. Truth be told, I was rather hopeful that she would ask me to stay with her, for I was very young and lonely, but perhaps it was better that I was disappointed. After all, making my own way in the world has served me well. I have often thought of her. If she had known for certain that John had died, she could have understood—she could have grieved—but for him just to vanish seemed impossible for her to fathom. It was soon after John vanished that the boys began talking of . . ."

"Yes, Mr. Markham?" Anne prompted him.

"It seems foolish, but you coming here today has reminded me that it was after John vanished that the boys began whispering of a child-snatching monster, and they've never stopped since."

"A monster?" Anne did her best to hide the tremor in her voice.

"Yes, a monster that would stalk the halls at night and choose a boy to steal away," Mr. Markham said. "The strange thing is that though it was thirteen years ago, the story still persists, and many are still so afraid of the monster that Mrs. Poole even uses the story to scare them into obedience."

"How very frightening for them." Charlotte shuddered.

"What does the monster look like?" Emily asked. "Does it have a name?"

"A name, no—and as for what it looks like, well, whatever a boy imagines, I suppose." Markham shook his head, bemused. "In any case I've worked and lived here now for three long years, and though boys die—more than we would wish—there has been no visit from a monster."

"No more strange disappearances?" Anne asked him.

Markham was silent for a moment and acutely uncomfortable.

"There was an incident. A few weeks ago, but . . . it's unrelated, I am sure. It led to the departure of the other tutor, Miss Goddard, who used to work here, and with her she took one of the boys."

"Please tell us, Mr. Markham," Anne asked. "Anything you remember might be helpful."

"I can't tell you more, except that Miss Goddard seemed very agitated, perhaps not in possession of her full wits, and she was dismissed. I was sorry, for Lucy was a good friend and . . . well, a good friend."

It was frustrating to have glimpses of moments that, if they could all be seen at once, might reveal the truth, but there seemed little more that Mr. Markham could tell them.

"One last thing, Mr. Markham," Anne said, holding out in her palm the medallion that had been left in Joseph's bed. "Have you ever seen an item such as this before? Exactly like this, I mean to say."

Mr. Markham leant over her palm, examining the medallion for some moments.

"I do not recall that I have," he said.

"Thank you, Mr. Markham." Charlotte stood, nodding to her sisters. "We are most grateful for your time. Next we need to talk to Cook—please, will you direct us?"

"Not I," Emily said at once. "I should like to talk to the children."

"Whatever for, Emily?" Charlotte asked sharply. "None of these children was even born in the year that concerns us."

"That may be true," Emily said, "and yet when it comes to monsters, children are the greatest experts of all."

38

✤

Emily

Emily had always found that the best policy when it came to long hallways full of whispering shadows was to walk as briskly and purposefully as possible, so as to dissuade any lingering ghosts from attempting to waste one's time. It was not that she was afraid of ghosts—indeed, under normal circumstances, she was always very pleased to meet one—but not today. Today she did not have time for ghosts, not when there were monsters on the loose.

As Charlotte, Branwell and Anne headed towards the kitchen, following the scent of boiled cabbage, in search of the aforementioned Mrs. Seed, Emily took the first flight of stairs she found and ascended to the second floor. It seemed unlikely to her that in a house as large as this, the boys they had seen in the classroom were the only inmates. Sweet, young Mr. Markham had mentioned something about the departure of a member of staff recently. If that personage had yet to be replaced, it was likely there was a good quantity of boys elsewhere in the building awaiting their turn to drink at the font of knowledge.

Sure enough, as Emily reached the upper floor, sounds of muted, whispered conversation and brief bursts of laughter drifted down the windowless corridor—little snatches of fellowship amidst all this gloom and oppression. Standing still for a moment, Emily listened for more telltale sounds, but it seemed as if the children were alert to her approach, as they suddenly fell silent. Opening one door she observed one long room crammed with beds, so icy cold that her breath misted before her. The room was empty of all except one small boy, who, though his cough was fierce enough to make the bedframe vibrate, did not wake. Dragging two paltry blankets off neighbouring beds, Emily laid them over the boy, before quietly retreating, offering up a prayer that whatever it was that ailed him might be gone by morning.

Crossing the hallway she opened another door, only to hear the scuttle of feet and whispers, as boys hastened to sit bolt upright upon their beds, each with a tattered-looking book of prayer on their laps. The all-pervasive chill had this dank room in its grasp too, and many of the children had their thin bedclothes wrapped around them like makeshift cloaks. They did their best to look absorbed in their reading.

"You need not be afraid," Emily said in the same way she might have addressed Keeper when he knew he'd done wrong but she was trying to tempt him inside anyway. "I have not come to scold you or to test you. I have only come to talk to you for a little while. And to ask you to tell me a story. You may close your books."

At least two dozen pairs of watchful eyes observed her as she walked into the heart of the room, taking a seat on a bed next to one of the bigger boys, though he was probably no more than ten years old, and a wisp at that.

"My name is Emily," she said, offering him her hand, which he rather hesitantly held for a moment, staring at it as if it were a wonderfully precious object. "And what is your name?"

"William—William Gower, miss," he said, regarding her with great wary eyes.

"How long have you been here, William?" Emily asked.

"Since I was six, I reckon, and I'm around ten now, miss." William stared at Emily as if she was fearsome, which she supposed she was rather, especially to a boy who hardly knew kindness.

"William, your tutor Mr. Markham told me that you children tell one another stories, and I am wondering if you will tell me a story."

"Which one, miss?" William asked. "We were just telling the story of the parting of the Red Sea, miss. Is that a good one?"

"That is a very fine story indeed," Emily said with an encouraging smile, "but I am more interested in the story of the Crossed Keys monster."

A ripple of concern swept through the group of children slowly gathering around Emily, who felt their scant weight depressing the pitiful mattress even deeper every time one of them ventured onto the bed.

"We are not allowed to tell that story, miss," William said gravely. "Mrs. Poole says it's a lie and that it's a sin to lie, miss."

"Mrs. Poole also says she'll send the monster to take us when we're bad, so is that a sin too?" came another voice from behind Emily.

"It *is* a sin to lie," Emily replied, "but it is not a sin to tell a story—that's another thing altogether, for a good story is a wonderful thing, even stories that may scare you a little. Why, even the Bible is full of stories, allegories and parables."

William and his friends remained silent, entrenched in reluctance.

"If you tell me the story of the monster, I promise that Mrs. Poole will never find out. And I am a person of my word, William—you can rely on that."

William looked for a long moment into her face, then at his companions for their approval. Emily pretended not to notice the nods of tacit agreement that encircled her.

"Very well, miss," William said, his hand stealing into Emily's. "Well, there's a monster that comes to Crossed Keys, miss—not every night, not even every year, but sometimes, when the moon is dark and the monster is hungry, it visits and steals a boy away. Only I am lying to you, miss, because you wanted me to tell you a story, and it isn't a story, miss—it's real."

Emily looked down at his small hand in hers. Smiling, just as she remembered her mother doing, she put one arm around William and, releasing her hand from his, the other round the boy sitting on her right, drawing them in closer.

"Now, what makes you think it is true? Have you ever seen the monster, William?" Emily asked.

"No, miss," William said. "And I'm glad. For if I had, it would have been the last thing I ever saw." He hesitated, frowning deeply. "But I have heard it. All of us here have. For it came not so long ago—that's how we know it is real."

The boys nodded and murmured in agreement, and a very small boy, perhaps no more than three years old, climbed onto her lap, winding his arms around her neck. These worried, vulnerable little boys touched her heart in a most unexpected way. They reminded her of the day she had first set eyes on Keeper, dirty and bloody, lost and unloved. All they wanted was for someone to tell them all was well and keep them safe, the poor little pups. For all the sorrows of her life, at least she had always had that.

"When did you hear the monster?" Emily asked. "Perhaps it was a sort of dream."

"Weren't no dream, miss—it happened two weeks since." William's voice dropped to a whisper as if he were afraid of being overheard. "You know when the monster comes because it sings a song, miss—the same song every time. You have to close your eyes, tight as you can, and not move an inch, miss. If it sees you so much as *breathe*, then you will be the one it chooses."

"Chooses?" Emily asked.

"Yes, miss." William shuddered, his gaze turning inward as if he was indeed remembering something terrible that had truly happened. "When the monster stops singing, you know that it has chosen the boy it will eat."

"I must confess that I have never heard of a monster that sings, William." Emily did her best to lighten the atmosphere. "Tell me, what song does it sing?"

"It's an old song, miss, called 'The Cruel Mother.' Mr. Markham said it was a song older than Halifax, older than this house, even, and that is very old."

The old ways, Emily thought. *Old magic, old superstitions, even old folk music seems to swirl around this mystery like a thick fog.*

"Can you sing it to me?" Emily asked the boys as one by one they shook their heads.

"We're afraid to, miss, in case it calls the monster back." William swallowed hard. "But I will hum the tune to you if you want."

Emily nodded, and William turned his head until she could hear his breath in her ear.

She felt him tremble against her, and felt the skin prickle and rise on the back of her neck, as if the strange, sad melody called to her from very far away. A long-distant dream, something like a memory, filled her with a profound sense of dread.

"And after the singing stops, the boy is taken up and out of the window," William told her. "The monster spreads its great wings and flies away with the boy to eat him up and chew on his bones."

"The monster *flies* away?" Emily repeated.

"Yes, miss," William said very seriously. "With great black flapping wings."

"And a boy was taken just two weeks ago?" Emily frowned. Was this a fairy tale after all? For surely if that had been true, Mr. Markham would have been sure to speak about it, if not the duplicitous and guarded Mrs. Poole.

"Yes, miss," William said. "Only this time it was different."

"How was it different, William?" Emily asked him.

"The boy—Tom, it was—he got taken, but he got away, miss," William said. "His name is Tom Hawthorne, and though no one will let him, he lived to tell the tale."

39

Charlotte

Charlotte, Anne and Branwell found Mrs. Seed alone in the huge kitchen, boiling something grey and unpleasant smelling. Despite its size the kitchen was the only room in the great house that was thoroughly warm, and the heat was welcome, though the stench of rotting vegetables was not.

"You've come, then," Mrs. Seed said, crossing her large arms under her considerable bosom. Though all the inmates were but a wisp away from starvation, it seemed to Charlotte that Cook found the means to feed herself quite well. Round faced and red cheeked, regarding them with suspicion, this formidable-looking woman had already received a visit from Mrs. Poole and almost certainly been briefed on what to say in answer to their enquiries—Charlotte was in no doubt about that.

"Good afternoon to you, madam," Charlotte said politely. Though Mrs. Seed was an imposing figure, her own small frame could be played to an advantage here. It was almost certain that Mrs. Seed would dismiss her at a glance as being small and inconsequential, as so many had throughout Charlotte's life. Just like most of those unfortunate souls, Mrs. Seed would soon learn to regret such an error in judgement. "Please, may we beg for a moment of your time?"

Charlotte was deferential, her voice light and feminine.

"Poole told me why you were here, but I don't know owt that will help you with your enquiries."

"Are you certain?" Charlotte looked up into Mrs. Seed's ruddy face, searching out her eyes within the spare fold of flesh that curtained them. "Or is that how Mrs. Poole advised you to reply?"

"She did." Mrs. Seed nodded, her gaze slipping over Charlotte's shoulder to where Anne was walking slowly about as though searching something out, while Branwell was sprawled in a chair near the oven. "Not that I care one jot for her opinions. I have despised her with all my being since the day I stepped into this hateful place. Even so, it makes no odds—I don't know anything about what happened back then, except for what I know, and that's what everyone knows."

"If you would be so kind as to tell us what you know so that we may corroborate it with other accounts?" Charlotte smiled.

Anne paced, pausing every now and then to stare very hard at nothing in particular; and Branwell, well, he was lost to thoughts that Charlotte could not fathom, though she was certain Mrs. Robinson would be at the bottom of them.

Mrs. Seed sighed. "The boys had been sent out for the summer, up to a farm Scarsdale way. I weren't needed, so I went to my brother's for a visit, and I should have stayed there. When they came back, there were some gone. Some died, as children are wont to do. And one ran away, which weren't no surprise, because he was a right little"—Mrs. Seed sighed again—"article. I reckon he got a taste for fresh air and sunlight, and that's all there is to it. I don't suppose he came to a good end, but there's no mystery there, and if anyone has been left any money, it won't have been him."

"Except that's not all there is to it, Mrs. Seed," Charlotte said as Anne stopped in front of the locked pantry door. The key was still in the lock.

"What do you mean, that's not all there is to it?" Mrs. Seed asked, still looking at Anne.

"A child's remains were recently found at Top Withens Hall, where John was last seen," Charlotte said, watching as Mrs. Seed's eyes widened, her ruddy face reddening even further. "There seems little doubt now that it is his bones found hidden there, just as there is little doubt that whoever took him that night has also taken another boy from our village. We believe John Rafferty was murdered, Mrs. Seed, so you would do well to tell us of anything else you might know now. Before charges are laid."

Mrs. Seed sat down in a chair with a great thump, and now it was Charlotte standing over her.

"I swear I thought he'd run," she said, her eyes darting this way and that. "Poole singled him out, seemed to take delight in inflicting her cruelty on him. When I heard he'd gone, I thought he'd bolted for sure—didn't want to come back to that. And that is all I know. Though . . ."

Mrs. Seed wouldn't meet Charlotte's gaze.

"Boys die here sometimes from causes other than illness—from a beating or another punishment like not being given water for three days or getting locked in the coal shed, and . . . well, she always lists them as dead of consumption, so as to make it more palatable for the patrons' report. She don't want to be distressing great ladies and gentlemen."

"How can you be part of this establishment, knowing that Poole uses it to cover up her attacks on these boys? Why have you not gone to the patrons, to the law, and demanded she be held to account for her evils?" Charlotte demanded.

"Because isn't it just the way of the world?" Mrs. Seed said.

Anne surged forward, but Charlotte caught her sister's arm, shaking her head slightly.

"What can you tell us about the monster the boys speak of?" Charlotte asked, wondering exactly what it would have been that Anne would have done if she'd let her reach Mrs. Seed.

"Well, it's nonsense, all stirred up by another troublemaker. A fortnight since one of them turns up just before dawn, all cut up and beaten. He said he'd been taken out of his bed by the monster. I ask you. He'd more than likely got himself into trouble in the town, and now he wanted a way back. He got a beating, but he wouldn't change his story. He said he could prove it, and that just made Poole beat him all the more, even though the boys in his dormitory reckoned they'd all heard it too.

"It was Miss Goddard who believed him. She's a soft one, too gentle for her own good, and she stepped in between the lad and Poole. There was quite a tussle until Markham threatened to go to the patrons. Miss Goddard took Tom to the constable, but the constable saw Tom's 'proof' for what it was: nonsense. Tom Hawthorne is a born liar; he'd swear night were day soon as look at you. The constable gave him a whipping for his lies, and Poole put him out on the street. She didn't account for Miss Goddard going with the boy, taking Tom into her care that very same night. If you ask me, I think she hoped Mr. Markham would go with her, but I heard them talking, and he told her he couldn't leave these boys alone here unprotected."

"Do you know what happened to Miss Goddard and Tom?" Charlotte asked. "We need to speak to them urgently."

"What, have they been left the money, then?" Mrs. Seed asked dryly before sighing again. "I heard she is a ladies' companion now, to some old maids out on Scar Top Lane, past Stanbury. The boy is with her. I don't know more than that, but I will tell you one thing more, and you will never say you heard it from me."

"What will you say, Mrs. Seed?" Charlotte asked.

"That Mrs. Poole keeps a great deal of the food and fuel and sells it on for profit. Mr. Markham wrote to the patron once, but nothing came of it, and I know why.

"Mrs. Poole is a blackmailer. She discovers secrets and holds them on account. She knows that the do-gooders who fund this place will not sack her. So I beg of you, misses, sir—if you have the power to remove her from here, then pray do it, and you will have saved more than one life."

40

❧❧❧❧

Anne

"The day is growing very late," Charlotte said as the four of them walked on, Crossed Keys Orphanage and all of Halifax some distance behind them now. "I rather wish we hadn't dallied to question Mrs. Poole, for I never met a more odious and evasive woman."

Charlotte was entirely accurate in their assessment of Mrs. Poole. For no matter how they questioned her, she turned this way and that, as slippery as an eel. They had thought it best to keep the discoveries they had made from Mr. Markham, Mrs. Seed and the children to themselves, for the sake of those poor souls, but also to prevent Mrs. Poole from understanding the true nature of their investigation and taking flight. Despite that, they had asked her all they could about the orphanage and its practices, and Anne had been sure that every answer Poole had given was a lie.

Anne could hear the worry in Charlotte's voice, and indeed she shared it. Under usual circumstances the ten miles from Halifax to home was a walk they would have thought nothing of, but now, with the last transport gone and the afternoon dimming by the minute, it seemed as if the road grew longer with every step they took, and Joseph Earnshaw was lost one minute more.

And it was entirely possible that they were on the wrong path altogether. Mrs. Seed had told them that Miss Goddard had taken a position the other side of Stanbury, but with no further detail.

These were homes and families that the sisters knew, and yet they were hard-pressed to think of one that was likely to have employed a companion, for that particular position was normally advertised by lone women of some standing. Anne could not think of one household in that area to fit that description. She could only hope that some inspiration would present itself to them before long; otherwise this long detour they had taken following Miss Goddard would prove to be nothing more than a waste of precious time.

"I fear I may not own the strength to continue for very much longer," Charlotte said. "Branwell, may I take your arm?"

Branwell let Charlotte lean on him with a sombre smile.

"Branwell, you have been such a good, stoic companion today," Charlotte said. "Though you have been silent and kept your thoughts to yourself, I hope you know what comfort your presence brings me—brings us all, I daresay. These past days, when we have been companions just as we used to be, have reminded me how much we need you, brother."

"Have they?" Branwell asked with a bitter laugh. "You need me to escort you—to protect you—though I'll wager that Emily Jane could land a harder punch than her wasted brother. You need me to lend your little rabble authority, perhaps, for as brilliant and as brave as you each are, you are still but women. But you don't need me, Charlotte—far from it. You have left me behind, all of you."

With a jerk he freed himself from Charlotte's embrace and marched on a few quick steps.

"You would think," Emily called after him, "that there were more important events happening than your own discontentment, Branwell! We are not the architects of your misery. Indeed, we do all we can to bring you back to life when you yourself have courted death just as readily as you did Mrs. Robinson."

"Emily, don't speak her name aloud," Charlotte muttered.

"None of this matters a jot," Anne told her sisters. "All that matters is that we locate Miss Goddard and the boy as soon as we can."

"No," Branwell said, marching back towards them out of the dark. "That's right—nothing I do matters. Nothing I do is right or worthy or good. I am a joke to you—a laughingstock. That the whole world looks upon me as a pitiful fool, I can bear. That my beloved Lydia must adhere to her cruel marriage when she longs to be with me, I can endure. But that you, my sisters, have sought the publication of your poetry without *me?*" Branwell shook his head. "That is intolerable."

"How . . . how do you know?" Charlotte asked, aghast.

"The letter Martha gave me after we returned from Ponden was addressed to a Mr. Brontë, but it was meant for you, Charlotte. It was from an Aylott and Jones, offering to publish your collection if you cover the cost."

"Oh!" Charlotte stopped in her tracks, reaching out for Anne. "Emily, Anne—we are to be published!"

The three sisters caught one another's hands and, a moment after, clasped together in an embrace.

"I can hardly believe it," Anne said. "Can it truly be real?"

"I believe it," Emily said. "I knew it would take only the right editor to see my genius, though I shall not enjoy the fame that will surely follow."

"To hold a printed, bound book with our words in it." Charlotte's voice was soft with awe. "I hardly dared dream it possible, but now . . . now the whole world shall see who we are."

"I offer you my felicitations," Branwell said. "I will just go and die in a ditch over here, and you can forget I ever existed."

"Branwell"—Anne grabbed her brother's hand, but he snatched it away—"we did not mean to leave you out. It is more that we never considered that you, accomplished as you are, would want to be associated with our little efforts."

"No," Emily said. "No, Anne. I know you want to soothe Branwell's hurt, but don't do that. Our work is not small or unimportant. We are very fine poets, as that letter proves. Whatever we write has equal merit, equal worth to any words written by any man. Don't make yourself less to make him feel greater."

"Thank you, Emily, dear—you always know exactly how to ease my soul," Branwell replied.

"Branwell, you are your own man," Emily told him furiously. "Why, have you not just published two poems, and were you not talking of writing a novel and telling us all how it would make your fortune? You have within you the means to triumph, to succeed—and a much greater chance at both than us mere women. We did not think of you, not to exclude you, but because you have a great future ahead if you will only put away your gin and self-pity long enough to grasp it."

"Well, as you do not require me for your collection, Messrs. Bell, then presumably you do not require me to escort you any further this night."

"Branwell, please," Charlotte said, "we meant no harm or hurt to you. We know only that you will find greatness—that you were born for it. And that we three must support ourselves somehow. That is all. Please understand that."

"But I don't," Branwell said. "And yes, I know a child is missing, and you three are doing your best to save the day; I know that my pain and suffering matter very little compared to the fate of that boy.

I am not proud of my anguish, Charlotte, but it torments me, every waking moment—and now this? To have you cut me out as though I am a tumour? It is too much. I am going home to join the search parties as I should have done this morning, for I am clearly no use to you."

Branwell was lost in the night within a few more strides, his three sisters standing in the road, looking after him.

"We should follow," Charlotte said.

"We should not," Emily countered. "He is nothing but a spoilt child."

"No," Anne replied. "No, he is more than that—so much more—and we didn't think of him when we sent away the poems, not once. We have hurt him, and even if it wasn't our intention, we must make amends, because I am very afraid that he cannot take much more hurt. But not now—now we must find Miss Goddard, and I cannot fathom where she might be in the collection of farmhouses and workers' cottages."

"I believe Mrs. Seed was lying to us," Charlotte said.

"One moment." Anne stopped on the road as a thought struck her. "There is a house just past Stanbury that used to be workers' cottages, but they were bought up years back and made into one home—now occupied by two lone spinsters."

"You mean the Sladden sisters, out at Tewit Laithe," Emily said. "They are hardly ever seen—one of them not at all—not by anyone for years and years. It seems hardly likely that they would employ a companion in their crumbling little cottage."

"Unlikely, perhaps," Anne said, "but not impossible. You said yourself that there are no other properties for us to call on that we do not already know, and perhaps such a forgotten place as Tewit Laithe might prove appealing to a young woman and a boy who believe they are in hiding from a monster."

"It's another two miles," Charlotte said. "I cannot feel my feet."

"But we must be thorough, Charlotte," Anne told her sister. "Surely the central tenet of detecting is that we miss not a single detail that might lead to the truth. If you will not accompany me, I will go alone."

Anne waited as her sisters exchanged glances.

"We shall come with you," Emily said after a moment, "as you knew we would. For if we did not, Tabby would never let us hear the end of it. And besides, Anne who is the baby no longer, you are quite right. True detectors leave no stone unturned."

41

Emily

Tewit Laithe had been so long neglected that it had almost fallen back into the hillside from which its stones had been hewn three centuries earlier. The house was a long, uneven concoction, made up of four workers' cottages that sat halfway up the hill, shielded from sight by a thick copse of trees and briars. The local legend went that Ned Sladden had acquired the three other cottages that adjoined his own soon after his younger daughter was born. The child was grossly malformed, they said, and ought not to have survived, but it was the mother who had died from loss of blood, and desperate to keep the cruel world away from his twisted child, the farm foreman had somehow bought the whole row of cottages from the landowner and made a sanctuary for his daughters. None knew how it was done, for Ned Sladden was a man of modest means, but there were rumours—there were always rumours.

Within ten years Sladden had passed, and since then—a period of time Emily was not entirely sure of, but was somewhere close to forty years—the sisters had taken care of themselves, refusing all offers of outside help. Scarcely seen and mostly forgotten by those who lived and worked around their little island of solitude, halfway up the hillside, they wandered their realm like a pair of lost ghosts.

The land surrounding Tewit Laithe had long since returned to the wild moorland, and the path that led to it from the road was barely visible even in daylight. On this frozen winter evening, it was near impossible to navigate; all they had to guide them was a vague idea of where they remembered the building being in relation to the peak of the hill, and even those memories were uncertain.

On they walked, upwards to where the dark brow of the hill met with the velvet blue of the night, stars appearing one by one like faraway lanterns. At last Emily saw the shadow of a building crawl out from the darkness and make itself known, as it unfolded into view. From without it appeared entirely dark and uninhabited, lacking the discernible flicker of a candle or the glow of a fire, but it could not have been any other house but the one they were seeking, not in this area.

"It seems utterly deserted," Charlotte whispered, though there was no one to overhear the sisters talking. "Perhaps the sisters have moved on after all."

"It may just be that they are at the back of the house," Anne said as she pushed open the rusty gate with some effort. "I shall knock on the door."

Anne banged firmly once or twice on the low oak door set into thick walls. There was no reply, no trace of movement from within.

"It is hardly surprising," Emily said. "Those who go to such lengths to avoid the company of folk are hardly likely to cheerfully answer the door, especially after dark. I rather sympathise."

"Well, we have come this far," Anne said. "We shall walk around to the back and investigate further."

"I'm not sure that we should," Charlotte objected. "It would be very much like trespassing, and there might be"—Charlotte hesitated—"hazards."

"Charlotte, dear," Emily reminded her, "it has been quite some months since we indulged in such a transgression. I shall lead the way, for I have some experience in this area. If there are hazards, then they shall accost me first."

"Very well," Anne said, "but should we meet the sisters, don't frighten them, Emily. They are not used to everyday folk, and so they are certainly not prepared to meet one such as you."

"One might argue that I am exactly the sort of person they are prepared to meet," Emily said.

Carefully they began to make their way around to the back of the property, Emily tracing her freezing fingertips along the roughly hewn walls of the cottage as a guide. It seemed that with every step the night grew darker and quieter, as if even the owls in the trees were holding their breath.

At last Emily could make out the faint bloom of a light coming not from within the house, but from one of a huddle of outbuildings bunched together to make a cobbled yard. Feeling a little as though she were stepping out into thin air, she detached herself from the safe harbour of the wall and headed towards the light. It was a creaking henhouse door that she pushed open, and as she did, she caught sight of a hunched, strangely balanced figure standing over the animals.

"Miss Sladden?" Emily asked very quietly, hoping her sisters would know to stay back. "My name is Emily Brontë, from Haworth. Please accept my apologies for calling on you so late and uninvited, but it is concerning a really quite important matter."

"You must go now," Miss Sladden spoke, keeping her back to Emily. "Please, turn away and leave."

"Miss Sladden," Emily began again, "I quite understand that I am here uninvited and unwelcome, but I am urgently trying to find a young woman and boy, formerly of Crossed Keys Orphanage: a Miss Goddard and a boy called Tom. Perhaps you could tell me if you have recently taken either into your employment?"

"Please go," Miss Sladden repeated, and Emily heard the distress in her voice. "I am not to be seen. I do not wish to be seen. Please go."

The pleading in her voice was such that Emily began to push open the door, before hesitating.

"Miss Sladden," Emily said, her eyes lowered, "you may not know me, but my papa is the parson at Haworth. Perhaps you know of him and know he is a good man, and that his children seek only to be as like him as they can be, to treat all as equals under God. You, your sister or Miss Goddard have nothing to fear from me or from my sisters, who are waiting outside."

"I do know your papa," Miss Sladden said, the discomfort in her tone easing just a little. "I read his letters and sermons in the paper. Your father is a good man, Miss Brontë, I am sure, but even so, I do not wish to be seen, so I beg you, miss, for my sake, please go."

"I will," Emily said. "Please, if you have heard of a Miss Goddard and her boy, Tom Hawthorne, please ask them to come at once to the parsonage, for it is very urgent we speak to them. We believe they may know something about a most dangerous person abroad this very night—a person who causes great harm to children, and who has, we are certain, a Haworth child in his despicable hands as we speak."

"Which child?" Miss Sladden asked, taking Emily aback a little.

"Joseph Earnshaw," Emily replied, uncertain as to why it mattered. "He has been gone one night already, and we are very afraid for him."

"I know Joseph," Miss Sladden said. "Full of mischief but bright—has promise."

"Indeed, Miss Sladden . . ." Emily was curious. "May I ask how it is you know this?"

"I do not wish to be seen, but my sister and I are God-fearing folk, Miss Brontë. Your own father visited us regularly once, before his sight failed him. Since then his curate, Mr. Nicholls, will come and visit us once a month to lead us in prayer. He brings us books and papers, and tells us stories from the schoolhouse. He speaks often of a Miss Charlotte. I trust he never speaks of us or our lives, for we have begged him not to."

"He never has," Emily said very quietly, "believe me."

Very slowly Miss Sladden turned around to face Emily, who after a moment lifted her eyes to meet the other woman's and held her steady, appraising gaze.

"I do believe you," Miss Sladden said, "but why do you think your Miss Goddard is here?"

"My sister has a feeling," Emily said honestly, "and we all of us believe that feelings can be compasses pointing towards the truth. Anne thought that perhaps a life as secluded as yours might prove a refuge for Miss Goddard and Tom."

"Refuge? No." Miss Sladden picked up the oil lamp and walked a few steps closer to Emily, holding the light up to her face.

Emily met her gaze steadily. Yes, Miss Sladden's spine seemed to be twisted, her cheek resting on one hunched shoulder, and the whole of that side of her face tugged down. But all that Emily saw was a fearful woman, doing her best to be brave for the sake of others.

"This house has been my prison all my life, Miss Brontë. My only escape is books and my own imagination. But now my sister is dying, and as I cannot go out, I must invite help in. Miss Goddard and the boy are within. You may speak to them."

"Miss Sladden, I am truly grateful for your trust," Emily said.

"Then you will call me by my name," Miss Sladden said. "You will call me Rose."

42

❧❧❦

Charlotte

Anne had been right in her assessment that the main living at Tewit Laithe was done mostly at the back of the house. Rose led them into a small kitchen that was warmed with a bright fire and several lamps. Boughs of evergreen firs and holly adorned the mantel top, oak beams supported the ceiling, and it was cheering to remember that in every hidden corner, it was still Christmas.

The convivial atmosphere disappeared at once the moment Emily and her sisters were seen standing behind Rose Sladden. A young woman who Emily imagined had to be Lucy Goddard stood up abruptly, her sewing sliding off her lap, and with one look, the boy who had been sitting opposite her at the kitchen table scrambled up some thick stone stairs.

"We have not come to harm you in any way, Miss Goddard," Charlotte said. "We don't have time to explain ourselves, but please, we need to talk to you and Tom about his escape from the clutches of the creature the boys at Crossed Keys call the monster."

Miss Goddard observed each sister carefully, and Charlotte could see how easy it must have been for sweet Mr. Markham to lose his heart to this delicate, copper-haired creature, her eyes so large and expressive.

"You believe his story?" Miss Goddard asked uncertainly.

"We do," Charlotte said.

"For the most part," Emily added. "A boy called William told me the monster flew away with his captives, and I must admit to some reservations about that part."

"It's a cloak." It was a boy's voice that came from deep in the stairwell. Eventually Tom Hawthorne came back down into the room, crossing at once to Miss Goddard, who folded her arms around him as if he were her own beloved child. "A great hooded cloak that flies out behind, for they walk very fast. It might look like wings at night to the little ones."

"But, Tom, it was a human being who took you from your bed?" Emily asked him, sitting down.

"Yes, miss—a monster but in the form of a man," Tom said.

"Can you tell us more of this monster and of what happened to you that night?"

Tom looked from Miss Goddard to Rose Sladden with a great deal of uncertainty and reluctance. It was clear that the memory frightened him deeply, the anxiety of reliving it clear in his expression. For most, childhood was not a halcyon time of innocence and protection: children worked, they died, they suffered. But whatever this boy had experienced had altered him forever.

"You can talk to them, Tom," Rose said. "They are friends. And there is another boy who has been taken—one who might not be as lucky as you. We must try to help him if we can, Tom."

Just then there came a thudding on the wall from the next room.

"My sister, Alice," Rose told them. "You stay with Tom, Lucy. I will go to her."

Charlotte took a stool by the range so that she was at eye level

with the boy, who even after several days in the care of Miss Goddard was pale and thin, his eyes huge with worry and fear. Charlotte
was in no doubt that he had seen something terrible—it was almost
as if a reflection of what he had endured was still imprinted within
his eyes.

"Your friend William told me that you had been sent to bed as
usual," Emily said, "though it was hard to sleep, for you were all so
cold and hungry, but that eventually he must have done so, because
he woke to the sound of an old song being sung—a song you all
knew of as a warning."

"We knew the monster had come then," Tom said. "We'd been
taught that by boys who had come before. 'Just don't open your eyes,'
they told us. 'Don't look, don't make a sound, don't breathe and
perhaps, if you are lucky, the monster'll pass you by and take your
friend.'"

"Did you look, Tom?" Emily asked him.

"Just a crack," Tom said. "I just wanted to see."

"And what did you see?" Emily asked him.

"Boots," Tom said. "A pair of black boots, the swirl of a cloak.
The second I looked, the singing stopped and then . . ." Tom fal-
tered. "It's all in pieces in my head, miss. There was a gloved hand
across my mouth for a second, so I could not cry out, and then a rag
stuffed in with summat on it that smelt of violets and tasted of burning. Before long it was as if I were half awake, half dreaming." Tom
looked into the fire as he talked, and the dancing flames dappled his
face. "It felt like the monster was strong—very strong—throwing me
up onto his shoulder and carrying me like an empty sack, like I was
hardly nothing. I tried to tell myself to fight, miss, but my arms and
legs wouldn't do owt. Next thing I remember, I was thrown hard
onto the floor of a carriage. The boots were on me, one on the back
of my neck, pressing down. I was afraid I'd choke—I nearly did!

Then a breath was allowed. I was too afraid to cry, for fear of being choked again. I had never known how much I wanted to live until that moment, miss. Then—I don't know why—the coach stopped quite sudden, with a jolt. I heard shouts from the road. The monster took his boot off me, perhaps to see what the trouble was, and I knew that was my chance. I kicked open the door and tumbled out of the carriage, scrambled up on to my feet. I had no shoes on, but I ran. We were high up—I know that—it was cold, and the wind was behind me. I ran. I didn't care where, nor did I mind the pain in my feet. I just had to get away. There were footsteps coming after—more than one set. I kept going, even though they were upon me, and then . . . then there were no ground under my feet. I was falling. I hit rock and was beaten from boulder to boulder as I tumbled. I don't remember when I stopped falling, but dawn was breaking when I came to. I suppose the monster thought me dead when I fell—I half supposed myself dead and all. I knew if I stayed where I was, I would be, so I got up, and somehow, though my leg were proper injured, I walked and walked until I found a road, and then a cart. I wasn't more than three miles from Halifax, the driver told me. He gave me a pile of sacks to keep warm under and took me back to Crossed Keys. I went to Miss Goddard. I told her—I said, 'The monster is real.'"

Charlotte looked at Miss Goddard, who had pressed her hand to her mouth as she listened to Tom recount his tale.

"And you had no reason to doubt his story?"

"Not one," Miss Goddard said. "Besides, his person told the truth of it. He was bruised and scratched all over, his head cut, arm and ankle broken. He still smelt of ether, a scent I know from my time working in an infirmary. And he still had about his neck something . . . I had never seen before—something he said the 'monster' must have put on him."

The sisters looked from one to the other. Could it be . . . ?

"Do you still have it?" Charlotte asked.

Still holding Tom's hand, Miss Goddard went to a bookcase and, taking out a prayer book, opened it to where a chain was enclosed between the pages. There lay a miraculous medallion atop the words of the Lord's Prayer.

Emily picked up the pendant, running her thumb over the clumsily etched date—the same date that was on the pendant left in Joseph's place when he was taken.

"What can it mean?" Anne asked. "Why is the year marked?"

"I believe it represents the year a boy is taken," Charlotte said, a great sense of dread spreading through her. "Tom was meant to be taken and kept until tonight's new moon, but he escaped. . . ."

Charlotte looked up at her sisters with dismay.

"And it would seem that our Joseph is a replacement."

43

❦

Emily

They were bone-tired as they finally reached the back of the parsonage. Then Emily heard a cry from somewhere beyond the house, followed by a shout of something like terror and fury combined.

"Papa! It's Papa!" Recognising his voice at once, Emily gathered up her sodden skirts and broke into a run, followed at a similar pace by Anne, Charlotte lagging somewhat behind.

"Keeper!"

Emily called to her dog as she passed the backyard, and as he joined her, he yelped with joy and then perhaps a little fear as they bowled down the alley that ran alongside the parsonage and found a crowd of people thronging between the schoolhouse and the graveyard, jostling and shouting.

"What is this?" Emily demanded, shouldering her way into the angry mob. "Out of my way at once. Where is my papa?"

Emily elbowed, and Keeper, considering it all a marvellous game, nipped at shins as he and his mistress fought their way into the eye of the storm, the centre of the crowd that had spread between the graveyard and the schoolhouse At last Emily set eyes upon the poor creatures who were the subject of such vitriol: it was the Brontë men—well, for the most part anyway.

Sprawled on the cobbles, cradled in her brother's arms, was the young man Charlotte had met at Ponden, Eamon Riordan, bloody and beaten. Branwell had apparently thrown himself into the fray, for his nose was bruised and his bent and broken spectacles hung off one ear. Papa stood before them blinking in the dark at the howling crowd, bellowing for calm, but to no avail. The blood of the mob was up, and they would not quieten, not even for their parson.

They might for a lady, though, Emily thought—but seeing as her sisters were still trapped at the back of the crowd, she would have to do.

"What is this?" Emily raised her voice as she planted herself firmly in front of her brother. "Why are you hounding my brother and my papa? Explain yourselves this instant, or have me and this ferocious hound to answer to."

Keeper's tongue lolled menacingly out of the side of his muzzle, and Emily wished he didn't look quite so much as though he were a grinning lunatic. Still, at least he was drooling excessively—that was something.

"Well, speak up!" She assumed her old, hated mantle of a teacher addressing an insolent child.

"It's for Joseph," Samuel Wright called out from the crowd.

It would be him, Emily thought, for he was the sort of man who was always angry, even when there was no cause—the sort of man who thought life had robbed him of something he'd never had in the first place.

"We've hunted for Joseph all day, and we've still not found him, but we know the necklace is a Catholic trinket and this Irish scum Riordan is Catholic."

"There is freedom to worship God as you choose in this

country!" Patrick spoke up once again, and this time there were only murmurs of dissent that answered him. "This man's faith is no business of yours, and his nationality of no relevance here."

"Filthy Irish scoundrels!" Abel Sutcliffe called out. "They are a curse on this land."

"No better than human apes!" A woman's voice this time, Susan Martin, if Emily had heard right.

"Crawling all over our land like vermin." Peter Milton—Emily would have thought better of him. "The papers say they will cause another famine here if we don't turn them away."

Emily shook her head slowly as she stared at them, looking as many of them in the eyes as she could, though many would not lift their gaze to meet hers.

"It is the English who are a curse to Ireland—what Christian nation would let people starve in their own homes?" she said, igniting a collective gasp from the would-be attackers, who were fed what little they knew about the Irish famine by the screaming headlines of the gutter press. "In any event, this young man was not even on these shores when the Top Withens child was murdered. He cannot be guilty of these crimes."

"They all huddle together as one, don't they?" another voice called. This time Emily could not discern its owner. "Breeding and keeping one another's secrets, like rats in a nest."

One moment passed, and in that single beat of silence, all gathered there saw the lightning ignite in Emily's eyes, and each of them cowered.

"Your own parson, your own curate are both Irish." Emily did not shout. She did not roar with all the burning fury and injustice she felt within her chest. And yet her voice rang out so firmly and so clearly that all there shrank back even further. "My papa, who serves you tirelessly, day and night, though he can barely see his hand ahead of his face, who has never wavered, even at the death of his daughters, my sisters, or our dearest mama—he has always been your faithful protector. My papa, who has taught you by his example kindness, justice and decency. My papa, a near helpless old man whom you pin into a corner as though he is a fox and you a pack of hounds. And Branwell who . . ." Emily looked down at her brother. "Well, let he that is without sin cast the first stone. Shame on you. Shame on you for treating those who are not able to stay in their homes, if they want to survive, like animals. Shame on you for pouring scorn on those who are not able to stay in their country and find shelter or safety for their children. Shame on you all. You think yourselves good Christian people, and yet it would have been *you* who turned Mary and Joseph away from the inn. It would have been *you* who told Herod where to find the Christ child!" She balled her fists on her hips and advanced towards the now subdued crowd. "You presume a man a killer because he is an Irishman? Or you presume him to know and harbour a killer for the same reason? You, who are all sinners, every one of you. We know who killed the Top Withens child, and now we have proof. You will depart to your houses or else keep looking for Joseph and caring for his family, and *we*, the Irish Brontës, will resolve the matter this very night."

There was a moment's hesitation—a moment, no more—and then one by one all who had gathered peeled slowly away, at which moment Keeper found his voice and began barking most ferociously.

"Better late than never, I suppose," Emily said, patting his bony head.

"Mr. Brontë, please accept my apologies." Mr. Nicholls burst onto the scene, almost knocking poor Charlotte over in his haste not to be altogether too late. "I tried to pierce through the crowd, but they would not let me pass!"

"All is well, Arthur," Papa said. "My daughter Emily dealt with the matter."

"May I take Eamon home, miss?" A pretty young woman, heavy with child, came forward. "God bless you for your kindness. The mob came and dragged him out of our house, and I feared him dead, and our babe not yet born."

"I'm all right, Mary," the lad whispered. "I'll be well and at work tomorrow."

"Branwell will help you back to your rooms with him, Mary," Charlotte said, bustling about as if the dispersal of the crowd had been entirely down to her. "And we shall ask the doctor to call on him tonight—and settle the bill on our account."

"Actually," Branwell slurred, "I'm not altogether certain I can stand up. I was in the Bull with the search parties when this fight began, consoling myself over my sisters' treachery. For now I will put aside our differences and endeavour to stand."

"How noble of you," Charlotte said, "and you had better stand, or you will find yourself sleeping in the gutter tonight."

"Would not be the first time," Branwell said, easing himself up and collapsing into Eamon, who was equally unsteady on his feet. Nevertheless together they seemed to keep each other upright.

"I could see nothing, but I heard it all, and you really were magnificent, Emily," Charlotte said as she took Emily's hand and guided her past a rather dejected-looking Mr. Nicholls, who had Papa by the arm. "Terribly coarse but magnificent nevertheless."

"Yes," Anne agreed, taking Emily's other arm. "You were as courageous as the knights of Gondal."

"Well, you know me, sisters dear," said Emily, lifting her chin, "no coward soul is mine."

44

Anne

"Though I am a man of peace, I was indeed ready to fight on your behalf," Mr. Nicholls said as he helped Papa navigate the steps into the parsonage. "I was prepared to take them all on in your defence, sir."

"It was just that you were prepared at the back of the crowd, out of harm's way," Emily said mischievously, as she grabbed Keeper's collar and dragged him to the kitchen, where, by the sounds of Tabby's cries, she stole something not intended for dogs with which to treat him.

Anne went into the dining room, where an agitated Flossy leapt onto her lap, and waited for her siblings to return, the door open just a crack. She could hear Charlotte pacing the hall.

"Are you coming in, Charlotte?" she called. "Time is short."

Charlotte ignored her, and within a moment, Anne knew why. Mr. Nicholls emerged from Papa's study, smoothing down his wild hair and straightening his cravat. Ever so slowly Anne leant back on the sofa, better to covertly observe her sister and the curate through the narrow gap in the door.

"Charlotte, I know what you must think of me," Mr. Nicholls said. "I promise you I would not have let your father come to harm."

"I know you would not."

Anne's eyebrows rose as she watched her sister take a step closer to Not-Her-Mr.-Nicholls.

"Sir, you need not apologise for being a man of peace and a good man. We visited with the Sladden sisters just this past hour, and I learnt from Miss Rose Sladden of your great kindness, compassion and discretion towards them. I wanted to thank you for bringing those women into the parish, despite their difficulties."

"It is no more or less than any of the people of this parish deserve," Mr. Nicholls said, his voice a little raw, as if he had been caught off guard by emotion. Perhaps there were hidden depths to Arthur after all.

"Mr. Nicholls," Anne heard Charlotte say, "will you fetch my brother, bring him home and stay close to us? We will need you both to swell our number this night if we are to find Joseph safe and well."

"I would do anything for you," Mr. Nicholls said, "and for your family, of course, Miss Brontë."

"Thank you, sir," Charlotte said.

There was one more moment when Anne could not precisely see, but she suspected it was filled with Mr. Nicholls's longing gaze.

"Well, you'd better be off, then."

A moment later the front door closed, and Charlotte came in and took a seat at the table, followed by Emily.

"Right, to the matter in hand," Emily said, catching a little late the way Anne was looking at Charlotte.

"What has happened?" Emily asked Anne. "Has Charlotte fallen in love again?"

"We are dealing with a most serious matter; a life hangs in the balance, and you and Anne wish to behave like foolish girls?" Charlotte said crossly.

"Charlotte is quite right," Anne said, full of reproach. "Nothing happened, Emily, save for Charlotte sharing a rather tender moment with her Mr. Nicholls."

"He is not . . ."

"To the matter in hand," Emily said. "For Charlotte is right, we must find Joseph tonight."

"Emily, you told the crowd that we had proof and that we knew who held Joseph," Anne said, "but the only proof we have is that the monster both harmed the Top Withens child and took Joseph. We still cannot be sure who it is."

"Mrs. Poole was up at Top Withens that summer, and we know she is a cruel woman," Charlotte said. "Could it have been her, taking out her anger on a boy? And without the shelter of the orphanage to hide her sin somehow, she concealed his remains in the chimney?"

"Cruel, yes, and duplicitous," Emily said, "but this madness, the rituals—it feels beyond her banal acts of barbarity. And besides, if Mrs. Poole had carved those runes, it would be as a deception, but Lizzy Goode says that whoever made them meant them, had studied them, even though they were blended with other elements. Do we think Mrs. Poole has the imagination for that?"

"I do not," Anne said. "It seemed to me that Mrs. Poole feels perfectly secure in her situation, and not likely to resort to the acts of a madwoman."

"Mr. Barraclough, then," Charlotte suggested. "A member of the order of Freemasons, which is closed and secretive, full of ritual and theatre: there are elements of both those in this mystery. And he was at Ponden just before Emily found the book that seemed to be left out for us. He installed a rare longcase clock at Top Withens in that same year that Mrs. Bradshaw died. Agnes, who came down from Top Withens to his employ, seems wary of him."

Their brother entered the room, a little unsteady and smelling like a brewery, but otherwise in possession of his faculties.

"Branwell, was Eamon well, when you left him?" Charlotte asked.

"Bruised, and he will be stiff tomorrow, but well enough," Branwell told her. At least it seemed that he was a good deal more sober now.

"What do you think, Branwell? Of Barraclough—you know him better than we do. Could his interest in ritual have turned into something more sinister?"

"It's been some time since I was at the lodge," Branwell said, "but Zerubbabel always seemed to me to be honest and plainspoken, if a little terse. Is it possible he could hide such derangement? Well, he is a very private man—I suppose it is possible."

"I am almost certain that it was he who left the books for us," Emily said. "But as friend or as foe? I cannot be sure."

"Then let us return to the most likely suspect. We know it was Clifton Bradshaw himself who paid for the use of the Crossed Keys boys—a deal done with Mrs. Poole," Charlotte said. "We know that the only certain link between these crimes is the medallion: an identical one connected with each certain crime, each with a year engraved upon it. The only person we can link both to John Rafferty and to Tom is Mrs. Poole, so . . ."

"So we must take into account the runes, the rituals in the woods close to Top Withens Hall, the rumours of conferring with the devil and all that Lizzy Goode told us. It takes a particular kind of evil to steal away and harm a child. And it takes control to keep such impulses in check for long periods of time—years, even." Emily hesitated as, at that moment, all of them thought of the children, including young Joseph. "Tom was taken before the bones were discovered—and escaped. So even if our actions have excited the monster, there must be something else—something apart from the discovery of the Top Withens bones—that urges them to act, a darker need than a new moon that we are as yet unable to comprehend."

"And what about the song that the children heard being sung? They said it was very old. Can that tell us anything more?"

"Tabby?" Emily called to the kitchen. "Will you come to us?"

"I suppose I must," Tabby said, "though I was expecting you to be out leading the constable to where poor Joseph is hidden, as you told the rabble out there."

"We will be directly," Emily told her. "Listen to this refrain the children sang to me, and tell me if you know the words of the song."

As Emily sang the melody, the room grew still, darkness gathering in every corner.

"I do," Tabby said, shuddering. "Dreary old misery of a song it is too. Why would children know such a horrible dirge? It's a tale to strike fear into your heart."

"They only hummed it," Emily said. "Could you perhaps sing it for us, Tabby?"

"I will, but be warned, it's about a mother who kills her own babes." Tabby looked most aggrieved, but even so she obliged, clearing her throat before she began.

And she didn't care how much it hurt.
There she stabbed them right through the heart.
She wiped her penknife in the sludge,
And the more she wiped it, the more blood showed.

"Heavens," Charlotte said. "What awful words!"

"Folk songs were the newspapers of their day, don't forget," Tabby told them. "That's how we'd learn about the rest of the world that weren't ours. It can't all be folderols and falling in love."

"Bess!" Emily stood up abruptly, slamming her hand down on the table. "I have heard those words before, whispered into my ear. I thought it was just nonsense spoken by an old lady with a gone-away mind . . . but it was Bess—Bess of Top Withens—who whispered the words of the monster's song in my ear."

"Then could it have been mad Old Bess who killed the boy?" Anne said. "We thought she was addled by age, but perhaps it was guilt that drove her mad, her strange ways and violent thoughts. She's like a living ghost."

"And yet Liston has always spoken of her fondly," Emily added. "Is it not more likely that she knows the killer, that her madness masks what she knows, but even so, now and then she speaks the truth, and was trying to show it to us all along?"

"It *must* be Clifton Bradshaw who knows that song. He *must* be the culprit," Anne said. "The first killing took place shortly after the death of his wife. We know he had dealings with Crossed Keys and also dabbled with the devil. Perhaps he was so desperate at the bones being uncovered and losing Tom that he could not wait any longer— perhaps he hopes to be caught."

"Are we certain?" Charlotte said. "For though the evidence is compelling, a misstep now may cost Joseph his life."

"We are as certain as we can be, and now there is no time to lose," Emily said. "We must go to Top Withens now, this instant. All of us: Branwell, Mr. Nicholls and John Brown. We must send Martha for the constable, for all the good he is. At least he will be able to arrest Clifton. But most urgently we must secure Joseph's safety before all is too late, for then, truly, our efforts would be for nought."

"I'll fetch our boots, and we will have to ask Mr. Nicholls to bring Papa—"

"I am here already," Mr. Nicholls said, "in the hope that I might be of service."

There was a knock at the door, and somehow, through the mass of people in the hallway, the door was opened to reveal not only Martin Earnshaw but Hemming, Lady Hartley's coachman.

"Is Lady Hartley here?" Charlotte asked, seeming to struggle with the pace of events, and no wonder. They must have covered twenty miles today and barely eaten.

Anne felt not one whit of exhaustion but she suspected the imperative nature of their quest was all that kept her on her feet, and yet Charlotte looked like a stiff wind might blow her away to particles at any moment.

"Her ladyship asks that you come to Oakhope at once," Hemming said. "She has heard of the unrest in the village and wishes for news and the comfort of your company."

"You will have to tell her ladyship that Charlotte cannot go now," Emily said. "We have a fiend to capture and a child to rescue. Lady Hartley will just have to wait."

Charlotte looked at her sisters. "I . . . I don't want to go with you, Emily, Anne. Forgive me, but I dread to go. I should like to go and wait with Catherine until there is news. I know you must think me very weak—"

"We do not," Anne said. "You need not come, Charlotte, if you are sure. You should rest and replenish."

"You go on—go now while there is still time."

Emily would have argued, but Anne prevented her by a single shake of her head, for there was no more time for talking. Outside, the cart from the Bull was waiting for them. Papa had on his greatcoat and hat, John Brown held the reins, and Mr. Nicholls and Branwell were set to accompany them.

"That Charlotte would turn away from the conclusion to our

detection is . . . It just makes no sense," Emily said. "She will not be present when we find Joseph, Anne—and you let her stay behind."

"It is her right to protect her mind and heart as best she can," Anne said as the cart began to roll away. "I know that you have faith that all will be well, Emily, but steel yourself, for we may be too late. When we find Joseph—if we find him—he may no longer be alive."

45

✤

Charlotte

As the carriage pulled away, Charlotte drew within herself, doing her very best to prevent her mind from asking the same frantic questions over and over again, the answers to which she could stand neither to know nor not know. The truth was, though she would own it only to herself, that Charlotte had been relieved when the invitation had arrived from Lady Hartley.

When she had first heard of the discovery of the Top Withens bones, it had not been the human soul that had once occupied them that was uppermost in her thoughts; it was her own desperate need to find a place of refuge and space in her mind that was not occupied by the name Constantin Héger. For a short while after the Chester Grange matter, the need she felt for him that previously seemed to have endured without end seemed to ebb a little, and there had passed whole hours—even days—when her entire self didn't burn for him. And then as the night drew in, and winter took hold, her love had leapt into flame once again, and all that anguish that she had hoped was dead and withered away was born again in a new spring of longing.

That first snowbound walk to Top Withens had been so much

more for herself than for that poor lost child—until she had seen the bones laid out, and how a life had been stolen. In that moment, though she felt the shadows gathering around them all, all else had faded far away in favour of this single-minded pursuit, even Monsieur Héger.

This detection had cost her a great deal of her spirit. At Chester Grange there had been a terrible sickness: an infestation of unhappiness and discontent that had inhabited the hallways and stalked the bedrooms, born out of betrayal and loss from generations before. If Charlotte had learnt anything from that particular adventure, it was that all we do, every action we take, every word we speak, has a consequence, perhaps not that very day, but one day, and it might be far beyond what one could ever imagine.

When it came to the monster, she could discover no human reason for its cruelty, at least not one she understood. The vast chasm of howling fury that must occupy that fiend terrified her beyond measure. It weakened her to know that such pure evil could be all too real. To her shame Charlotte discovered she did not have the strength to face such a creature. So she had let her dear family, Mr. Nicholls, and those from the village who had joined them in the cart take that stand without her.

Bowing her head as the carriage rattled up the driveway to the grand entrance of Oakhope Hall, Charlotte examined her conscience and found herself wanting. All her life she had battled to do what she believed was right, to make a path and place in the world that was better and more promising than any expected of her. Each day she did her best to be good and decent. Yet now, facing the greatest test of her faith she had ever encountered, she had retreated as fast as she could to the safety of a well-appointed parlour and a roaring fireside.

If Emily and Anne brought Joseph home safe and well and caged the monster successfully, then in time Charlotte would find a way to reconcile herself with such bitter disappointment. But if they did not, then she would never be able to forgive her own failings.

"Miss?"

A gust of freezing air billowed inward as the coachman opened the door and offered her his hand as she stepped down. Oakhope Hall was ablaze with light. Lamps shone in seemingly every one of the dozens of windows, and even the pillared portico boasted a pair of burning torches that stood as tall as she did.

"Miss Brontë?" A maid seemed to be waiting for her by the door and took her cloak and bonnet at once, eyes lowered all the while as if she expected to be admonished at any moment.

"Thank you," Charlotte said warmly, afraid she must seem terribly aloof and unpleasant.

"My mistress is waiting for you in the red room, miss," the girl said. "Please follow me."

Charlotte paused for a moment, looking around at the splendid opulence: the polished marble floors and the gold-framed paintings that seemed to shine in the lamplight. It was dreamlike somehow, and she could not help but feel that such grandeur was never meant for her, in her tired, muddied gown frayed at the hems. And yet there was an exhausted, wrung-out part of her that longed to be lost in this fantastical world, to surrender to it as one might to a dream and give up all thoughts of ever waking.

"Miss?" the maid prompted her anxiously, glancing towards what Charlotte presumed must have been the red room. "My lady is waiting, and she is most eager to see you."

Charlotte followed her at once.

"Oh, Charlotte, dearest—at last!" Lady Hartley was standing before the fire, looking intently into a little trinket box as Charlotte entered the room, a luxuriant apartment decorated entirely in scarlet. At the sight of her guest, Lady Hartley snapped the box shut and crossed the room to greet Charlotte, taking her hands in hers and kissing each cheek very warmly. She was wearing a rather fine deep green riding habit that seemed a little curious, given the hour, but perhaps, unlike Charlotte, Catherine was preparing to ride up to Top Withens herself.

"Oh, but you are quite frozen," Lady Hartley said, horrified, her soft hand cupping Charlotte's cheek. "Come, sit with me by the fire. You must think so terribly badly of me, summoning you forth as if you are under my command, but I could not wait a moment longer to discover what has become of the poor child who was taken— Joseph, was it? I heard your sister said you had proof that would name the culprit. Is that right?"

"It was." Charlotte was heartened at once by Lady Hartley's kindness, her distressed heart eased by Catherine's bright eyes and sweet countenance. "Oh, Lady Hartley—Catherine—I am so glad to see you. I have felt quite depleted, but the sight of you gives me such heart."

"You are too kind," Lady Hartley replied. "You could have refused me, you know. I didn't really consider what I was asking of you, to come to me at once this late at night when we should all be in bed. But I have been sick with indecision, uncertain whether to act or not, as you can see." She gestured at her attire as she led Charlotte to a scarlet sofa. "It is only that I have been quite ill since our visit into the wilds: unwell in my heart, body and mind, worrying about the poor dear child. It has troubled my thoughts so very grievously that I fell into a fever. Lord Hartley took one look at me and said that I must send for you or go quite mad. The moment I thought of your dear little face, I felt better, and I knew my husband was right to counsel me so."

"Is Lord Hartley at home?" Charlotte asked her.

"He is with his books somewhere," Lady Catherine told her. "The beauty of a house this enormous is that one can make a terrible din in one wing, and not a jot of it will be heard in the other. Why, with many of the staff sent home for Christmas, you and I could shout at the top of our voices and not disturb a soul."

"I cannot imagine wanting to." Charlotte smiled.

It seemed to her that Lord Hartley had been quite right in his assessment: Lady Hartley wasn't quite herself. There was an excitement, a kind of restlessness about her, that reminded Charlotte of a schoolgirl with a secret she was bursting to reveal.

"Tell me, Charlotte—whatever you know, tell me all."

"I do have news." Charlotte took a breath and straightened her weary back. "My sisters and I have discovered a great deal in the hours since Joseph was taken. We have uncovered much about the creature that stole him, and we fear perhaps there are other children."

"Others?" Lady Hartley's eyes widened in horror, her hand raised to her mouth. "Oh, dear Lord, Charlotte, how terrible. Who could do such a thing but the very devil himself? Have you been able to locate them?"

"We have not, conclusively," Charlotte said, "but we have collected a sufficient amount of evidence to point towards Clifton Bradshaw. Top Withens was searched, but his property spans many acres, and within it there are ravines, abandoned dwellings, woodlands. We must trust that we will find him in time, before . . . Well, it is very cold. A party is travelling up to Top Withens as we speak. In fact they will almost be there."

"Goodness." Lady Hartley seemed exhilarated by the news. "And you came here to tell me rather than go and vanquish the demon?"

Charlotte held her gaze for a moment before dropping her chin.

"I must admit I was glad not to go, Catherine," she said. "I was afraid—afraid of what we might find and what we might not. I suppose I still am. You must be very disappointed in me. I know I am in myself."

"Of course I am not, dear Charlotte." Lady Hartley was gentle, and Charlotte was put in mind of the murmured kisses her mother used to place on her forehead when she was a very small child; she had to force herself not to rest her head on Catherine's shoulder. "You are quite a remarkable young lady. I have never met another such as you. I do believe if I had known you in my younger years, I would have benefited from your great influence. And as for fear . . . well, I myself am no stranger to it. My life has been full of terror."

"It must have been terribly hard to lose your father so young."

"Harder to live with him," Lady Hartley said. "He was an unkind man, Charlotte. But the terror I speak of is one far greater. I had a lover before I married Leonard, you know."

"Oh," Charlotte said, feeling suddenly very much out of her depth.

"We met when we were barely more than children, and really so far apart in society that I shouldn't have noticed him, but I could not help it. He was so dear to me, so fierce and protective. He'd fight any who hurt me, and I had never known a love like it. I was very young, scarcely fourteen when I took him to bed. We had a few perfect months together, hiding our passion from those who could harm us and then . . . those who could harm us were gone, and it was my turn to be cruel. I cast him out. He was too lowly, too rough ever to be a husband, and as much as I loved him, I wanted the life that I had earned by enduring such cruelty. So I cut him out of my life, Charlotte, but not out of my heart. He lives there every day, and each day I am in terror that he never thinks of me, never cares for me, never imagines what my life has been without him. Can you imagine the constant fear of wondering if the only man you have ever loved considers you at all? Sometimes, I am driven to distraction with the need for just one sign from him that I am not forgotten."

"Indeed, I can understand that particular madness exactly," Charlotte said, thinking of Constantin. "But your life with Lord Hartley is such a fine one, and a good one with purpose. That must be of some comfort."

"It affords me the freedom to do as I must," Catherine said, her expression still for a moment before igniting into a dazzling smile. "And tonight I can see that what I must do is take care of you and your dear, perfect mind. The intellect that has solved a terrible crime is in my hands. I must ensure it is properly cared for."

"Lady Catherine." Charlotte blushed, turning her face towards the fire. "I am just myself, a person who feels rather little and insignificant in this great sphere tonight."

"Not at all. Why, my dear, you are *everything* to me." It was said with such passion, and Lady Hartley's gaze was so intense that for a moment Charlotte felt caught quite off guard. "To find you, to know you and see inside your great thoughts, has been like drinking at an oasis in a desert of buffoons."

"Please forgive me." Charlotte withdrew her hands from Lady Hartley's grasp as the room swam and tilted. "I find I am a little faint. I haven't eaten in an age, and perhaps the warmth of the fire and the great emotion of events has overwhelmed me. . . ."

"Let me call for refreshments at once," Lady Hartley said. "Charlotte, please do forgive *me*—I fear we were both quite swept away for a moment, weren't we? I shall correct that at once."

Charlotte smiled, uncertain as to why a strange kind of queasiness simmered in her chest. It felt a little as though she were already lost in that never-ending dream. Lady Hartley rang for her maid and then rang again.

"I do so like to give our people Christmas at home, but I must say it is rather tiring when one simply cannot get one's maid's attention!" The last few words were shouted into the hallway.

"I cannot think what has happened to Maude." Lady Hartley stood up again. "Perhaps she is on the other side of the house seeing to Leonard. I can see that I shall have to go and find her. The trouble is, Charlotte, I am altogether too soft on my servants. They take such liberties with my good nature, stride around the place as though they own it."

Charlotte thought of the timid girl who had greeted her at the door. That had not been the impression she had received.

"Please do not—not on my account, Catherine," she said, feeling suddenly very much in need of the humble familiarity of her own home. "In actual fact I think I must return to the parsonage to wait there for news. Perhaps you could call your carriage instead?"

"I shall, the moment you have had food and drink," Lady Hartley said, returning to the sofa once again. "Look at you, poor child—you are as pale as a snowdrop, likely to fade right away at any moment. Please excuse me, dear, while I go and fetch you something myself. Please rest. Lay your head upon a cushion and be at ease."

The sofas were deep and inviting. Nevertheless Charlotte stood up the moment Lady Hartley departed, wringing her hands as she tried to fathom what had just taken place.

Something was amiss, out of place, but what? Or was it her own emotional exhaustion casting shadows from embers?

Charlotte stood in the centre of the great wound of a room, turning her gaze into every corner. In the candlelight it almost seemed that the walls rippled and bled. Pressing her thumbs into her temples, she did her best to make sense of this strange sensation: a kind of half-formed thought, an intuition, a little voice in her ear that whispered, *Leave.*

Catherine had been staring into that little box on the mantel quite intensely when Charlotte had entered. Perhaps it contained a clue to her strange demeanour. After all, if Branwell could take the pharmacist's handmade pills that sent him into a trance, then perhaps Catherine had taken something—some kind of tonic that had the opposite effect. It would not do to be caught snooping, but Charlotte had to know. Glancing at the door that stood ajar, she hastened to the little box and picked it up. It was beautifully made of polished rosewood, inlaid with other woods, ivory and mother-of-pearl. As Charlotte tipped the lid of the box towards herself, she was confronted with the eerie grimace of an exquisitely rendered skull and crossbones. The theme of memento mori wasn't such an unusual discovery, but the little box just seemed so at odds with this beautiful room and with Lady Hartley herself.

A deep pull of curiosity arose within Charlotte. Music began to chime as she opened the lid, a melancholy little tune that took her a moment or two to place. As she remembered where she had recently heard it, it was as though a great rock had been placed on her chest; she was pinioned with dread. For the box was playing the song Tabby had sung for them not an hour since.

That strange song that she had never heard before this night, she had now heard twice.

Fear rising in her throat, Charlotte made herself look into the box. At first glance it appeared empty, but as she tilted it, she heard the metallic slide of hidden contents. Turning the box over in her trembling hands, she fumbled for a secret opening that must have been there.

Run, her thoughts told her urgently, and yet she did not. She could not run from the drawing room of a great lady and out into the snow without her cloak and bonnet, solely based on the reprise of a particular folk song and an overexcited imagination.

After what seemed like an age, Charlotte found a wooden pin

that she hooked out with her thumbnail. The side of the box slid open, and she tipped the contents into her palm.

For several long moments, it was impossible to move, to think, to act. All Charlotte could do was stare and wonder.

For in her hand there were half a dozen miraculous medallions, each with a date inscribed on the back, two of which were the twins of the ones they had discovered. Whoever had hidden them there must have been the same person who had taken the children, and there were six medallions in here. Copies, they had to be copies or doubles of the medallions that she and her sisters had already recovered. They were mementos.

Charlotte gripped the mantel as her knees buckled beneath her, and at that moment she caught sight of a face staring at her from outside the window. It was Hemming.

"Oh dear," Lady Hartley said as she swept into the room, "I see you've found my treasure. I had hoped to spare you distress, but I should have realised, Charlotte, that you are not one to turn away from an opportunity to know. What is it they say? A little knowledge can be such a dangerous thing."

46

Anne

Papa sat straight-backed and stoic as the cart clattered its way up the roughly hewn track to Top Withens Hall. Anne had wrapped his cloak tight around him and tucked a blanket over the top, yet whenever she looked at his face, set in resolution despite the howling, bitter blizzard, she was overwhelmed with a sense of deep comfort. As long as her papa was in the world, then all would be well, for Papa would make it so.

On the journey, Anne linked her arm through his and laid her head upon his shoulder, turning her face away as best she could from the full brunt of the wind. Emily flanked Papa on the other side, always forward facing, looking into the blizzarding snow as if she could see something in the endless whirl of flakes that no other could discern. John Brown drove the cart while Branwell, Mr. Nicholls and Martin Earnshaw and his brother huddled in the back. Nought was said, for there was nothing to be said until they had Joseph safe and well, and Clifton Bradshaw under lock and key.

At last they reached Top Withens, standing square against the elements, feet planted firm with resolve. So strong were the gusts of furious cold that Anne felt she might be lifted from her feet and snatched into the air at any moment, as she and Emily helped Papa to find his feet. John tethered the cart horse in the shelter of the courtyard, and the small party stood at the door of the house.

"What's this?" Molly asked, opening the door. "Miss Anne, Miss Emily—come in, Mr. Brontë, sir. Come in, all. Why, what a night to be abroad! Is it that they have found the boy?"

Anne was glad of the shelter, though the hall was hardly warmer within than without. The fire had gone out, and there was no sight to be had of Old Bess. Liston appeared from upstairs, wearing a coat and over that a kind of shawl. Molly went at once to his side.

"Where is your father, young man?" Papa asked him. Anne was glad to hear his voice strong and firm. "We must speak with him at once."

"I am here, Brontë." Clifton's voice rang out of the dark, and Anne realised that the older Bradshaw had been sitting in the shadows all along. "What do you want with me?"

"Tell me where my son is, you devil!" Martin Earnshaw flew at Clifton, dragging him out of the chair he had been slumped in and into the meagre candlelight by the collar of his shirt.

Anne gasped at the man she saw there, gazing round at them half-crazed. His face was gaunt and grey, his lips and hands fair blue with the cold. He looked no more than an hour or two away from death.

"Where is he, you demon?" Martin's voice cracked with his own emotion as he seemed to try to shake some into Bradshaw. "Or have you done away with him already?"

"I do not have the boy," Clifton said, gruff and yet calm at the sight of their party. "I've been out all day and half the eve looking for him, same as you, I don't doubt. I'm just back, sat down in the chair to take my boots off, and I found myself too exhausted to make a fire. You searched my property already. The boy is not here, nor is he on my land. I have looked over every inch."

"And why would we take your word?" Martin shook him again. "Where have you hidden him? My boy will die if left out much longer. Please, have you no mercy? I beg you. Tell us what you've done to him so that I may know the fate of my child!"

Martin let go of Bradshaw, turning away. Clifton's whole body shook, his knees buckled, and Branwell caught him, sinking to his knees on the flags, the larger man in his arms.

"Tell us, sir," Emily commanded, her eyes flashing, "for you are caught and you will hang. Your only hope for redemption is to help try to save the boy while we still may."

"Why cannot you believe that I don't have him, nor do I know where he is?" Clifton howled, his voice as elemental and as raw and wicked as the wind that tore at every stone and tile of Top Withens Hall.

"There is more than enough to draw the conclusion of your guilt," Papa spoke, lifting his hand forward as if he might somehow search Bradshaw out by touch, or perhaps even bless him. "Confess your sins, and I will pray for you before the constable arrives."

"Any path that you have followed to find me guilty has been laid false," Clifton said bitterly. "I did not kill that poor child who was hidden in my walls or any other. I did not take Joseph, and I wish with all of my rotten heart that I knew where your son is hidden, but I do not." Shaking Branwell off, Clifton staggered into a chair, convulsed with a fit of coughing.

"Father, are you ill?" Liston asked unhappily. "Pa, it's me, your Liston. I know you are not what they say you are, Pa. Mother could never have loved such a man, and she loved you."

"But I am," Bradshaw told his son. "My sins are many, and I should hang for them. I could have saved Joseph if I'd spoken up earlier."

"What do you mean, Pa?" Liston shook his head, kneeling at his father's feet. "Spoken up about what?"

"What you must understand is how much I loved her, love her. Not a normal kind of love either, not the good healing kind that I felt for your mother. No, she were like a sickness that gets into your blood and poisons everything. I knew what she did back then, years ago, and I never spoke of it. And when she came here, then I knew too that it must have been her who killed the boy and hid him here. But I didn't say anything, because to see her again was to love her again, just as I had when I was a boy. She always knew I'd die for her, and she was right. I was ready to. I was ready to until tonight and the thought of that poor lad, lost out here somewhere. It was like I awoke from a dream that's kept me captive half my life, even when I didn't set eyes on her for years on end. But not tonight. No longer will I let her keep my heart in her clutches."

Bradshaw looked up, meeting the gaze of everyone who stood around him so that they might see the truth in his eyes. "I know who took Joseph."

"Why, why in God's name would you not speak of such atrocity? What manner of coward are you that you would protect such a creature?" Anne hardly knew what she was saying until her eyes met Liston's, and she saw the hurt and fear there.

"Liston, he must speak of what he knows, or another life will be on his conscience," Anne begged. "Will you not make him speak?"

"Liston, make him speak," Molly cried. "For God's sake, I beg you!"

"Father, tell me—tell all those here what you know. For if you do not, what manner of man are you?"

"A damned one," Clifton said. "Long ago, when I was a lad, I met a fine young lady, and she became my obsession. Before long I would do anything for her, and I did. I did terrible things. When she told me she had drowned her father while he bathed, I kept silent, for I knew what a brute he had been. When she asked me to help her stop her cousins from tormenting her, I did, though I could not know what lengths she meant to go to until it was too late and they were dead. I could have spoken up then, told the world my love was a murderer, but she was still just a girl of no more than fifteen. And she was my religion, my every act of violence on her behalf a prayer to her. Though the things she did might seem wrong to the rest of the world entire, I knew it was only because of the horrors she had endured. She told me she had never known kindness until I had laid my eyes upon her." Clifton cradled his own chapped and cracked hands against his chest as if he were holding another's over his heart. "I was no witness to the death of her uncle and aunt, but . . . I suspect she had a hand in it. We should have been free then, the two of us. To marry and live a good life at last, now all those who had sinned against her had suffered her vengeance. But it was in that moment that she cast me out and cut me off. She wanted more than this, more than me. She told me she deserved a finer life than I could ever give her. I was no use to her anymore, half beast and brute that I was. For a while I thought I might die, but a man must live, and a man must marry, and I married your mother, Liston. After some years, I loved her too. For she was everything the other was not: kind, gentle, brave and good. I don't know what prompted her to hide her secrets here or to take Joseph. But I know it was her."

"Explain yourself at once," Emily demanded.

"What is this to-do, then?" Old Bess shuffled out of the back, blinking at the rabble that stood in the hall, her white hair standing tangled and wild about her head, as if she must just now have risen from her bed. "And now the fire's gone out, and there's the parson stood in the cold. Mrs. Bradshaw must not hear of this! Liston, light the fire. I'll make us tea."

Liston did not move. It seemed to Anne as if all of them had been struck dumb, made immobile by Bradshaw's strange confession. Poor Bess, who trod every step in the past, seemed blind to the horror of this present moment. How fervently Anne wished she could have walked with the old servant in happier times.

"Liston, are you senseless, boy?" Bess snapped, clipping the young man sharply about the head. "Come on now, do my bidding, for your ma will be home soon from market, and she loves to come in to a good fire, she does."

Slowly, his face as white as the snow that sheeted the land without, Liston left his father and walked stiffly to the mantel, where he took up the kindling box. After a few moments, the fire burnt fiercely, though no warmth could be drawn from it.

"Well, come over here before you catch your deaths, won't you?" Bess smiled and beckoned. "It's just like it should be: guests at Christmas come to bid us season's greetings. Why is there no holly up, Liston? Your ma loves to see the holly up."

"Bess, dear Bess." Emily approached the maid with a carefully composed smile stretched over her fear. "When I was here last, you whispered the words to an old folk song in my ear. Do you remember?"

"I am always singing," Bess said brightly. "Always have, since I was a lass."

"'And she didn't care how much it hurt.'" Emily said the words softly, but her gaze was fixed on Clifton Bradshaw, who flinched at them. "'There she stabbed them right through the heart.'"

"'She wiped her penknife in the sludge,'" Bess answered. "'And the more she wiped it, the more blood showed. The more she wiped it, the more blood showed.' Strange old song that, not one of mine— one of hers, for only one such as her could want it sung."

"Who? Who sings that song, Bess?" Emily asked. "Where did you hear it?"

288 Bella Ellis

"Well, his mistress, of course," Bess said, her expression suddenly sour and full of loathing. "I hear her singing at night. They think she's long gone, but she ain't. She comes back here in the dark and casts her spells. She's as wicked as they come, is the mistress. I saved one boy from her, but I couldn't save them all. But I can't talk more. I mustn't. She said if I spoke a word, she'd come back and take my Liston, and I cannot allow that. I must keep my silence though it will send me straight to hell, where his mistress will be waiting for me."

"The mistress?" Anne stepped forward. "Bess, Mrs. Bradshaw has been dead these thirteen years."

"I know that, you silly fool," Bess snapped. "*His* mistress, I said. *His.*" She pointed at Bradshaw. "Born a witch, and she'll die a witch, I don't doubt. The devil is waiting for her in hell—she asked him to invite her. She's wicked, that Cathy. As wicked as they come."

"Cathy?" Emily demanded. "Whom is she speaking of, Bradshaw?"

"Please, before it's too late"—Anne turned back to Clifton—"who is the monster who takes these boys?"

"My Cathy," he sobbed. "My Cathy took Joseph and perhaps others I do not know of, but you don't understand. She's broken—abused and ill in the head. The sins she commits are all inherited from those who sinned against her."

"Cathy?" Anne whispered, looking up at her sister as dread dawned in her expression.

"Lady Catherine Hartley," Emily said.

The sisters came to the same terrifying conclusion at exactly the same moment.

"Charlotte," they whispered as one.

47

Charlotte

"Why, Lady Hartley." Charlotte found herself smiling, the disjointed nightmarish fear she had felt dissolving into crystal clarity. "You did not tell me that you had found such an important link in the chain of this mystery. Please tell me at once how you came upon this evidence."

It was all Charlotte could do to hope that Catherine was fooled by her pretence, at least enough to give her the opportunity to get away. Hemming was still stationed outside the garden doors, cutting off one exit. Catherine had claimed that only Maude was left of her staff. If it was Maude who blocked her way out of any other door, Charlotte resolved to charge her to the ground.

"Send Hemming to fetch the law, and surely you will lead us straight to the culprit and to Joseph. You will be the hero of the hour!"

"It is an abiding annoyance that even the most independent woman must sometimes call on a man to do her bidding. Hemming certainly was a wonderful find: a man of unshakeable countenance, he will always do as I ask. But I shall not be sending him to fetch help, Charlotte. I'm certain you realise that."

Lady Hartley tilted her head to one side as she watched Charlotte, rather as a cat watches its prey. She was standing between Charlotte and the door, the only other means of exit from that opulent room. And what was more, she was holding something that glinted in the firelight. Charlotte's eyesight was ever failing her, but now she cursed it more than ever, for she was very afraid that Lady Hartley was in possession of a knife.

"You have been wrong at every turn," Lady Hartley said, her face taut, stretched into a grimace. "But you are not now, Charlotte. You do me a disservice to think I will be taken in by your playacting. I applaud your courage and ingenuity, however. You see, you are really much more remarkable than you know. I wish you could see for yourself how very splendid you are. But let's speak plainly now as friends and kindred spirits. I am the monster you have been searching for, and you ought to be very afraid of me."

"I am very afraid of you," Charlotte said. And then, in the space of but three seconds, she picked up a vase from a small table and swung it with all her might, hitting Catherine in the cheek, shards of the shattering china exploding outward.

Her face badly cut, Catherine shrieked in fury; the blade sliced through the air.

Charlotte gathered her skirts and ran.

48

Emily

"The cart," Emily said to John Brown. "We need the cart to take Anne and me at once to Oakhope Hall."

"Daughters," Papa asked them, his voice trembling, "where is Charlotte?"

"She is with Lady Hartley, Papa," Anne said, "and she doesn't know the danger she is in."

"We must go to her at once," Emily said. "I have not driven a cart before, but I imagine it cannot be very hard."

"But what about my boy?" Martin asked. "What about Joseph?"

"The only one who can answer that is Catherine Hartley," Emily said. "The cart will go faster with just me and Anne. We'll go at once."

"You cannot go alone," Mr. Nicholls said. "I will accompany you."

"You will stay with Papa," Emily ordered. "Branwell, you may come, and do not tarry."

"And I," Liston said, his eyes blazing. "And none shall dissuade me."

Molly wept, turning into Bess's embrace.

"Then take this." Clifton reached up, took down his old sword from over the fireplace and offered it to his son. "Even as much as I have loved her, I have always known how dangerous she can be. That day she came to Top Withens, it was to frighten me, to threaten and to test me. To let me know that she would make sure all believed I had killed the child in the chimney, and that if I said owt against her, there would be vengeance. The truth is, if she hadn't taken Joseph, I would have let her have her way. I would have hung for her."

"Pa!" Liston shook his head. "I cannot fathom anything you say."

"Because you are not mad, and you have fought against my brutality to become a good man. Don't let her destroy you too, my son. Whatever she says to you, remember you know what is true."

As it was, Liston took the reins and slapped the cart horse into a gallop.

The earth seemed to disintegrate beneath them, falling away as if the world were coming to an end. Snow whirled all around, and somewhere beyond she felt the stars wheeling madly, above and beyond. Emily held on for grim death, turning her face into the cold, until her cheeks and fingers were numb and she could fool herself that she was not afraid anymore.

In the tumult and tumble of the descent, she felt Anne's fingers reach for her, and they held each other's hands tightly. Liston drove the cart on through the village, and at last they arrived.

"Charlotte!" both women shouted, scrambling out of the cart. The grand front door to Oakhope Hall stood wide open, and though the house was bright with candles, all was quiet. Grasping Anne's hand, Emily advanced into the house, followed by Branwell and Liston, holding his father's sword before him. "Charlotte?"

"Emily." Anne tugged at her hand. She was pointing towards a bloody handprint that had been pressed against a pillar.

"Charlotte, in God's name, answer me!" Emily shouted, turning around. Letting go of Anne, she ran to the only room where the door stood ajar and found it empty, shards of broken china scattered across the polished floor.

Returning to the hallway, Emily caught a glimpse of movement in the shadows beyond the sweeping staircase. Furiously she plunged forward and dragged out a young maid by her arm.

"Where is my sister?" Emily demanded, her eyes glittering dangerously.

"She ran out," the girl said, tears running down her face. "She ran out into the snow, and the mistress has gone to find her. She . . . she means to do her harm."

Emily let go of the girl, and the four ran out into the night.

All was silent, but as Emily held a lamp aloft, she could see a trail in the deep, deep snow and imagined her sister stumbling through it, her skirts slowing her down, the trail leading towards the cover of the woodland that enclosed the grounds. Beneath those woods were the secret caves and passages, the follies that had been built there long ago. Emily hoped that they would be a good place for her sister to hide, for following the trail there was a set of hoofprints. It seemed Lady Hartley had given Charlotte a head start while she mounted her horse, and as the trail reached the edge of the woods, all Emily could do was pray that her sister had not yet been caught.

49

Charlotte

It was utterly black in the woodland, and every sound seemed amplified by the pristine snow. Very soon Charlotte realised that her skirts in the snow revealed her path, no matter how fast she should run, which was not fast at all. The heavier and wetter her skirts became, the slower her frantic progress, and yet when she dared to glance over her shoulder, it seemed Catherine was taking her time in following her. Well, there was no need to hurry—her escape route was well signposted.

She had managed to travel quite far amongst the trees, to where the canopy was thick enough to prevent snowfall from betraying her, before she heard Catherine gee on her horse, and saw the snow-topped branches tremble at its gallop.

This could not be the end of her life, Charlotte determined. This would not be her fate, not now before she had even made her mark on the world. She had so much to do, so much greatness to shine forth. No longer would she feel so small and insignificant. She refused to succumb, no matter what it might take. She had been so afraid that she was not brave, that she had no strength for a battle.

But in this moment Charlotte discovered that Lady Hartley was right about one thing: she was made of courage.

Charlotte knew that there were entrances to the caves in amongst the trees. If she could find one, then she could evade Catherine in the tunnels and perhaps find a way out. It was an imperfect plan, but she had had to run away from the village road when she had made her desperate bid for escape, and beyond the tree line there were only moors.

"Oh, Charlotte." Catherine's voice rang out in the clear night, sounding much closer than Charlotte had hoped. "Do stop running, my love. Come and greet me with your arms outstretched, and let me cradle you as a mother would."

Her only chance was to act—to remain passive now would be the cause of her demise. Forcing herself not to panic, Charlotte retraced her last few steps and hopped onto a fallen trunk, swaying precariously for a moment or two before she regained her balance. Crawling along its length, she flung herself as hard as she was able into a deep thicket, and found herself caught as a fly in a web, thorns snatching at her skirts, her hair, her hands.

"Charlotte, show your dear little face to me," Catherine called. "So serious and plain. Let me explain it all, for I'm sure you will understand. I never meant to become the creature that I am. I was made this way by the men who abused and hurt me: the father who beat me, the uncle who attacked me, the cousins who tortured me, all of them injuring me so grievously that I was forced to stop them dead. I had no choice if I was to survive."

Charlotte realised that any movement she made now would betray her position, and worse, she was stuck fast. Closing her eyes, she did her best to concentrate on remaining perfectly still.

"I arrived at Oakhope aged a little more than eleven years old. I was so miserable and afraid; I ran away up to the moors, and I thought I should never come back. And I met him, standing by the crossroads. It was as if he had been waiting for me." Charlotte held her breath as the branches around her bent and rebounded. "We were friends at first, playmates and confidants, and then one summer afternoon just after I turned fourteen, we became lovers. It felt as natural as the water running down the hillside. It was just before I rid myself of my uncle and aunt that I discovered I was with child. I did not tell anyone, not even Clifton. Instead I told him that I could never marry a man like him, so dirty and lowborn, that I must have a life of greatness. I told him that I was never meant to be a rough farmer's wife. A London solicitor who had been appointed to manage my estate sent me two matronly companions to watch over me. It took only a small portion of my fortune to offer them freedom and an independent income in return for their discreet departure. I appointed my own staff with great care, often at the prison gate, and paid them handsomely to keep my secret. After my child was born, I hired a nursemaid who knew not to talk and kept him here, my precious secret, my darling boy."

Catherine was just a few steps away. One moment more and Charlotte was certain she would be discovered. And then, from a long distance away, she heard her sisters calling her name, their voices carrying on the cold, clear air.

"Blast them!" Lady Hartley moved away to investigate, and seeing her chance, Charlotte tore herself free from the thorns, refusing to feel the burning pain of her shredded skin and ripped-out hair. On she ran as fast as she could, gathering up her skirts around her, and suddenly there it was—a great, yawning mouth, solid black against the glinting trees: the entrance to the caves.

50

Charlotte

For a moment all was pitch-black, and yet Charlotte could not risk standing still. Reaching out to find a rough stonelike wall, she used it as a guide and kept moving forward as quickly and as quietly as she could. She heard movement behind her and quickened her pace still more. As her eyes became accustomed to the dark, she saw a flicker of light ahead: lamplight. Somewhere not very far ahead, parts of the cave were in use. Charlotte longed to run towards the light, like a moth to a flame, but she stopped herself. Instead, as Catherine's footsteps drew closer behind, she ducked into a narrow, entirely dark passage, pressing herself against the walls. She held her breath as Lady Hartley stalked past.

There wasn't a moment to lose. As soon as Lady Hartley passed the bend, Charlotte began to follow her. The sensible thing would have been to turn around, to run out the way she had come in, and find her sisters, whom she knew were nearby. But there was a light down here for a purpose, and Charlotte was certain that purpose was Joseph. She had to get to him before Catherine could complete her awful task.

Every step took every ounce of her strength. Fear coursed through her veins. She could feel her pulse pounding at her wrists and temples. Yet Charlotte had never felt so alive, so powerful, as she did in the moment. Taking care to make her every movement silent, she kept a steady pace, catching glimpses of Lady Hartley's cloak as she turned a corner, rounded a bend, and then Charlotte stopped as she heard the sound of Lady Hartley's footsteps recede. Cautiously, Charlotte peered around the corner. There was the source of the glow—a torch bolted to the wall lighting the entrance to a flight of descending steps. It seemed she was about to follow Catherine into the very bowels of hell.

Before she could move forward, a hand snaked around her neck and clamped over her face. Charlotte's eyes bulged, and she struggled until her assailant turned her swiftly around, and they were face-to-face.

"Anne," Charlotte whispered, pulling her sister into a tight embrace. "Thank God you are here. Where are the others?"

"Last seen above, looking for you in the woods," Anne told her. "They will find their way in and follow the light, as I did. Help will soon be at hand."

"I believe that Joseph is down there." Charlotte nodded at the steps. "We can't wait another moment, Anne."

Anne nodded, determined. "We shall not."

Hand in hand, the two sisters went on.

51

Anne

They crouched down behind a low wall that bordered the entrance to the chamber. Another Oakhope folly, it had been built in the style of an ancient temple, hexagonal in shape with pillars at every corner, and a mosaic floor and walls depicting creatures and gods from a fusion of Greek, Roman and even Egyptian mythology. Images of snakes seemed to slither in the flickering light; twin wolves raised their heads to howl at an invisible moon. And yet the chamber seemed to be empty. Wherever Lady Hartley had gone, it was beyond this strange ceremonial room.

"We must go on," Charlotte whispered, but Anne shook her head.

"No, wait. See there on the altar—fruit, bread and, I'd guess, mead. We saw an identical offering at the stones at Top Withens. Whatever she means to do, it will be here. Wait, and let her bring him to us."

Anne glanced at her sister, who gazed at the darkened passageway across the room. She could feel her sister's urge to charge, and yet Charlotte stilled herself. She heeded Anne and waited. It was only two minutes more before Anne was proved right.

Lady Hartley returned, the blood trickling down her face making her an even more fearful sight. With her was Joseph Earnshaw.

"Am I to go home now, miss?" Joseph asked as he wandered, untethered, into the middle of the room, turning slowly as he gazed around.

"In a little while, Joseph," Lady Hartley said. "First you will eat with me—eat and drink—and then I will take you home."

Joseph took the cup she passed him, and looked into it.

"I'm not thirsty, miss, nor hungry," he said, and Anne could hear the tremble in his voice. Joseph always was a quick one—no man's fool even at eleven years old. He knew that Lady Hartley meant to render him senseless or worse.

"Eat and drink," his captor urged him. "I can't let you go if you don't, Joseph. All that will happen is that you will fall asleep, and when you wake, you won't remember your stay with me, and we will both be safe."

"I see," Joseph said, his voice so small that Anne had to strain to hear it. "But you said you were bringing Miss Charlotte to take care of me."

"And I have," Lady Hartley said, glancing towards where the sisters were hiding. "Would you like her to be with you now?"

"Very much," Joseph said, tears in his voice. "I would very much like to see her."

Before Anne could move, Charlotte stood up.

"Here I am, Joseph," she said.

Anne watched as Charlotte made her way to the middle of the room, her shoulders back, her head high even as her skirts hung in tatters, and there was blood on her hands and face. Despite her appearance, Joseph flung himself into her arms, wrapping his arms around her waist and hiding his face in her fallen-down hair. Anne watched as her sister kissed the top of Joseph's head and whispered something in his ear.

Had Lady Hartley guessed that Charlotte was not alone behind the balustrade, or did she simply count on her sister to surrender the moment she saw the boy's desperate fear?

"There." Lady Hartley smiled, smearing her own blood across her face as she wiped it with the back of her hand. "Sit, both of you, and I shall serve you. We shall have a picnic."

Charlotte kept her arm around Joseph as Lady Hartley began to divide up the fruit with her gleaming knife.

"There are people close by, Catherine," Charlotte said. "You will be discovered at any moment. It would be so much better for you if you were to lay down the knife and let us go."

"You do so remind me of my boy, Joseph," Catherine said, ignoring Charlotte. "He was a little older than you, but small for his age. We had such a happy time together when he was a babe. But as he grew older it was harder to keep him hidden away. I couldn't risk his being discovered—it would cause my ruin, and his. So I moved him down here, into the caves. I really believed it was the best thing for us both. The caves became his nursery, his whole world. Each night and day was spent within this labyrinth. I found a nurse to take over his care, one who could be trusted as long as she was paid well enough. You've met, I believe—one Mrs. Grace Poole. At first I visited him often, but it was so damp and cold down here I found leaving him behind more and more difficult. After a while it seemed unkind to unsettle him with my presence, so I trusted him to Poole, gave her more than enough funds to provide him with everything he needed to be happy. Poole brought me weekly reports and told me all was well. I chose to believe her. I wanted to believe her. But I knew that the moment I turned sixteen, I had to marry, and quickly.

For if I did not, there would be all manner of fools desperate to acquire my fortune. I agreed upon the first good prospect my solicitor sent to me, and it was a good match. Leonard never even guessed that there was a boy, growing up in darkness beneath his feet. Then there came a time when I was taken to Paris for a number of weeks, and while I was there, I saw true miracles performed." Lady Hartley's eyes glowed with the memory. "I saw with my own eyes how those who were about to die were saved by the Virgin Mary and her miraculous medal, and I realised the power of motherhood—that a mother's love is capable of surmounting any barrier. Leonard truly loved me, and I determined that as soon as we returned to England, I would bring my son forth into the light and that somehow Leonard would accept him."

"Catherine." Charlotte spoke gently. "You weren't born a monster—the hate and suffering you endured have made you one, but beneath it all, there is still a human heart beating. Please, look at this little boy and understand that he is loved, just as much as you loved your son."

"I didn't love my son enough—at least not during his life." Lady Hartley shook her head. "My son starved to death while I was in France. Poole tried to tell me it was consumption that took him, but I could see the truth of it. I could see that it was her fault for leaving him alone down here to waste away and mine for abandoning him. I was his mother, and I hid him away so that I could have the life I desired. I loved him too much to let him live with others who might have cared for him, and not enough to claim him as my own. Poole fled, taking my secrets with her, and has used them to her profit ever since. And I took my boy back to his father's house. It seemed fitting somehow. After all, Clifton had abandoned me. He'd let our son die just as much as I had. If he'd only stood up against me, forced me to marry him, then perhaps . . . Well, it was too late. I had heard what had become of Clifton. The more his wife ailed, the more the guilt of our past consumed him, and he was lost to bad men and evil ways, trying to drown away his horror by revelling with his cohorts and whores amongst the trees, fancying themselves bacchanalians. So in I went, quiet as a mouse, with my little boy in my arms. I had the secrets I needed. I gathered them all, all the female gods, the wise-women and the moon, and wove them together as one. All I needed was the right place and a sacrifice. A child's life for my son's. If I can find the right boy, the right soul to please the old gods and the devil himself, I can bring my boy back to life, you see. I know I can."

Anne watched as Lady Hartley talked, walking around and around her captives, her knife hanging loose at her side. As she passed in front of them, Charlotte tipped both her and Joseph's cups across the floor, using her tattered skirt to cover up the pool.

"How did you get John Rafferty there?" Charlotte asked.

"I have never heard that name," Lady Hartley said. "I went for Liston—he was to be my sacrifice, the babe born barely a year after my son. I wanted Clifton to feel the pain that I did, to see that no matter how much you drink and fight, you can never escape your sins. I underestimated Mary. I'm certain that Clifton never mentioned my name to her, but somehow the moment she saw me, she knew who I was.

"'You are the one who drives him to madness,' she told me. 'You are the one I could never free his heart from.'"

"I told her simply that my son had died, and I'd come to kill hers. The woman was on the verge of her death, but still she fought me like a lioness. I almost admired her. Mary barred me from her son, hard enough that the maid Bess could lock Liston out of reach. Clifton's wife died in my arms. It seemed the decent thing to do, to speed her on her way. And, of course, I needed a sacrifice, and though she was not the child the ceremony called for, she was all I had. I took her to her room and performed the ceremony. If she had just let me have Liston, it might have worked, but a sick woman already dead wasn't sacrifice enough for the mother gods.

"The night wore on, and I buried him there in the chimney breast, kept him safe with all the magic I could muster and knew that one day my time would come again. I whispered to Bess on my way out of the door. I made a bargain with her. If she kept her silence, I wouldn't come for Liston again. Only one other saw me leave: the clockmaker. Perhaps he had an idea of who I was and what he thought I might have done, but he had secrets of his own to keep. And I have always escaped discovery, because I am careful and sure. I wait for the right soul to present itself, and then I wait for the dark moon, and though I haven't succeeded yet, tonight I know that I am close. Joseph, as poor and pointless as he is, has a joy of life that makes him shine very brightly. A feast fit for the old gods."

"A feast?" Joseph turned to Charlotte. "Am I to be eaten?"

"No." Charlotte held the boy's hand in hers. "Why are you so proud to be such a proficient murderer, Catherine?" Charlotte asked. "How can taking the lives of others possibly honour the memory of your son?"

"You, who have never been a mother, you cannot understand the love that drives me! It was easier after I persuaded Leonard to fund the orphanage and had Poole installed there. It kept her quiet and suited my needs. Those boys Poole found for me, they would have been dead before they were twenty anyway—poor, sickly and worked half to death. I allowed them to serve a greater purpose than to be mere fodder for the factories. I honoured them and him every time I tried to bring my boy back to me, and I will try again and again until either he is in my arms or I am taking my last breath."

Anne watched as Lady Hartley looked up.

"And now the hour is upon us. The dark moon has ascended and I have two bright and brilliant souls to offer to the mother gods tonight. So eat, drink and dream, my loves, and I promise you that you will know nothing of what comes next."

"Mother?"

Suddenly Joseph tried to pull away from Charlotte; she stared at him open-mouthed. The boy hadn't taken any of the tainted food—she was sure of it—so what on earth was happening? And then she realised the brave little soul was creating a diversion, a chance for them to escape. She let go of his hand as he reached out towards Lady Hartley.

"Mama, is it really you?"

The boy was speaking with a terrible faux-upper-class accent, and yet in her crazed state of mind, it seemed enough to stun Lady Hartley, for she stopped still and stared at Joseph, lifting her arms towards him, her face softening with joy, tears of happiness glittering on her cheeks.

The knife clattered to the floor.

"My darling? My Edward?"

"Joseph, *run!*" Charlotte shouted, flinging herself at Lady Hartley, catching her enough that they both tumbled to the floor.

In an instant Lady Hartley grabbed for her fallen knife. At the same moment, Anne sprang from her hiding place as Joseph raced past her.

"Bring the others here!" Anne called to him as she ran to Charlotte and was forced to a standstill.

The knife flashed and glinted in the mêlée, and Anne could not tell who had control of it—she was afraid that to lunge into the fight would cause harm to her sister. And yet she must get the knife before it could be used.

"Stop this now!" Liston bellowed as he ran into the room, just at the moment that the madwoman flung Charlotte on to her back and, pinning her to the floor, raised her knife to strike. In the very same split second, Anne grabbed the hilt of Liston's sword and, dragging it from its sheath, swung it towards Lady Hartley.

"Let my sister go." Anne levelled the point of the sword at the assailant's throat.

Lady Hartley turned to look at her. "You do not have the stomach for killing, Anne Brontë," she said.

"If you believe that, then you have never known the love one sister has for another," Anne replied. "Do you wish to test it?"

It seemed as if every second were an hour, and then at last Lady Catherine Hartley dropped her knife and climbed to her feet.

"Catherine!" Lord Hartley entered with a half dozen men. He stood staring at the scene that confronted him, disbelief and horror etched across his face. It seemed that he was an inattentive husband indeed. "Dear God, woman, what have you done?"

"Leonard, my dear," Lady Hartley replied. "I have got myself into a spot of trouble."

"Misses Brontë? Liston Bradshaw?" Lord Hartley peered at them each in turn. "Please forgive my wife. She is quite unwell. I will take her into my custody, and as soon as I understand it all, I will make all good."

"You cannot make good murdered boys," Liston said, his eyes burning, "or the lives she ruined." He pointed at Catherine, who simply smiled at him in return.

"It must be hard to know your pa never really loved you or your mother," Catherine told him. "His soul was always mine, and it always will be. I'll keep it beside me, even in hell."

"You're a liar. My father loves me, and he loved my ma." Liston lunged at the woman, held back only by Anne and the difficulties of the confined space.

"You are." Clifton Bradshaw appeared from the tunnel, looking like a wraith, already half gone from this world to the next. "I loved you once, Catherine. I loved you when you were a sweet girl and a terrible woman. But it was no more than a fever, an infection. And tonight I am cured. I don't love you now. I hate you."

Tears stood in Catherine's eyes as she looked into Clifton's.

"Then our eternity together will be very long indeed," she said. "Leonard, please take me away from these people. I'm terribly tired."

Quite suddenly they were alone.

Anne dropped the sword and gathered her sister into her arms, as Liston sank to his knees, burying his head in his hands, and Clifton rocked him in his arms.

"Dear God!" Anne heard Emily exclaim as she and Branwell raced down the stairs, then collapsed to their knees to embrace both her and Charlotte.

"Is Joseph safe?" Charlotte asked.

"Yes, he is above with his father, who followed us," Branwell said. "Nicholls led a party of men from the village—they are all above waiting to rescue you."

"Well, waiting never did prove very beneficial," Charlotte said.

"I do believe I missed the whole adventure," Emily said, looking at her two sisters in turn. "This is intolerable, for I shall never hear the end of it."

"That is likely true," Anne said, lifting her chin. "But for now, please may we go home and have a glass of sherry?"

52

❧

December 25

Emily

Emily rose before dawn and, swathing herself in her favourite silk shawl, crept quietly downstairs with Keeper at her heels. For she had only one true present to give her family this Christmas morning, and that was the gift of music.

Settling herself at the piano, she opened her sheet music and began to play Haydn's introduction to "Winter" from *The Seasons*.

The piece began softly, at a measured pace, gentle, and as full of grace as the snow that continued to wrap their home in swaths of white. Soon Tabby would be busying herself lighting the fires, and Papa would be readying himself for church. Her sisters would be up, exchanging homemade trifles and drawings, and this little house would be full of love and the warmth of family.

Emily leant into the music, tilting her cheek towards the gentle rise and fall of the melody as she played. As her fingers travelled over the keys, she let the last of the darkness of the previous few days rise into the air with the music.

Lord Hartley had placed his wife in an asylum the very same

night that Anne and Charlotte had vanquished her. It was better than she deserved, but Emily supposed that a man with as much power and influence as Lord Hartley would never have let his wife stand trial. At least now she would ever more be prevented from doing harm, lost in a world of her own insanity. Hartley had come to the parsonage the next morning, having seen off the law with reassurances and, no doubt, sizeable bribes, and he had sworn that he had known nothing about Catherine's madness. Emily had been moved to believe him, for he listened to the whole dreadful tale sitting by their fireplace, his face as white as marble, his hands trembling despite the heat of the fire.

Lord Hartley promised each of the Brontës that he would not rest until the name and burial place of each stolen child was found. He removed Mrs. Poole from the orphanage and, upon searching her office, found a quantity of material that she kept to blackmail and threaten the good names of local gentry, and letters of agreement selling the boys into short and brutal lives for profit. In some ways, Emily had thought, Mrs. Poole was worse than Catherine, for she was not mad, simply utterly devoid of compassion and driven by greed. No one had been sorry to learn that following a swift and private trial, Mrs. Poole was to spend the remainder of her life in prison. In contrast, they had all been delighted that Lucy Goddard was to take her place. Emily smiled to herself as she played, imagining how much better things would be at the orphanage now, and how happy Mr. Markham would be to see Lucy Goddard and Tom return. And how much further joy there was to be had in knowing that there was a new tutor and matron at Crossed Keys. A kindly if shy woman who was beginning, only now that her sister had passed, to live her life to the fullest: one Rose Sladden.

As for Clifton Bradshaw, after that night of searching for Joseph, he had fallen gravely ill. None expected him to see the new year, but when Liston visited, he told them his father seemed at peace at last, in a way he had never known him to be before. Papa had been taken to his bedside and prayed with him.

Soon after Clifton passed, Liston had come to the back door of the parsonage and sat with his head in his hands in the kitchen.

"All I can think is that he is there with her now. That she has his soul, and she will never let him be at peace," he told them in anguish.

"Then you must cease such thoughts at once," Anne said. "Your father confessed his every sin to our papa. They prayed together before he died. There is only one who has command over his soul, and it is He who watches over your father now. If he was truly repentant, which I am certain he was, then he is redeemed and at peace. And as for you, Liston, you have a whole life ahead of you to live well and justly. To make good your corner of the earth."

Liston took great comfort in Anne's words, and afterwards, though still hardly speaking to his sisters, Branwell had escorted his friend home.

Last night they had all gathered for the Christmas Eve service, the church full of candlelight and song, warmed by the companionship and community of the whole village, and it seemed to Emily that whatever darkness had stalked their lives was entirely gone away—in fact had been chased away by the brave Brontë sisters.

After the service, Emily had found Zerubbabel Barraclough waiting at the door, intent on avoiding small talk with the other parishioners.

"Are you and your sisters, quite well?" he asked.

"We are," Emily replied.

"I did not ever come to see to your clock," he told her. "Events overtook me, and I was out looking for Joseph."

"The clock is working perfectly," Emily confessed with a small smile. "But I think you knew that, Mr. Barraclough."

He nodded. "I didn't suspect her of anything until the bones were discovered," he said. "I saw her that night, the night that Mary Bradshaw died, and supposed she had been drawn into the goings-on in the copse. I considered it no business of mine—we all have our secrets. Then I remembered that years ago, just before Mary Bradshaw died, when I'd been installing a clock up at Ponden, she'd been there in the library, and when she left, her eyes were glittering as if she had a fever, and she raced past me without a word. I recalled those books, and my suspicions led me to seek them out again that morning we met at Ponden. There was nothing there that enlightened me, but you, Miss Brontë, you understood it, did you not?"

"I suppose I understood enough to take us a little closer," Emily said, "though we didn't so much solve this mystery as vanquish it after it uncloaked itself. If I had lost my sister to that fiend, I would never have been able to forgive myself for not seeing it all. You see, Mr. Barraclough, I didn't understand until then that a woman could be capable of such cruelty."

"It seems we underestimate females in every quarter," Zerubbabel said with a small smile.

"What were you doing that night, if I may ask?" Emily's eyes widened. "Were you part of Clifton's debauchery?"

"I most certainly was not." Barraclough examined Emily's face for a moment, weighing her up before he went on at last. "I was visiting my beloved, my Agnes, who, forgive me, I have loved as a man loves a woman these last fifteen years."

"Oh," Emily said. "And now I see why you are such a private man, Mr. Barraclough. But why will you simply not marry Agnes? You are both free?"

312 ec Bella Ellis

"Agnes was married already—she'd done so very young and regretted it at once," Zerubabbel said. "Every so often I check for the man's health. As yet, he is still living. Still, we are settled as we are and hurt no one."

Emily thought for a moment. "Mr. Barraclough, may I tell you a secret of mine in exchange for yours?"

"You may," he replied gravely.

"I did solve one mystery entirely, but it is such a delicate matter that I have vowed to speak of it to no one, and it is most vexing because none shall know that I am terribly clever."

"You may burden yourself upon me," Zerubabbel said with the merest twitch of his mouth.

"The mystery of John Rafferty." Emily lowered her voice. "A boy we assumed for good reason to be the child discovered in the chimney. However, once it was established that the poor child was Lady Hartley's unfortunate son, I could not stop thinking of what had become of John Rafferty. And then I remembered something Mr. Markham had told me, about the workers' cottage where John's mother still lived. I wrote to her at that address and asked her a simple question. The reply came this morning, and I am proved to be correct, though I burnt the letter at once and will carry its contents to the grave. Just as soon as I've told you."

"What did you discover?" Zerubabbel asked patiently.

"John was not missing. He was living with his mother in the guise of her lodger all this time. It seems that he decided he could wait no longer to be with her, and as weak and little as he was, he was cunning. He ran away from Top Withens to go to her. Knowing his mother would be worried about how they would cope, he attempted to alleviate the situation with some ill-judged theft. He was caught in Keighley and taken before a judge and sentenced to ten years. But he escaped. Mrs. Rafferty's lodger is her son, though he leads a respectable life under another name now, and he is soon to be married. Isn't that wonderful?"

Zerubbabel thought for a moment.

"Yes," he agreed. "I believe that it is. Any happy ending or second chance in this world is wonderful indeed."

After Emily had bade good night to Mr. Barraclough, she began her walk home through the graveyard, only to stop dead in her tracks, for but a few feet away was a figure she had seen before—the woman dressed from head to toe in black.

"Who is it?" Emily called out, holding on to Keeper's collar as he emitted a low growl. For one moment more, the figure stood there, perfectly still, and then a cloud passed over the moon and she was gone.

Catching her breath, Emily ran to the spot where she thought the figure had been standing, and, brushing the snow away from the headstone, she read a woman's name. The grave belonged to Mary Bradshaw.

53

❧❧❧

Anne

Anne met Charlotte at the top of the stairs, and together they went down to find Emily playing. Flanking her on either side, Anne began to sing, her sweet, high voice rising to fill the room, and Charlotte joined her in singing the harmony.

In due time Branwell too appeared, and at his side their papa, followed by Tabby and Martha. Emily's music flowed from one song into another, and now they sang "Hark! The Herald Angels Sing," filling the whole of the parsonage with song.

Anne looked upon the faces of those she loved with all her heart, and felt a deep and precious kind of peace that, despite the cruelty and madness of this world, she would never forget. For in that room stood her family, her faith and her love. And no matter what might come next in this life, she knew that none of them would ever fail her.

"I have been thinking of a novel," Emily announced a little later in the dining room, after they had dressed for church, "a novel of such barbarity and infamy that the world will tremble at its pages, a novel that shows what evil and depravity men—and women—are capable of."

"I believe that there may be at least four novels' worth of stories in the events of our last detection," Charlotte said. "Now that we are to be celebrated poets, we should not waste a moment but follow up our literary success with three stories, as exciting and thrilling as we can make them."

"But will people ever believe that we have drawn our plots from experience?" Anne asked.

"No," Charlotte said, going to the mantel, where she retrieved four letters from behind the clock, each one containing a new case that required the services of a detector. "And God forbid that they ever should."

Music on Christmas Morning
by Anne Brontë

Music I love—but never strain
Could kindle raptures so divine,
So grief assuage, so conquer pain,
And rouse this pensive heart of mine—
As that we hear on Christmas morn,
Upon the wintry breezes borne.

Author's Note

As ever when I am writing a Brontë Sisters Mystery novel, I endeavour to keep biographical facts about the Brontë family accurate. In *The Diabolical Bones* I've included a scene in which the book of poems is accepted for publication by Aylott and Jones; although this did happen, it didn't actually take place until a month later, in January 1846. Charlotte wrote to Aylott and Jones on January 28, and before the end of January was making arrangements to have the books printed at the sisters' own expense.

Charlotte always claimed that Branwell didn't know about his sisters' secret writing careers; however, we do know that on March 28, 1846, Charlotte wrote to Aylott and Jones asking them to address all correspondence to her real name in the future, as there had been "a little mistake" with proof copies addressed to "Mr C Brontë Esq." Could it be that Branwell had opened the post by mistake? It is possible.

If you are familiar with famous Brontë locations, you will know that Top Withens is a real place. Top Withens was originally a farmhouse dating from the early sixteenth century. In 1591 it was divided

320   *Author's Note*

into three farms: Top, Middle and Lower Withens. The farms were occupied until the 1930s, when Lower and Middle Withens were pulled down, and Top Withens blocked up. In creating Top Withens Hall I have followed Emily's lead in *Wuthering Heights*, using the beauty spot that is widely believed to be the geographical position of the house in the novel, but replacing the humble farmhouse with a much grander building. There is a great deal of evidence pointing to beautiful Ponden Hall as the model for Wuthering Heights, particularly internally—it is a place where Emily spent a great deal of time—with some of the gothic splendour of High Sunderland Hall thrown in for good measure. I feel sure Emily, like every author, took elements of what she knew to create something unique to her novel.

Oakhope Hall and the Hartley family are entirely fictional; however, Oakhope Hall is based on a real location, Oakworth House, built for textile manufacturer Sir Isaac Holden between 1864 and 1874, the grounds of which did contain an eccentric network of man-made tunnels, grottos and caves. You can still see the remains of these amazing follies if you visit Holden Park today, though sadly the house was lost to fire in 1907. If you'd like to see images of this amazing house and others (including High Sunderland Hall), I recommend Kate Lycett's *Lost Houses of the South Pennines*.

Crossed Keys Orphanage in Halifax is fictional, though the perils and conditions endured by orphans at this time are well documented.

The Barraclough family was a real family of clockmakers local to Haworth, and there is in fact a John Barraclough clock in the Brontë Parsonage Museum, Haworth. One of three brothers, John's son Zerubbabel became one of the most celebrated clockmakers in the area. Zerubbabel never married, but he did live with his mother and housekeeper, who was actually called Martha. We do not know the nature of their relationship.

As for prejudice against Irish people fleeing the potato famine, and indeed the Brontë family itself, this was sadly commonplace. In 1860, novelist Charles Kingsley (author of *The Water Babies*) referred to the Irish people he saw on a trip to Ireland as "human chimpanzees," and the press regularly portrayed the Irish as parasitic freeloaders who were lazy and stupid. In 1837, after Branwell intervened at a local hustings where his father was being shouted down by an enraged crowd, the locals burned an effigy of him holding a potato in one hand and a herring in the other, a reference to his Irish origins. Though, in a bid to improve his chances of progression in England, Patrick changed the family name from Prunty to Brontë, prejudice and intolerance meant that their Irish roots were never entirely forgotten.

Bella Ellis
May 2020

Acknowledgements

It is impossible to write a Brontë Sisters Mystery novel without the help, knowledge and insight of a great many people who are so generous with their time and expertise.

Thank you to all the staff at the Brontë Parsonage Museum, particularly Ann Dinsdale, who has been so encouraging and kind. And to Steve Wood, Haworth historian and author extraordinaire, who helped me, particularly with matters pertaining to the crypt and the schoolroom. And to Dr. Jian Choe, whose paper "The Brontës and Christmas" was so useful in helping to create the right atmosphere in *The Diabolical Bones*. And to all my fellow Brontë geeks, but particularly to Graham Watson, who is a wonderful source of knowledge. I've been lucky enough to make some great friends in Haworth, including the wondrous Diane Park, whose enthusiasm and energy is always welcome.

Hugest amounts of gratitude go to my dear, dear friend, brilliant Julie Akhurst of my beloved Ponden Hall, who is the first to read my manuscripts, and who proofreads them and often helps me with research. Julie and her husband, Steve Brown, have made me feel like part of their Ponden family, and I count myself so lucky to have them in my life.

I have many reference books constantly on my desk, chief amongst them *The Brontës* by Juliet Barker; *A Life in Letters*, edited by Juliet Barker; *At Home with the Brontës* by Ann Dinsdale; *The Letters of Charlotte Brontë*, volumes one through three, edited by Margaret Smith; *A Brontë Kitchen* by Victoria Wright; *The Letters of The Reverend Patrick Brontë*, edited by Dudley Green; and of course the complete works of Charlotte, Emily and Anne, which inspire me constantly.

Thank you to my marvellous publishing teams on both sides of the Atlantic. Melissa Cox, Lily Cooper, Maddy Marshall and Steven Cooper at Hodder in the UK, and Michelle Vega, Lauren Burnstein, Jessica Plummer and Jennifer Snyder at Berkley in the US.

And huge thanks to everyone at David Higham agency, especially Lizzy Kremer, Maddalena Cavaciuti, Georgina Ruffhead, Alice Howe and the whole of the rights team, whose hard work on my behalf I am always grateful for.

During the course of finishing this book, the world changed forever due to a global pandemic, giving us all a less than welcome insight into what life was like for Charlotte, Emily and Anne, living day to day with an unseen illness that could prove to be fatal. Heartfelt thanks to everyone, everywhere, who is working to keep us safe and to find treatments and vaccines, and to all of those in publishing who are doing their best to get books to readers around the globe. We all need a good story in our lives now more than ever, and I really hope that by the time this book is published our troubles are behind us.